I0590013

Challenged By You

Kate Sweden

Wild Magnolias Press

Copyright © 2025 by Kate Sweden

All rights reserved.

No part of this publication may be reproduced, distributed, or transmitted in any form or by any means, including photocopying, recording, or other electronic or mechanical methods, without the prior written permission of the publisher, except as permitted by U.S. copyright law. For permission requests, contact Kate directly at kateswedenromance@gmail.com.

The story, all names, characters, and incidents portrayed in this production are fictitious. No identification with actual persons (living or deceased), places, buildings, and products is intended or should be inferred.

ISBN-13: 979-8999002525 (Paperback)

For the readers who know that foreplay starts with snark,
that sarcasm is a love language,
and that nothing pairs better with filthy smut than a perfectly timed punchline.
This one's for you.

Contents

Chapter 1

Excited to Collaborate. Truly.

I F MY MARGARITA GLASS had eyes, it would've looked concerned. Possibly judgy. Maybe even preparing to stage an intervention.

I took another sip—salt rim, top shelf, exactly the way I liked it—and narrowed my gaze at the glowing laptop screen in front of me.

The screen's light caught my hazel eyes, probably amplifying the unholy rage behind them. My dark brown hair was twisted into a topknot, and my sun-kissed skin—freckles thriving despite my twin's campaign for daily SPF—was already plotting revenge.

There he was.

Jerrick Thorne.

Chief Marketing Officer of Adventura Luxe, based in Austin, Texas, where stress is a flex and people pay ninety bucks for bottled air.

And the smug bastard had done it again.

Unveiling the Future of Elite Travel: Elevation. Curation. Obsession.

I slammed my laptop shut. The pen cup rattled. The margarita sloshed. Wilder Horizons wasn't a travel agency. We curated perfection disguised as spontaneity for billionaires—honeymoons, retreats, events. My scoreboard wasn't bookings—it was repeat contracts and referral deals. Which meant this panel wasn't just PR. It was currency.

"You've got to be fucking kidding me," I muttered, sinking into my chair, the picture of a villain who'd upgraded to Manolo Blahniks. "Obsession? That was my line, you tan, expensive-looking thief."

Across the room, Bali, my long-limbed tabby with an attitude problem, lifted her head, blinked, yawned—her version of flipping me off—and resumed her coma.

I flipped my laptop back open. The press release was still there—cocky little shit.

That pitch? I tested it on Daisy—our disaster-certified intern—at last month's strategy roundtable. She squinted, chewed her pen cap, and called it "expensive cult energy." I told her that was the point.

As Chief Marketing Officer of Wilder Horizons, the luxury adventure travel company I run with my five sisters, I don't sell high-end vacations. I sell escape. Fantasy. Bucket-list dreams, gift-wrapped in glitter and just enough danger to keep your therapist employed.

Cue the Oscar-worthy sigh.

Right as I launched into a very professional, extremely justified rant—to Bali, obviously— Rayann's face lit up my screen, mid-eye roll, already judging.

"Babe. You spiraling again?"

Rayann. My mirror image. The slightly less unhinged one. She knows every thought I have before I've even cursed it into existence.

"Define spiraling."

Rayann snorted. "You're drinking at your desk. Alone. Murder-vibe playlist. Skulls and crossbones all over your pitch notes. That's a yes."

"I'm not spiraling. I'm spiraling *strategically.* There's a difference."

"Right. Please don't set anything on fire. Again."

"That one time was a birthday candle malfunction."

Controlled experiment, thank you very much. Who knew the smoke detectors were wired like CIA satellites?

Rayann laughed, equal parts comfort and trouble, the human version of my favorite dirty latte.

"So what'd he do this time?"

"He hijacked my launch language. The 'obsession' angle we ran in last quarter's Mirage package? He dropped a campaign teaser that reads as if my PowerPoint presentation had a baby with his jawline."

There was a pause. "Okay, gross, but also impressive."

"I hate him," I growled. "We're talking tropical parasites and papaya-in-a-salad level hate. I hope a howler monkey pegs him with a rotten mango mid-press conference."

Rayann cackled. "You've been working too hard. When's the conference?"

"Next week. Osa Peninsula, Costa Rica." I jabbed at the screen, unapologetically hostile. "And guess who they announced as my co-host?"

I swiveled toward the giant whiteboard on the far wall of my Maris Key condo, the Florida sunlight still blazing like a spotlight through my floor-to-ceiling windows. My condo was the ultimate paradox: sleek white walls and minimalist furniture paired with shelves crammed with tropical trinkets and gold pineapple sculptures that collect dust I pretend not to see, color-coded binders, and no fewer than four aggressively scented candles. I think of it as "Tropical CEO Chic." As though I led a silent retreat for Type-A control freaks who flowchart their inner peace.

I was curled up barefoot in my lemon-yellow silk pajama set—a tank top and matching shorts I justified as office attire because from the Zoom frame up, I looked like I might invoice you for something expensive.

The laptop blinked back to life. Right there, beneath the words **Luxury Travel in the Social Age**—our names. Together. **Wilder & Thorne**. Wild ambition. Thorny history. What could possibly go wrong?

"He's not just attending," I said. "He's co-presenting. With me."

Rayann let out a low whistle. "Want me to come? I can pack a taser and an emotional support bottle of tequila."

"Tempting, but no. I've got this."

Because I did. I always do.

Some days I was two clicks from madness—but I'd still set the whole game aflame before anyone clocked the fractures.

I wasn't just the *spirited* Wilder twin. I was the deal closer. The mind behind every viral campaign Wilder Horizons had launched in the last three years. I played dirty with guerrilla charm, and I sealed deals in heels that could double as weapons.

Last quarter, I talked a billionaire's assistant into signing a five-figure add-on package in the time it took her boss to finish a smoothie. I'd smiled, dropped the word "exclusive" twice, and handed her a pen. She didn't even look at the line item—she just signed. Guerrilla charm in action.

Thorne might've stolen a few words—but I had ideas. Big ones.

And maybe—maybe—a prank or two up my sleeve.

I grabbed my Santorini pen—dark green, gold logo, stolen with flair from a cliffside resort that charged extra for sunshine, and faced the blank whiteboard.

"Oh, Jerrick Thorne, you son of a bitch," I whispered, lips curving into a smile that would've terrified my therapist. "You made this personal."

Morning light poured in as I traded my silk pajamas for wide-leg white linen pants (still warm from the dryer), a silky halter top, and enough dry shampoo to constitute a federal offense.

The Wilder Horizons office shimmered as always—perched on the sun-drenched Gulf Coast of Maris Key, Florida. Coastal views. Glass everything. And enough tropical greenery to suggest our CFO might secretly be a houseplant.

The scent of lemongrass diffusers, high-achieving humidity, and sister-induced anxiety hit me the second I stepped inside.

"Brynn," my sister, Emme, called, catching me outside the break room with a folder in one hand and a green smoothie that resembled something you'd cleanse a colon with in the other.

She was all crisp lines and early morning efficiency, with her black hair slicked into a no-nonsense ponytail and her phone already buzzing. *Vendor Relations Barbie*, if Barbie carried a stun gun for delayed shipments.

"Don't touch the frogs in Costa Rica," she said.

I blinked. "That's... oddly specific."

"They look cute. They are not. They're wet demons in disguise."

"Noted," I said. "Have a magical day, sunshine."

"Don't get arrested," she called over her shoulder.

"I said magical, not criminal."

Summer's door was already open. Of course it was.

I stepped in and found her seated behind her desk, posture straight, laptop open, a single pen aligned with military precision on her legal pad. Her blazer was beige. Her soul—laminated.

"You're late," she said without looking up.

"I'm exactly four minutes early."

"Exactly four minutes behind *me*."

God, I loved her.

"Relax," I said, sliding into the chair across from her. "I'm not going to light anything on fire before the Costa Rica trip. Probably."

She looked up. Summer Wilder, our oldest sister, Chief Operating Officer and wielder of the sacred highlighter system, had the kind of stare that could freeze a volcano mid-eruption.

"This isn't a vacation," she said. "The conference is a high-stakes PR opportunity. We'll be in front of our competitors, clients, and possibly international royalty. Please don't embarrass us."

I smiled. "I never embarrass us. I make us memorable."

"You are a one-woman crisis management department, Brynn."

"Flattering."

She clicked something on her screen with extra aggression. "I need your deck finalized by tomorrow. You'll be co-presenting with Jerrick Thorne. And before you ask, yes—I approved it. He's already confirmed."

"Oh, I know," I said sweetly. "We've been emailing."

"Brynn..."

"Strategically spiraling," I said, holding up a finger. "Not emotionally combusting."

Summer closed her laptop like she was resisting the urge to throw it at me. "Remember, you're representing the brand. Not one of your Instagram reels gone rogue."

I stood, already halfway out the door. "What if I represent both?"

She didn't answer. She was already typing.

The air shifted the second I crossed into my end of the hall—Rayann's office directly ahead, mine tucked to the left, and Summer's command center looming diagonally behind me like a boardroom Bat-Signal, ready to summon doom. Focused. The kind of energy that said someone was about to lose it—and odds were good it'd be me.

Daisy, stationed at the floating desk just outside our offices, popped up like a meerkat who'd sensed a disturbance in the Force. I gave her a breezy wave and kept moving.

Straight into my office.

Glass door.

Controlled slam.

Instant relief.

I dropped into my chair, flicked open my laptop, and clicked on the blinking icon of doom: Email (17 Unread).

Jerrick fucking Thorne.

There he was again—smug, sharp, and lurking beneath a subject line that practically smirked: **"Panel Content Framework – Updated Flow Suggestions"**

I opened it. Read. Stared. Rage cracked its knuckles somewhere behind my eyes.

FROM: Jerrick Thorne

SUBJECT: Panel Content Framework – Updated Flow Suggestions

Brynn,

Attached is my proposed structure for our segment next week. It aligns with the original event goals but streamlines the talking points for clarity and cohesion. Happy to discuss adjustments if needed.

– JT

I massaged my neck. Picked a pen. Clicked it twice, purely for effect.

Then I replied:

FROM: Brynn Wilder

SUBJECT: Re: Panel Content Framework – Updated Flow Suggestions

Hi Jerrick,

Thanks for the reminder about structure. Your version is... admirably safe. I'll be revising on my end to add back some of the actual excitement people came for.

Warmly,

Brynn

He replied three minutes later—three.

FROM: Jerrick Thorne

SUBJECT: Re: Re: Panel Content Framework – Updated Flow Suggestions

Brynn,

Noted. Let me know when to duck and when to smile. Shall we keep the word *obsession* off the table?

– JT

Duck and smile? Tempting. Maybe I'd build him a presentation slide that "accidentally" looped a cat meme in the middle of his graphs.

Death by PowerPoint, Thorne-style. I stared at his bullshit PowerPoint foreplay. Bali's judgmental spirit echoed in my mind. I flexed my fingers, took a steadying sip of cold coffee, and fired back:

FROM: Brynn Wilder

SUBJECT: Re: Re: Re: Panel Content Framework –
Updated Flow Suggestions

Only if you promise to keep your ego in a carry-on.
Excited to collaborate.

Truly.

BW

When I hit send, my lips curled as if I was about to sell
him a dream and shove him off a cliff.

Wilder Horizons wasn't just a travel company—it was
our father's masterpiece. He built it from nothing but
charm, grit, and a refusal to settle for ordinary. When
he died, the six of us stood in his office staring at the
contracts and the aftermath, and we had two choices:
take it on together or walk away. Nothing halfway. We
chose together. Our name. Our lifeline. Dad's legacy to
protect—or torch.

As Chief Marketing Officer, my job was to make sure
the world still believed in Wilder magic. That meant
dazzling new clients, locking down the ones who already loved us, and making damn sure no rival agency
stole what was ours. This Costa Rica conference isn't

just a networking event—it's open season. Competitors like Adventura Luxe—and every other high-end agency—would be circling, hungry for any slip. If we lost ground here, it wouldn't just bruise my pride. It would tarnish Dad's legacy.

Which meant babysitting Jerrick Thorne wasn't just a punishment—it was a test. And if he thought I'd roll over while he flexed his spreadsheets, he'd seriously underestimated how feral I could play.

Rayann and I were twins, but somehow she'd become "the strategist" while I was branded "the sparkler"—the one guaranteed to light things up and maybe set the curtains on fire in the process. People remembered my antics, my jokes, the bad-timing pranks... not the planning that went into them. Sitting in my office, staring at the Costa Rica briefing packet, I couldn't shake the worry that I was more mascot than mastermind. The Wilder twin you invite to the party—then hire someone else to clean up after.

My pen tapped an uneven rhythm against the desk, undecided between building a strategy and starting a fire.

Across the glass, Daisy clocked the look and immediately busied herself with her keyboard.

Smart girl.

Chapter 2

Undecided Danger

MARIS KEY'S FAVORITE ROOFTOP lunch spot, Breeze, was where influencers came to pretend they discovered ceviche—and where locals came to critique them for it. The air was thick with salt and charred lime, the kind of coastal breeze that carried both sunscreen and grilled fish.

My phone buzzed with a Wilder Horizons family-flavored doom ping before I could sit down. Summer's name flashed, which meant this wasn't optional.

"Quick check-in," she said the moment I answered.

Summer was technically the oldest, but Chief Operating Officer suited her better—steady, practical, crisis-control incarnate. Juliette, three years older than me and the sister most likely to beat God at chess, was CEO. Titles fit the personalities, not the birth order.

"Juliette's buried in contracts, I'm wrangling three appointments, and you're about to be on a stage with our biggest rival. Everyone good?"

"Define good."

"Not spiraling, not drinking before noon, and preferably wearing pants."

I swirled my mezcal margarita. "Two out of three." The smoky bite of the tequila clung to the back of my throat, salt crusting my lips as I tried not to grin.

Her sigh could've powered a wind farm. "Remember why Dad built Wilder, Brynn. It was never just trips—it was proof that travel can be both unforgettable and intentional. We carry that. Don't let some CMO with a smug LinkedIn smile make you forget it."

"Copy that. Build legacies, not enemies."

"Please. You'd stencil that on a crop top if I let you. Go kill lunch with Emme. I'll see you on the prep call tomorrow."

The line clicked off.

Emme slid into the seat across from me, phone already in one hand, a sleek folder in the other.

"Tell me you didn't start drinking already," she said without looking up.

"It's a lunch cocktail. It's called balance."

"Mezcal margarita. Two salt rims. A lime wedge the size of your ego."

I grinned. "See? Balanced."

The waiter arrived and took Emme's order—grilled shrimp salad, dressing on the side, naturally. I ordered the mango ceviche with house-made tortilla chips—my favorite.

I waited until he walked away before dropping my elbows dramatically onto the table. "I need to vent. No judgment."

Emme's mouth twitched. "Already judging."

"Perfect." I leaned in. "Do you remember that arrogant prick Jerrick Thorne?"

Emme's eyebrow twitched—just enough to say *pot, meet kettle*. "The CMO from Adventura Luxe? Tall. Sexy. Talks like he's narrating a branding documentary?"

Yeah. Him. With the voice that sounds like smoked honey and a fucking smirk that makes me want to throw a stapler at his forehead.

"That's the one."

"You mean the guy who beat you out for the Vanguard Award last year?"

I narrowed my eyes. "I was robbed. My campaign had live parrots."

"Exactly."

I ignored that. "He's back. And not just back—he's my co-presenter at the conference next week."

Emme's eyebrows rose for exactly one second before settling into professional curiosity. "That's not ideal."

"It's a hostile takeover of my mental health."

She sipped her sparkling water. "What did he do this time? Besides exist."

"He emailed me a proposed deck outline this morning. It was—" I waved my hands in the air like I was crafting a dark spell. "Streamlined. Organized. Uninspired. It reeked of beige—like if khakis were a personality. "

"He's from Austin," she offered.

"Exactly," I said, like that explained everything.

Emme tilted her head. "Didn't he also pitch the same Maldives concept you pitched to The Alta Group?"

My jaw twitched. "Yes. After I mentioned it during a joint panel. He claims he'd 'already been working on it.'"

"You do speak in soundbites."

"I can't help being brilliant. But apparently, I also moonlight as a volunteer strategist for men who ghost originality."

"So... are we packing vengeance or subtlety?"

The waiter returned with our food, and I busied myself twisting mango salsa onto a chip like it might pass for strategy. The ceviche was tangy and bright—mango sweet against cilantro and briny shrimp, the chips still warm enough to sting my fingertips.

"You hate him," she said eventually. "But you also… don't *not* enjoy this."

I scoffed. "That's ridiculous."

"Is it?"

"I didn't come for joy. I came for blood."

And if there were sparks? I'd burn them out with strategy.

"He's complicated. Smug. He writes emails like TED Talks. He has *opinions* about kerning."

"And yet you respond in five minutes flat and then refresh to see if he's answered."

I took a long, defiant sip of my drink.

"I'm preparing," I said. "Tactically. If I'm going to be stuck next to him on stage, I need to know what kind of polished hell I'm up against."

"Mmm." She stabbed her salad. "Do you think he knows you're spiral-planning?"

"Of course not. I'm a fortress."

Emme arched a brow.

"Okay, I'm a fortress with a cocktail bar and mood lighting. But still."

She smirked. "Well, just don't throw anything at him in Costa Rica. Unless it's a marketing award."

Back home, I lit one of my "calming" candles—citrus and sandalwood—and attempted to zen out on my sofa with a weighted blanket and a rerun of that baking show where everyone's teeth are perfect and their meltdowns are charming.

It didn't work.

At the twelve-minute mark, I picked up my phone.

Not to check email.

Not to scroll aimlessly.

Just... to confirm something.

I typed in his name: Jerrick Thorne.

LinkedIn popped up first, naturally.

His profile photo was exactly what you'd expect: suit, open collar, confident smile that said *I sign contracts before dessert and probably never forget your birthday just to assert dominance.*

Adventura Luxe – Chief Marketing Officer.

Eight years. Ivy League MBA. International keynote speaker.

There was a video embedded of him presenting at a marketing summit last year. I clicked it.

He started with a story about scuba diving with sharks in Belize and somehow connected it to user segmentation. I hated how good it was. I closed the app; it felt like an insult to my shoes.

Across the room, Bali lifted her head from the armchair, blinked at me once, then rolled over dramatically, tail swishing like she'd lost respect.

"Don't judge me," I muttered. I took another sip. "It's not stalking. It's competitive analysis."

The front door buzzed.

Rayann.

Perfect. Right on time for my mental breakdown.

Rayann stepped into my condo like she owned the place, tequila in one hand and a conspiratorial glint in her eyes. She brought a rush of night air and the smell of sun-warmed jasmine over coconut cream—summer in high heels and judgment.

"You look like you just drafted a revenge email and actually hit send," she said by way of greeting.

"I was doing research."

"You were doing emotional recon in a silk robe and your sad girl playlist. This calls for shots."

She shoved the tequila into my hands and kicked off her heels like she hadn't just come from some high-end event, looking flawless.

"I don't have limes," I muttered, turning toward the kitchen.

"That's fine. You've got trauma. That'll work." She leaned against the counter, pouring. "Max's spending his last free week pretending to be productive," she said, rolling her eyes. "Translation: he's reorganizing our storage unit again before we move to Rome."

I snorted. "You've committed to a man who alphabetizes his wrenches. You knew what you were signing up for."

"I thought it was foreplay," she said, deadpan, handing me the bottle. "Turns out it's just nesting with bubble wrap."

I pulled two mismatched shot glasses from the cabinet, one that said *#BossMode* and the other that said *It's Not Day Drinking If You're Networking*. I handed her the networking one. Fitting.

"Cheers to travel. And emotionally repressing things until they explode in a foreign country," she said.

We clinked. We drank. I winced.

Rayann marched straight to my open suitcase like she was about to conduct a federal audit—hands on hips, ready for battle.

"Why do you have six swimsuits and only one pair of heels?"

"Because I'm prioritizing versatility."

"You're prioritizing emotional avoidance. That, and your nipples."

"They're very persuasive."

She held up a skimpy black two-piece with gold rings at the hips.

"Is this a bathing suit or a boundary issue?"

"It's a resort. The networking starts at the pool and ends in someone's inbox."

Next, she grabbed a bright coral wrap dress and doubled over laughing. "Is this... silk?"

"It's *silk blend*."

"For the jungle?"

"It breathes!"

Rayann wiped a fake tear from her eye. "What are you trying to do—slide through the rainforest like a goddamn marketing panther?"

I crossed my arms. "I like to feel prepared."

She kept digging. "You've packed three bandeau tops, four strappy rompers, a leather mini skirt, and—oh my God—are these stilettos?"

"They're wedges."

"They're weapons."

"They're dual-purpose."

"Brynn. There are snakes."

"There's also Jerrick Thorne," I snapped.

She froze mid-rummage, then slowly looked up at me like she'd just cracked a case on *Law & Order: Sexy Crimes Division.*

I blinked. "I didn't mean it like that."

"Oh, you *absolutely* did." She held up a pair of gold hoop earrings roughly the size of drink coasters. "You're planning an outfit arc."

"I'm... what?"

"An outfit arc," she repeated, delighted. "Start strong. Dazzle mid-week. Destroy him emotionally by Friday."

I opened my mouth to argue but came up empty.

"You're dressing like a heatwave got a glam squad."

"I'm being professional."

"You packed an off-the-shoulder jumpsuit with cutouts."

"I like ventilation!"

"You're presenting next to Jerrick Thorne, who once wore a blazer to a beach mixer."

I groaned and flopped onto the bed. "He's so... unbothered. The human equivalent of a curated hotel scent. Polished. Controlled. Dead inside."

"You say that like it's a bad thing."

"It *is.* He's too smooth. Has opinions about presentation fonts and pretends they're world peace strategies."

"So you hate him because he's a threat to your throne."

"I hate him because he beat me out for an award with a pitch I mocked in a group chat."

Rayann climbed onto the bed beside me and handed me another shot. "So basically, you hate him because he's hot and competent."

"I hate him because he signs his emails like he's too busy for a full name."

"'– JT' is kind of sexy, though."

"Don't you dare validate him."

We drank. I glared at her glass like it had betrayed me. A beat passed.

Then she asked, way too casually, "So... you planning to bang him in Costa Rica?"

I choked. "Jesus. No."

"Not even hate-sex?"

"No!"

"Because you've *thought* about it. Don't lie—I can see the eyebrow twitch."

"I think about stabbing him with a clicker. That count?"

Rayann smirked. "Murder with tongue?"

"I hate you."

"You love me."

She held up the last swimsuit like it was Exhibit A in my inevitable HR complaint. "This one's see-through in the sun. Pack it."

I stared at her.

"Pack hot," she said, patting my shoulder as she stood. "Play hotter."

Then she raised her tequila and gave me a wicked grin. "To war."

And just like that, she breezed out of the room—leaving me with an open suitcase, a tequila hangover loading, and the haunting realization that maybe—just maybe—I wasn't entirely dreading seeing Jerrick in Costa Rica.

Her voice floated back from the hall. "Oh, and Brynn? Maybe pack your new belt for Jerrick. You might need it."

I smirked, reaching for my sunglasses. "For him or for me?"

No answer. Just the sound of front door clicking closed.

I stared at the see-through swimsuit still dangling from the edge of my suitcase, then reached over and flicked it off the bed.

It landed on the floor, a decision I didn't want to make yet.

The condo was suddenly too still, like it knew I was full of shit and was just waiting for me to say it out loud. No sister banter, no snark to ricochet off of. Just me, my questionable packing choices, and a suspiciously warm second margarita I no longer wanted to finish.

I stood up. Sat back down. Reached for my drink anyway, then pushed it away. This was fine. I was fine. Just casually emotionally unwell in a room full of strappy dresses and self-denial.

I looked at the mess I'd created.

It wasn't just the clothes. It was the intent.

The lingerie shoved in a corner, equal parts wishful thinking and denial. The lipstick that lasted through a board meeting and a nervous breakdown. The ridiculous earrings that made zero sense for jungle humidity but somehow felt like armor.

Why did I pack like I was going into battle?

Why did I care if he saw me coming?

Because part of me—the deeply annoying part that didn't listen to reason—still wanted to prove something. To him. To myself. To whatever version of me kept reapplying lipstick like it was war paint.

I rubbed my temples, exhaling slow like it might trick my body into relaxing.

This wasn't about Jerrick. It couldn't be. It was about the presentation, the company, the optics. I was going to represent Wilder Horizons with strategy, style, and possibly waterproof mascara, depending on the humidity index.

That's all.

And if I maybe—maybe—wanted to look hotter than necessary while standing next to a man who once called my campaign "commercially aggressive" in a keynote?

And if that made him sweat? Even better. Not that maddening tension that wrapped itself around every interaction with him, a ribbon pulled too tight. God, I needed to sleep. Or pack less emotionally. Or lie down in front of a speeding golf cart.

I glanced at the whiteboard in the other room, where my panel notes sat under a bold header I'd written in permanent marker: OWN THE NARRATIVE.

Right.

I would. I always did.

I stood, shoved half the swimsuits into a separate bag I labeled *Undecided Danger,* and marched to the kitchen to rinse my glass.

Tomorrow, I'd finalize my deck. Confirm logistics. Be a professional.

But tonight?

Tonight, I was a woman alone with her suitcase, second-guessing her motives and wondering why the hell the thought of sharing a stage with Mr. Fucking Perfect made her feel like she might spontaneously combust.

I wasn't going to hook up with that jackass.

Never.

Not even a chance.

... Obviously.

Which, in my defense, is exactly what someone who's absolutely in denial would say.

Chapter 3

Welcome to the Jungle

I GLIDED THROUGH AIRPORT security with the efficiency of a woman who packs emotionally but labels compulsively. Two checked bags. One curated carry-on. And an ensemble built for arrival impact: ivory linen pants, gold accessories, and a silk camisole I steamed twice, in case the universe tried me.

It did.

My gate had moved. My boarding group was a swarm of influencers in coordinated athleisure. And a man dumped a smoothie on the seat beside me before I could sit.

I took it as a sign that I was still better than everyone.

By the time I boarded the connection to Costa Rica, I was sweaty, dehydrated, and deeply offended that the plane didn't have a first-class cabin. It did, however, have overhead bins that barely tolerated my Undecided Danger bag.

The flight attendant wasn't impressed.

"I'm sorry, ma'am—this one may need to be gate-checked."

"Ma'am?" I repeated, tight smile locked in place. "Absolutely not. This bag holds silk, secrets, and my will to live."

"You've got two options—make it fit, or wave goodbye at the gate like it's a breakup scene."

I slid it into place with a sigh and whispered, *"You're so much better than this,"* as if I were sending a soldier off to war.

The flight was smoother than I deserved—no delays, no seatmate with halitosis or a loud TikTok habit. I even managed to get through customs without breaking a sweat or accidentally declaring emotional baggage.

Outside the Costa Rican air wrapped around me like a humid silk scarf. Thick and warm, it carried the scent of jungle and jet fuel.

A man in crisp resort whites held a sign with my name printed across it in bold, blocky letters. **WILDER.**

Underneath it, in smaller font, someone had scrawled *Welcome to Pura Vida!* with what looked like a gold paint pen. It was aggressively cheerful. I hated it a little.

"Ms. Wilder?" he asked with a friendly smile and an accent smooth enough to bottle.

"That's me," I said, pulling the Undecided Danger bag behind me with the authority of a woman pretending she had it together.

"I'm Mateo. I'll be your driver today."

Mateo led me to a sleek black SUV that looked far too clean for anything involving nature, opened the door like a gentleman, and even offered me a chilled eucalyptus towel and a bottle of water. Wilder Horizons didn't skimp. I'd give us that.

The ride to the resort was scenic and almost criminally serene. Dense jungle. Bright flowers. The occasional iguana doing its best runway walk along the road's edge.

"You here for work or pleasure?" Mateo asked.

"Bit of both," I said, knowing full well my past was about to check in at the same resort. "Let's call it... business. But the complicated kind."

He laughed. "That's most people here."

By the time we pulled up to the resort—an architectural fantasy tucked into the hills with wide glass windows—I'd almost convinced myself I was ready.

I'd seen luxury. Been jaded by it, even. But this place? Next-level. Palms and bougainvilleas everywhere. Stone paths curving around infinity pools and open-air suites tucked into the jungle curated squares on a billionaire's vision board. The air was thick with orchid bloom and humidity that clung like gossip. Even the shadows looked rich. The staff wore white linen and glided like friction was beneath them.

I tried to act like it was all beneath me, which was hard considering I nearly moaned when a handsome concierge greeted me with a model-perfect smile and a chilled rum punch.

Then I caught my reflection in a lobby mirror. Windswept. Dewy. Slightly murderous.

Time to relax. I adjusted my hoops, reapplied lipstick, and turned to face a well-dressed staff member with a printed itinerary and impeccable timing.

Summer had signed off on the partnership, sure—but this event?

This had my name all over it.

My vision. My timeline. My reputation on the line—with Jerrick's smirk stamped all over the fine print. The forum wasn't a casual mixer—it was where billion-dollar accounts shifted hands over cocktails. Resorts, agencies, even private island collectives sent their best to charm the same dozen ultra-high-net-worth clients. Win here, and Wilder wasn't just relevant. We were untouchable.

I couldn't let him finesse his way into controlling the narrative. Not this time. Not when the entire damn industry would be watching us present together on Saturday night.

There it was.

Day One. Jungle Lounge. 4:00 P.M. "Smart resort casual."

Co-host: Jerrick Thorne.

Because of course it was him.

I stared at the name. Bold. Centered. Owning the damn page.

Not *co-presenting*, thank God—that's reserved for Saturday night. Tonight? We're the assembled charm offensive.

I was still glaring at the font when a ripple of laughter drew my attention to the terrace behind me.

There he was.

Smiling, the kind of grin that knew exactly what it could get away with. Tan. Polished. Wearing a soft blue button-down, sleeves pushed up as though he'd been airbrushed into existence. Hair shorter than I remembered, styled with grooming standards and the ego to match. Jaw sharper. Smirk worse.

It should've been nothing. Just another good-looking man in linen. But my stomach dipped anyway, like my body remembered something my brain had politely buried.

And just like that night in Dubai—late pitch prep, not enough distance—I felt it all over again. The slow burn of almost. Dubai had been a perfect storm—city lights too harsh, tequila too reckless, and a rooftop too secluded for good decisions. By midnight, his shirt sleeves were rolled, my heels were dangling, and our shoulders pressed so close the air throbbed between us. He leaned in, I didn't pull back, and for one unbearable second his lips hovered over mine. We didn't cross the line. But I've replayed that almost more times than I'll ever admit.

Jerrick Thorne, in the wild.

Charming the group. Hands in pockets. Laughing like it hadn't been planned. As if he didn't rehearse his charisma in the mirror, Bond-villain style.

I stepped half-left and pretended to scroll my phone.

Don't look again.

I looked again.

His smile hit with all the kick of a double espresso and the heat of a dare. He looked better than the last time I saw him. Unfair. Men weren't supposed to age like private-label bourbon.

I straightened my shoulders, walked into the lobby like I hadn't just had a micro-crisis, and handed my itinerary to the concierge.

"Tell Mr. Thorne I'll see him at four," I said, already turning for the elevator. I wasn't going to combust. I was going to prepare. I was going to own the narrative.

And if that cocky grin slithered into my dreams tonight?

I'd sue him for emotional damages.

My suite was peak indulgence: polished teak floors, a private plunge pool, and bamboo ceiling fans spinning like they were too elegant to care. A fruit platter waited beside a bottle of champagne and a handwritten note with the suspicious cheer of a trap laid in cursive.

Brynn Wilder didn't get upgrades by accident. And if this was a bribe? I was listening.

I stepped inside just ahead of my luggage and let the quiet luxury wash over me—private terrace, hammock, and an open-concept bathroom with a rainfall shower I already knew would wage war on my hair.

I checked the mirror again. Not flawless. Florida humidity hadn't done me any favors. A little shine, a little frizz, a little *God, please let my moisturizer forgive me before someone important sees me.*

"Okay," I said aloud. "You are calm. You are cool. You are a high-functioning professional woman with strategically packed cleavage."

Bali wasn't here to keep me honest, so I kept myself in check, just enough to stay grounded.

I unpacked only the necessities: skincare, backup skincare, SPF 50 thanks to Rayann, and the sapphire silk wrap dress I'd labeled *backup power outfit*, but was clearly about to promote.

Then I pulled out my heels: Athena.

All my heels have names. Strategy, not quirk. Some women carry mace. I bring heels with an agenda. Athena was a pair of gold wedge heels with a low, silent threat. Just enough platform to say yes, I can move in these, and just enough arch to say but not away from you.

Sexy. Stable. Jungle-approved.

The obvious choice for a mixer hosted by a man who thinks humidity is no excuse for bad tailoring. I set them on the bed beside the dress as if we were prepping for a diplomatic ambush.

Then I spotted it. The itinerary. Again.

4:00 PM. Jungle Lounge. Jerrick.

God help me.

I considered ripping it in half—then remembered I needed it for directions. I wasn't above getting lost in a five-star jungle, but I'd rather die than ask him for help.

Air. I needed air.

A quick lap around the resort felt smart—mental reset, emergency exit recon, the usual. Cabanas, koi ponds, vines more filtered than a beauty influencer's feed. It was luxury overload, and I hated how much I wanted to tongue-kiss it.

Then I saw the Jungle Lounge.

Monday. Day One. Executive Icebreaker. Which meant four more days of smiling pretty and pretending not to imagine what his jawline would look like under cross-examination.

The lounge looked like the set of a travel magazine's wet dream. Floating lanterns. Carved wood. Elegant, low-slung seating. Live strings played by a man in all white who looked like he taught philosophy in Milan on Mondays.

It was full of beautiful people who looked like they had never sweat in their lives.

Beautiful. Romantic. Intimidating.

And Jerrick would be co-hosting with me there in under an hour.

My stomach flipped.

Get it together, Brynn. You're the shark here. They're just tourist bait.

Back in my suite, I executed pre-event prep like I was heading into battle.

- Hair: Swept into a casual-sophisticated knot. Polished, but not try-hard. A few pieces left loose—because perfection was suspicious.

- Dress: The sapphire wrap. Fitted. Fluid. The kind that moved like it had secrets. High slit. Neckline that hinted, not announced.

- Shoes: Athena. Obviously.

- Perfume: Two spritzes behind the ears, one for courage. Nothing floral. I was here to conquer, not impress.

- Earrings: Gold, subtle.

- Lipstick: Bold.

I stepped back and looked in the mirror. Head tilted. Jaw set. Eyes sharp. *Okay, Thorne. Let's see who blinks first.*

I grabbed my clutch, tucked a few business cards in the outer pocket as signature weapons, and headed for the door.

I entered the lounge as if it were a runway. Chin high, shoulders back, not a single wobble in my wedges. Athena held strong.

The air smelled of citrus, money, and just enough sex to make the velvet banquettes feel complicit. The live music wasn't background noise—it was orchestrated ambiance, layered into everything, down to the outrageously expensive air. A tray passed, and I snagged a drink with a flamingo-pink flower that would've looked unhinged on anyone else. I wore it like a crown.

The crowd had started to hum—industry elites, artfully disheveled as if they'd been styled by a drunk Vogue intern with a black card, sipping from coupe glasses and laughing like none of them secretly hated each other.

I clocked at least three competitors from last year's luxury travel summit, one fashion CEO, and a wellness exec from a startup called Lüme, specializing in vaginal crystals and "spiritual bio-resets." The Dunes Collective had a rep here too, already whispering to the same panel judge who'd sunk Wilder's Peru bid. And Ferox Experiences—Wilder's loudest, wildest rival—was working the room like it was Vegas. Everyone here wanted blood wrapped in a bow. I wasn't about to bleed first.

Wilder Horizons didn't sell vacations. We built escapes for the kind of people who counted Gulfstreams and private lounges as milestones. My wins weren't likes or ad clicks—they were repeat contracts and whispered referrals. Which made this panel less about a slideshow and more about survival.

Every brand here was chasing the same prize: kingmaker accounts. If a single investor on this panel signed, it meant seven figures in repeat business. Survival of the bougiest.

Then there he was.

Jerrick.

Freshly showered, clearly changed, and wearing a white linen shirt like it had been tailored by the devil and custom-fit to sabotage my last shred of common sense. Collar open. Signature sleeves rolled. Smooth smirk. A presence that brooded quietly and commanded every-thing else.

He turned.

Smiled.

Walked toward me.

Stay cool. Stay sharp. Don't punch him with your eyes.

"Brynn," he said, warm and unworried—like we were old friends, not seasoned rivals who nearly went to war over font hierarchy. "You didn't keep me waiting long."

"I like to leave just enough room for you to panic," I said, sipping. "It builds character."

His grin tugged wider. "You look..." His gaze swept down, then back up—slow enough to scorch. "Danger-ously prepared."

"I like to be remembered," I said, voice light, smile sharper. "Climates change. First impressions don't."

He chuckled.

Not laughed—chuckled.

A low, sinful sound that probably made interns bite their knuckles and spa attendants offer massages and their contact info.

"You've still got it," he said, tilting his head, admi-ration edged with intent—the look of a man already planning to steal the blueprint.

"I never lost it," I said with a sweet smile. "But thanks for noticing."

He leaned in slightly. "You know, you can relax. This isn't a duel."

"Please. If this were a duel, I'd already be holding the weapon."

A passing exec interrupted to shake his hand. I stepped back, using the break to reset my posture and remind myself: I was here for business. Not bloodshed. Not banter. And definitely not bone structure appreciation.

He turned back.

"Can I get you another drink?"

"I'm good," I said, lifting my glass. "But feel free to grab something stronger. You'll need it—after dessert."

His brow lifted, slow and curious. "Dessert?"

I smiled. "Oh, I never skip dessert."

And with that, I walked away like I had better things to do. Not because my knees went soft over a smirk.

Definitely not.

That would've been too easy. Too... honest.

I circled the perimeter, casing the place. Not for security. For exits. Pressure points. People worth engaging—or dodging. I spotted him again mid-laugh with the Dunes Collective rep, head tipped just enough to show off the column of his throat.

Show-off.

He worked a room without trying—let the impression land, then let it linger.

I moved toward the bar. Not to get a drink. Just to regroup. I leaned a hip against the polished wood, tracing the rim of my glass like I didn't care who was watching. I needed a minute to cool the heat under my skin and remind myself that I didn't fly to Costa Rica to be *that girl*—the one who forgets her name when the hot rival gets too close.

But I *knew* who was watching. His presence wrapped around me like heat off a bonfire: dangerous, magnetic, just far enough not to burn.

"Good turnout." Low. Casual. A hint of something unbuttoned beneath the surface.

"I plan well," I said, still not looking.

"I didn't say it was your doing."

"No, but you will. Once you realize this isn't your arena."

He exhaled—half chuckle, half hum.

Finally, he said, "You walked away earlier."

"I did."

"On purpose?"

"Of course. I'm not one to linger once the point's been made."

He sipped that in like it was smoother than the cocktail in his hand. "And the point was?"

I stepped closer. Not touching—just enough to lean into his space and lower my voice a hair.

"That I'm not here to orbit around you."

His eyes flared—just slightly. "Wouldn't dream of it."

"Good," I said, brushing past him. "Keep up."

I didn't wait to see if he followed.

But I knew he would.

And he did.

Three beats later, his voice curled just behind my shoulder. "You always this quick to pull rank?"

"I don't have to," I said without breaking stride. "It's already implied."

He laughed then, quiet and genuine and far too easy. "Careful, Brynn. If I didn't know better, I'd think you missed me."

I turned just enough to flash him a smile. "Then it's a good thing you don't know me at all."

And just like that, I slid back into the crowd, hips swaying, skin buzzing, high on the knowledge that I hadn't just won the moment.

I'd set *the tone*.

Chapter 4

Deck Me, Daddy

MY PHONE VIBRATED THE second I opened one eye. I reached blindly from beneath the covers, swatting at air until my hand smacked something plastic and glowing. Bali wasn't here to glare at me for sleeping past six, which meant no accountability—and three missed notifications from Summer.

The hangover had set up camp behind my left eye and pitched a tequila flag I didn't remember earning. The last thing I remembered was the swish of Athena's heels and me obnoxiously flirting with Jerrick.

I blinked at my phone again.

- 7:02 AM — **SUMMER:** Your calendar invite's been updated. Please review.

- 7:03 AM — **SUMMER:** Reminder: your panel pitch deck is due Friday. You and Thorne need to be aligned by EOD.

- 7:04 AM — **SUMMER:** Call me!

Of course the last one wore a red exclamation point. Summer was the queen of micromanaging microman-agers. I groaned, rolled to my side, and dragged the sheet with me like it could shield me from executive expecta-tions. It could not.

"Aligned by EOD," I muttered. "I haven't even aligned my soul yet."

- 7:10 AM—**ME:** Is that your way of reminding me that failure would reflect poorly on your Q3 board report?

- 7:11 AM—**ME:** I've got it handled. And I love you too.

I sat up slowly—regal in defeat—and opened the at-tachment she'd sent. The panel brief glowed like a chal-lenge. Bold font. Corporate optimism. At least three uses of "collaborative synergy." I immediately wanted to set something on fire.

The event was a joint production—Wilder Horizons and Adventura Luxe, tag-teaming their way through a week of luxury networking, forced-fun excursions, and high-stakes schmoozing in paradise.

The keynote panel? That was the crown jewel. And I was expected to share it—with him.

WILDER HORIZONS x ADVENTURA LUXE Closing Keynote Panel – "The Next Frontier: Redefining Luxury in a Post-Digital Age" *Featuring: Brynn Wilder, Chief Marketing Officer, Wilder Horizons & Jerrick Thorne, Chief Marketing Officer, Adventura Luxe*

Assignment: Together, the panelists will co-present an original concept or collaborative campaign that reimagines the future of high-net-worth client experiences. Must include visual storytelling, competitive innovation, and audience engagement.

Target: Billionaire investors, global media, elite partners

Time Slot: Saturday, 6:00 PM

Location: Main Pavilion

I stared at the screen. Then the ceiling. Then back at the screen. "Oh, hell no," I said aloud. This wasn't a panel. This was homework. With *him*.

Not just a headline and a smirk. This was align-ment—real, strategic, visible. And maybe that scared me more than I wanted to admit.

Not just talking points. Not just *vibe alignment.* A fucking full-blown, billion-dollar Shark Tank pitch. With my name right next to his.

I opened his last email—the one with the subject line that suddenly made too much sense:

Panel Content Framework – Updated Flow Suggestions.

Updated. What-the-Now-Fuck. Flow. Suggestions.

Pause.

How *dare* he.

I scanned his proposed structure. Bullet after bullet of uninspired corporate oatmeal.

Slide 1: Welcome & Brand Positioning

Slide 2: Three Core Drivers of Luxury Evolution

Slide 3: Comparative Innovation Timeline

"Comparative Innovation Timeline"? Is that even a thing? What the stupid fuck does that mean?

Seriously, we used to laugh about that kind of buzz-word bullshit. Somewhere between our second round of mezcal and the third draft of that doomed Dubai pitch.

Back when I almost kissed him.

Shut up, Brynn. Shut. Up.

Slide 4: Joint Value Proposition

Slide 5: Q&A / Engagement Summary

Like a TED Talk had vanilla sex with a Power-Point—and left the condom on the clicker. Perfect for him, perfect for Adventura Luxe: polished, safe, and dead inside.

I dropped my head back and groaned into the pillow like it could muffle my suffering.

"You're really doing this," I muttered to the ceiling. "A real project—a corporate trust fall between two people who should never be left unsupervised."

I swiped to Summer's messages and typed with one eye open.

ME: You're enjoying this, aren't you?

Her reply came in three dots and no delay.

SUMMER: Immensely.

By 8:10 a.m., I was striding toward the infinity pool in a red one-piece—plunging neckline, open.

It wasn't made for laps.

It was made for dominance.

I kicked off my sandals—Karma, the kind of casual that still knew how to make an impression—twisted my hair into a knot that said important but unbothered, and slipped into the water like a swan with a grudge.

I swam laps anyway. I needed movement. Direction. Somewhere to put the fire buzzing under my skin.

The pool was gloriously empty—just me, the breeze, and the simmering rage of being told to collaborate with a man who said *synergy* in a voice that could make you forget your safe word.

The sun still hung low, slicing through the palms in long golden streaks. The water shimmered. The air smelled like ocean breeze tangled with hibiscus, sunscreen, and the faintest whisper of coffee from the breakfast terrace. Everything felt slow here—lazy and luxe. Time ditched its deadlines and curled up in a hammock with a satisfied little sigh.

Lap one: composed.

Lap two: focused.

Lap three: rewriting Jerrick's deck in my head.

Slide 1: Welcome & Brand Positioning → *Hi, we're rich, hot, and spiritually allergic to all-inclusive resorts.*

Slide 2: Three Core Drivers of Luxury Evolution → *Cocktails. Climate guilt. Curated sexy people.*

Slide 3: Shared Vision for Experiential Impact → *Please enjoy this high-dollar fever dream while we pretend to like each other.*

One more lap. Then I flipped onto my back and floated, staring up at the sky as if it held answers—or at least a plausible excuse for this marketing ménage à deux with Mr. Stick-Up-His-Ass.

Fucking backstabber.

But I was already picturing his reaction. The blink he'd try to hide. The way his mouth would twitch as if he wanted to comment—and knew better. Which, for the record, was never a guarantee.

Finally, I planted my palms on the edge and pushed up, lifting myself out as cool water trailed down my spine in a way that felt vaguely indecent. My legs followed—deliberate, strong, built for the spotlight. I ran a hand over my thigh like I was manifesting a GQ ambush, not prepping for a pitch meeting.

The pool was empty, but if Thorne rounded that corner, I wanted him to see vengeance in a one-piece, poised like I'd been born to own the water and the room all at once.

I held the pose for a dramatic three-count. But then my calf cramped, and I turned into a sexy giraffe having a stroke. I dropped the act with a muttered curse, flicked water from my lashes, and tried to shake it off, just in time to *feel* it. That weird, hair-raising sixth sense.

Like I was being watched by someone pompous enough to monologue in a mirror. It felt familiar. That strange hum under my ribs, part instinct, part dread.

My stomach dipped. Not just because he caught me mid—sexy giraffe, but because every time he showed up, I felt that same dangerous hum—the reminder of how easily I'd let him in before, and how thin my armor really was.

I turned.

And—yep. There he was.

Speak of the devil... and poof—here comes the fuckery.

How the hell does he always appear like that? The man moves like a linen-wrapped Houdini—no warning, no sound, just smug apparition. Unnatural. Possibly witchcraft. I should've brought sage.

And holy shit. Did I just physically giraffe-malfunction in public? Did he see that? Of course he saw that. My fucking dignity just ghosted me in broad daylight.

Fresh off a run. Navy athletic shorts slung low. Fitted tee. Abs and arms sculpted like a warning label. Shoulders you could reasonably blame for making bad decisions. Skin glistening in a way that should've been illegal before breakfast. Dark hair damp. Eyes steady. And way too aware.

Not gonna lie—he looked like a man who fucked like he argued. Slow. Sharp. Dead sure he was right.

His gaze dropped fast. Recovered faster. But not fast enough to pretend he hadn't seen the suit. Or the hips. Or the business-class thighs.

His eyes narrowed. One blink, and control snapped back into place.

We stared.

Stomach tight. Brain short-circuited.

Nipples—traitors.

"Uh... see you in an hour?" His voice was low. Throaty. Spent in that disarmingly sexy way.

I nodded. "Sure." Like a normal human. Not at all like a woman one pelvic pulse away from disaster.

And just like that, he walked away—completely unaware he'd detonated my central nervous system.

Jesus, Brynn. You're a grown-ass woman with an international marketing degree, not the lead in a poolside porno. Get it together.

I grabbed Karma and walked as if I wasn't one breath from melting into a puddle of professionally inappropriate fantasies.

This was fine.

I was fine.

Totally normal behavior.

Two CMOs. A billionaire panel.

And mutual undressing before 8:15 AM.

I just needed caffeine, a stronger game face, and a priest.

I got to the rooftop a few minutes early, claimed a table with the best breeze, and ordered coffee strong enough to fix my life choices. By the time he showed, I was calm, caffeinated, and pretending I hadn't just considered exorcism.

Open-air workspace. Jungle backdrop. A carafe of water sweating in the center like it, too, felt the tension.

The table was sun-warmed teak—the kind that made you feel important just by sitting at it, like deals made here were meant to echo.

Laptop open. Iced coffee halfway to extinction.

A fresh doc titled: ***Panel Presentation – Things I Will Not Tolerate (Starting with Him)***

Item one: "Experiential impact" as a phrase.

Because who the fuck comes up with that shit?

Item two: His ever-present, shit-eating grin.

Item three: My reaction to said grin.

I crossed my legs like a woman in control, adjusting the hem of my high-waisted caramel shorts—tailored to intimidate. Paired with a breezy olive tank—just enough to say *effortless,* and just enough to say *I remember that sweaty morning ambush, thanks.* Gold hoops caught the light. My sandals stayed politely under the table, unlike my thoughts.

Then he appeared.

Fresh from whatever devil's grooming ritual he'd perfected, walking like the air bent to let him pass. Slate gray tee, fitted like sin—as if he'd dressed down for war but couldn't help turning it into theater. Black joggers clinging in all the right places. A dark watch. Darker scruff. And not a single sign he was bothered by heat, deadlines, or the woman actively plotting his downfall via bullet points and passive-aggressive caffeine sips.

He dropped a leather journal and a neatly clipped packet on the table between us.

A leather journal? Adorable. What was this—stationery kink?

Not even a flicker of recognition for the one-piece ambush. Professional. Ruthless. Possibly broken.

He slid a coaster under the wobbly table leg; the shim settled the shake I hadn't admitted was driving me insane. A small angle on the umbrella, a narrow twist of my laptop—five degrees left—so the palm frond in the background didn't sprout from my skull. A slim USB-C charger appeared at my elbow. "You're at thirty percent," he said, tapping the battery icon without touching me. "Power drop in ten. This saves the scramble."

Not a glance at me, but a precise sort of caretaking that betrayed habit. He wasn't just neat. He noticed everything. He always had.

He squared the chair to the table, clipped the packet so it wouldn't kite in the breeze, and nudged my glass an inch off the trackpad. "You'll thank me when the videographer decides we're B-roll," he added, eyes still on the setup. Logistics masquerading as neatness. Care, disguised.

"Print deck," he said. "Updated with a few refinements."

I looked at it.

Same soul-sucking structure as before.

Welcome—blah.

Joint value—double blah.

Q&A—kill me now.

He waited like I might burst into applause. I took a long, pointed sip of coffee, just to give my eyeballs time to roll. "I like that you still think 'timeline' is foreplay," I said.

"I like that you still pretend sarcasm is strategy."

We smiled at each other like diplomats who'd signed a ceasefire but sharpened their knives anyway.

"I brought some concepts too," I said, flipping my screen toward him. "They include a real story arc, emotional stakes, and absolutely zero PowerPoint sex crimes."

He leaned in, scanning the slides as if he wasn't mentally rewriting every slide out of spite.

Slide 1: The Psychology of Escape

Slide 2: Risk, Reward, and the Billionaire Brain

Slide 3: Desire, Delivered

He tilted his head. "You think 'Desire, Delivered' is strong enough to stand on its own?"

I blinked, because apparently we were critiquing genius now. "It's punchy."

"It's vague." His brow furrowed, a quiet tell only someone paying attention would see. It read more like concentration than criticism, his brain already reworking it behind his eyes.

I waved him off. "It's aspirational. Billionaires eat that shit up."

Fine. Maybe I'd workshop that one. Later. If I felt like it.

Slide 4: Fantasy, Curated

Slide 5: Why You'll Never Vacation the Same Way Again

His eyebrow twitched. "Bold."

"That's the point."

"It's also... provocative," he murmured, eyes narrowing, surprise flickering into interest.

"Exactly," I said. "And guess what media loves? A hook. A narrative. And maybe, if we're lucky, just enough tension between co-hosts to make it interesting."

His eyes lifted to mine. "You planning to weaponize our dynamic?"

I smiled. "I already am."

His gaze lingered a beat too long. Then he leaned back—arms folding with an ease that made me want to set something on fire.

"You always do this," he said.

I raised an eyebrow. "Be right?"

"Push boundaries. Make it theatrical. Say the things no one else says in a pitch room."

"That's what makes it land."

"It's risky," he said, eyes sharp. "It either hits hard, or it makes half the room uncomfortable."

"Good," I said. "Comfort never closed a deal."

He studied me, torn between argument, curiosity, and something far more dangerous.

"Do you ever wonder what would happen if you just... followed the formula?" he asked.

I tilted my head. "You mean your formula?"

"It works."

"It's safe."

He didn't blink. "And yours is a storm in heels."

I smiled. "Forecasted storm. High impact, limited warning."

He exhaled through his nose, the way a man does when handed a ticking bomb wearing lipstick.

Then, quieter—less polished.

"You know I've watched you pitch. Many times. You talk like you're telling a secret you shouldn't share."

"Because I am," I said. "That's the sell. That's the trick. Say it like it hurts, like it bleeds a little. Make it cost something. And they believe you—because part of you does."

He tapped a finger against the edge of my laptop. "I used to think you did it for the reaction. For the flash."

I raised an eyebrow. "And now?"

He smiled, the slow curve of someone who knew I'd underestimated him. "You cast it like a spell," he said. "Make the room lean in before they realize you've already won them."

I didn't answer. Mostly because I was busy pretending to be unbothered. I wasn't sure if he'd meant it as a compliment, a warning, or something worse—something that felt too close to understanding me.

And partly because—ugh, fine—the bastard wasn't wrong.

Which was rude.

He leaned back, elbows resting, completely at ease after dropping a verbal knife into my lap.

"Thing is," he continued, "you play like you've got nothing to lose. That's dangerous."

"To you?"

"To everyone else." He didn't blink. "But especially to someone who plays by the rules."

"So rewrite the rules."

He tilted his head. "Tempting. But I still play to win."

I leaned in, just slightly. "Then maybe it's time you followed my lead."

He didn't move. Didn't smirk. Just stared, memorizing me in real time. Then he reached for his packet, flipped the top page, and scribbled something onto Slide 2. "Let's see how the boardroom reacts to performance art," he said. "We'll try your version."

I blinked. "Who are you and what have you done with Jerrick Thorne?"

"Convince me. Right here. Right now."

"I hope you brought a pen, Thorne. Because I'm about to write your lines for you."

Chapter 5

Foreplay In Five Slides

I TILTED MY HEAD with a smile that wasn't even trying to be sweet. The kind that promised I'd ruin him—and enjoy every goddamn second.

"Slide one." I clicked through on my laptop. "The Psychology of Escape. We lead with desire, not demographics. Want inside their wallets? Start with their heads."

He arched a brow. "Risky start."

Then he jotted something in his journal—messy, hurried scribbles that read more serial-killer manifesto than CMO notes.

Huh. Who knew Mr. Precision had the handwriting of a caffeinated raccoon.

I kept going.

"Slide two. Risk, Reward, and the Billionaire Brain. These clients don't crave safety. They want stories that start with danger and end in exclusivity. Look at every brand they worship—there's always an edge."

"An edge isn't the same as a liability."

I leaned in, dropped my voice. "The only real liability?" 'Being forgettable.'"

He didn't blink, but I caught it—a shift in his jaw. Fingers curled, holding something back.

I clicked forward.

"Since you love frameworks," I said, tapping a key, "here's one you'll appreciate." A decoy slide flashed: **Slide 2B — Comparative Innovation Timeline (Now With 37% More Beige)**—khaki gradient, stock chinos, the works.

He huffed—half laugh, half warning. "Cute. Delete it before it scars me."

"Oh, it's staying," I said, smiling. "For morale." I killed the joke slide and snatched his printout. "Your 'Three Core Drivers' read like a panel syllabus. Try this."

I crossed out his bullets and wrote in thick black strokes, just like Dubai—me scrawling on his neat pages, him pretending to hate it while his pen kept circling back to my words:

Access — *doors money can't usually open* (after-hours ruins, unlisted runway, keys that don't exist)

Alibi — *make danger feel insured* (carbon offsets, medic on silent standby, security disguised as service)

Awe — *myth on command* (signature ritual, leave-behind artifact, legend that survives the NDA)

He went still, underlined Awe, then paused long enough to lock it away. "Access, Alibi, Awe," he said, low and certain. "That actually lands."

"You can take the credit," I said, handing the page back. "Consider it community service."

"Credit where it belongs," he said, already stitching my words into his outline—pen moving fast, precise, unshowy. That wasn't new. He'd said the same thing in Morocco, handing me the mic at the eleventh hour. Only this time, it landed differently. He meant it.

He flipped the page to face me, margins suddenly clean. "No sandbagging on stage."

"No gotchas," I agreed, and we were—briefly—on the same team.

"Slide three. Desire, Delivered. Not a vacation—a fantasy under NDA. Access without consequence. Gratification with turndown service."

He coughed. Or maybe choked. Hard to tell.

"Slide four. Fantasy, Tailored. We sell seduction with structure—personalized, exclusive, barely out of reach. Think Versailles in the jungle. Private chefs. Hidden beaches. Orgasms and offshore accounts."

He choked. For real this time.

"That's... blunt."

"It's honest. They're not buying a schedule. They're buying a feeling—worshipped and untouchable."

I clicked to the final slide.

"Slide five. Why You'll Never Vacation the Same Way Again. That's not a tagline—it's us. We don't just sell the dream. We *are* the dream. You and me."

I let the silence stretch.

He watched me like I'd sprouted horns. Or wings. Maybe both.

"I'll admit it," he said finally, voice low and rough. "You're not wrong."

I smiled. All teeth. All intention.

"Oh, honey." I closed the laptop with a clean snap. "I'm never wrong. Just ahead of schedule."

He didn't move.

Didn't speak.

He just stared, eyes flicking between a fight and something far less professional. Then he nodded, straightened, and forced his expression back into order. He leaned in, elbows braced, voice lower now. Controlled. Careful. "'Alright,' he said, slow." "Let's say you're the fantasy. The pull. The promise."

That was new. No sparring. No smirk. Just... surrender?

It shouldn't have thrown me. But it did—he dropped the rope mid-tug and I was still pulling against air. Not since that night in Dubai, when the words turned slow and soft, and he looked at me like I was something more than an adversary.

I'd buried that stare.

Until now.

I didn't answer. Just watched him—heart thudding louder than any rooftop should allow in the daylight.

His gaze dropped to my lips, climbed back up—and stayed there. No smile. Just heat. "Then what does that make me?"

And damn it, I wanted to answer.

With sincerity.

Which was horrifying. And absolutely not on the damn agenda. I opened my mouth—no clue what was about to come out—when the rooftop door swung open.

A cheerful voice shattered the tension, too perky for the emotional landmine it landed in. "There you are! Oh—"

We turned—slowly, as if yanked out of something dangerous and weren't sure it hadn't followed us.

Conference director. Forties maybe. Blazer. iPad. Frozen mid-step, eyes wide. Her look flicked between Jerrick's jaw and my flushed face, clearly debating whether to offer a fan, a high five, or a cold shower.

Her eyebrows did something wildly unprofessional. "Oh," she breathed. "Didn't realize you two were in the middle of... something."

Jerrick beat me to it—calm, dry, absolutely evil. "We were. She was selling me orgasms and offshore accounts."

I didn't blink. Just flipped my hair like it was my final word and dared her to say something. "And he was about to buy the whole damn package."

The woman made a sound—half gasp, half laugh—and spun so fast her clipboard nearly took flight. "Okay! I'll, um—yeah. I'll come back in ten!"

She vanished like smoke.

Silence.

We stared.

Then, simultaneously—

"Professional setting," I muttered.

"Totally appropriate," he said.

And then we both lost it. Full-blown, unhinged, face-cramping hysterics.

I doubled over and smacked the table. He leaned back too fast and nearly tipped his chair.

I wheezed.

He swore under his breath—'Fuck'—and immediately froze, like the word had just escaped without clearance.

Our eyes met. My mouth dropped open. "Did you just—"

He looked horrified. "I don't know where that came from."

Which only made me cackle harder. "You swore," I gasped. "You never swear. Oh my god, are you broken?"

His smile cracked wide. "You're broken."

"I've always been broken. That's not news."

He shook his head, grinning now. "You're contagious."

We both looked away—too aware, too flushed, too much. Silence ballooned between us. A full, mortifying minute.

"I need a Bloody Mary," I muttered. "Lunch is at the pool." I grabbed my bag and bolted—pulse pounding like I hadn't just sold this man sex and financial fraud in one breath and nearly passed out from the way he looked at me.

"Try not to look too humble," he called after me.

I didn't trust my mouth not to betray me.

Didn't trust myself to look back, either.

After a quick change into my reasonably professional bikini—if that's even a thing—and a flowy coverup, I made my way to the poolside gathering.

The infinity pool sparkled like a luxury thirst trap, tables lined with shaded cabanas and palm fronds, the buffet curated by someone with both a coconut fetish and a Michelin star. Even the shade had swagger. This wasn't a party. It was an aesthetic—curated sweat, intentional casual, vacation couture.

Guests drifted through in chic swimwear and linen that said *I yacht on weekends, bitch*. Laughter bounced off stone walkways. Every cocktail came in coral or turquoise. A steel drum band played something vaguely tropical—evocative enough to make everyone feel approximately 63% more relaxed and 12% hotter.

I claimed a high-top near the pool's edge and surveyed the buffet: ceviche, grilled pineapple skewers, lobster tacos, and a watermelon salad that whispered, *this is healthy, but also sexy*.

I filled a plate. Grabbed a drink with a flower in it. And absolutely did *not* look for Jerrick.

Did. Not. Look.

Until he appeared—sliding a mango mojito off the tray like it was a special order.

Black linen shirt. Those stupid, sexy rolled sleeves—like he knew I couldn't stop staring.

Am I seriously losing my shit over a sleeve kink now?

Swim trunks. Aviators. Flip flops—for some godforsaken reason. Strategic casual, not casual at all. Every thread screaming: *I wake up sexy and quarterly reports still fear me*.

Drink in one hand. A grin that said he'd either closed a billion-dollar deal in the past thirty minutes or just rearranged someone's spine against the mop sink.

Possibly both.

He dropped into the seat beside me—uninvited, obviously assuming our little rooftop giggle fit made us friends now. I gave him the kind of smile that said *we're not doing this again*—tight-lipped, civil, and about as warm as a conference room bagel.

He clocked it, though. The shift. Sat a beat longer than usual. Then he leaned back, thigh brushing mine, casual as ever. "What's going on, Brynn?"

I didn't answer right away. Just sipped my drink and watched the pool shimmer, a mirror full of truths I refused to name.

His voice dipped. Less smug now. "We were good up there. Felt like we were finally getting somewhere."

I didn't look at him. Couldn't.

"We agreed on the pitch," he said, quieter still. "So why do I get the feeling you're pissed at me again?"

God, that made it worse. He wasn't wrong. Because he'd shown me something real—and instead of leaning in, I was already halfway out the door. Right back into the comfort zone where Jerrick Thorne was the villain...

And I didn't have to feel a damn thing.

"You know what?" I smiled and stood—slow, wicked. Dangerous. "You're right."

He blinked as he stood too, wary now. "Wait—what?"

"It felt good," I purred, saccharine enough to rot teeth, "to see the human side of you." And then I shoved him. Hard. Both hands, straight to the chest. Jerrick Thorne—CMO, walking contradiction, and the one person who still knew how to throw my balance—toppled backward and crashed into the pool.

The splash was *majestic*. Mythic. Like a merman slap from the gods.

Gasps. Laughter. Someone definitely clapped.

And for one stupid, sparkly second, I wasn't even mad.

I was weightless. Like the universe had winked and handed me a win I didn't have to earn.

He surfaced, slicked his hair back, and smiled up at me like I'd handed him a love letter—not an assault.

Then he lunged.

"Don't you da—"

Too late.

His hands clamped around my waist. My cocktail launched skyward.

And in I went.

Fully submerged. Fully done. By the time I came up, sputtering mascara and lost earrings, he was already laughing like I'd just gifted him the win.

"You *pulled* me in!" I shrieked.

"You *pushed* me first!"

"That doesn't count!"

I lunged for him, fully prepared to dunk his smug, soaking face into next week. But he caught me—hands closing around my waist, steady and solid in the water.

Everything went still.

For half a second, there was no pool, no fight, no noise—just the press of his fingers and the pulse that jumped straight to my throat.

His grin faded, slow and knowing. Mine did too.

Dangerous territory.

Too much. Too close. And definitely too many people watching.

I splashed him in the face. "Easy, Thorne. We start making waves like that and HR's gonna need a snorkel."

Laughter rippled from somewhere behind me. He didn't let go. Not right away.

We were soaked. Ridiculous. And I was far too aware of how his shirt clung to those abs—like it had been painted on. Water streamed down his chest in smug little rivulets.

Oh sweet Jesus, Zeus, and every horny god above—do not let me orgasm in this pool.

It was infuriating—how quickly he could strip away my armor with nothing but proximity and waterlogged abs. Someone handed me a fresh cocktail from the edge. I drank it like it was vengeance in a glass.

"Truce?" he asked.

"I'm actively debating murder."

"You look good wet."

"Truce expired."

Chapter 6

Don't Touch the F*cking Frogs

B Y 7:05 PM, THE jungle buzzed with heat, torch-light, and the unmistakable sound of egos getting tipsy.

The Rainforest Connection Dinner was technically on-property, but it didn't feel that way. Between the woven lanterns, flickering fire pits, and citrusy citronella fighting for its life, it felt like we'd been airlifted into an upscale nature documentary. One where the predators wore wrinkle-free cotton and flirted as if it was a contact sport.

Long tables sat beneath canvas canopies draped in gauze and fairy lights. Ferns spilled from woven planters. A speaker played something Latin-leaning and shamelessly slow. A waiter handed me a drink with rum, mango, and either cinnamon or sin. I wasn't sure.

I took it anyway.

"Place cards?" I muttered, scanning the setup.

"Color-coded," said a staffer with a clipboard and an overachiever's smile. "Seating's randomized for team-building."

Of course it was.

I found my spot—dead center, directly across from Thorne.

Oh. For. Fuck's. Sake.

He was already there, tan forearms on the table, drink in hand, that infuriating smirk curled as if he'd conjured the ambiance himself. Dark green shirt, sleeves rolled—of course.

God forbid Jerrick Thorne just wear a goddamn short-sleeved shirt like a normal emotionally available human man.

Nooo. He had to roll them up—carefully, deliberately, forearms on full display, veins popping as if they had a personal brand deal.

And then those pants.

Snap the fuck out of it, Brynn. Mind. Gutter. Out.

Lightweight, sand-colored pants slung low on his hips. Leather belt.

Barely damp hair. No tension. No guilt. Not even a mosquito bite.

Wish I could bottle that level of audacity and fucking drown him in it.

But I looked damn good too. High-waisted linen trousers in sun-kissed coral—tailored, tapered at the ankle, cut to hug just enough curve to short-circuit Jerrick's brain.

Fitted black tank, square neckline, ribbed fabric. Thin straps. No bra—because the gods invented double-stick tape and the power of suggestion.

Gold layered necklaces caught the string lights with every subtle shift.

Minimal makeup—dewy, glowing. Lip gloss called "Collateral Lust."

Hair down. Loose, air-dried waves with just a touch of sea salt spray, as if I hadn't spent fifteen minutes perfecting the *undone* look.

Strappy brown leather sandals, casually luxe, with a gold anklet peeking out—because yes, that was intentional.

A gauzy white wrap slung over one shoulder, there solely to slide off when the air got thick.

"Evening, Wilder," he said, raising his glass in mock salute.

What I wouldn't give to peel all that off and put those smug muscles to better use. God, that smirk. That hair. That shirt—oh, for fuck's sake, Brynn.

Wanting him was the worst betrayal—of my brain, of my ambition, of every late night I'd sworn I'd never be that girl again.

"I would've kept walking," I muttered, sliding into my seat, "but the rum's free."

Other execs started filing in—meaning I had about seven minutes and thirty-two seconds before someone pulled out a conch shell and demanded feelings.

"I assume you've forgiven me for pulling you into the pool," he said.

"Forgiven you?" I sipped. "I'm still drafting my retaliation strategy. It involves a blow dart and plausible deniability."

He grinned. "Still thinking about it, though."

"You're not that memorable, Thorne."

His eyes flicked to my lips. "Could've fooled me."

First *zap* of the evening. And not from the bug zappers.

Just then, one of the activity hosts—a twenty-something team-building bruh in cargo shorts and a headset—called the table to attention. He clapped twice. "Fun fact," he announced, grinning as though he'd personally discovered wildlife, "a three-toed sloth was spotted on the trail this morning."

Everyone nodded like this was profound. I couldn't help myself. "Finally, someone I identify with. Slow, slightly disheveled, clings to trees for survival? Relatable."

Jerrick snorted, shaking his head, but the corner of his mouth betrayed him.

Tonight's post-dinner agenda: a rousing jungle-themed trivia game with "interactive elements." His tone said "fun and playful." His eyes said, "Please clap. I need this."

Jerrick leaned in as the host passed out hand-carved trivia tokens and brass clickers that belonged in a colonial museum. "I hope your memory's sharp," he said.

I smirked. "I hope yours is short."

He chuckled low. "You're going down."

"Already did," I muttered into my drink. "Right into the pool, if I recall."

He grinned.

I didn't.

The trivia started out all cutesy.

The first few rounds were easy. Tropical animal facts. Island geography. Something about cacao beans and mating rituals that made the British guy from accounting go pink to the ears.

Then someone brought out a tray of tequila shots—*thank the fuck God*—and that's when team-building went feral.

"Round three," announced the host, sweating in a way that suggested deep regret for every career choice that brought him here. "Truth or Dare: Executive Edition."

Groans. Awkward laughs. A few half-hearted claps. Then—like magic—a new round of shots.

My card buzzed first. The host lit up as though he'd just been handed a bonus check.

"Miss Wilder! Truth or dare?"

I narrowed my eyes. "Truth."

He grinned like I'd just walked into a trap he built himself.

"Name one person here you'd never want to be stranded in the jungle with."

Easy. Obvious. Practically baited.

I turned slowly toward Jerrick. "I'd say Thorne—but we all know he'd build a shelter, collect rainwater, and talk about scalable luxury solutions until I begged a jaguar to eat me."

Laughter rolled across the table.

He just smiled—lazy, lethal, and storing that comment like ammo.

The game circled the table, dropping secrets I mentally filed for future leverage.

"Your turn, Thorne," the host said, practically vibrating with glee.

"Truth," he said, eyes locked on mine.

The host scanned his card. "Have you ever stolen an idea and passed it off as your own?"

The whole table let out a collective *oof*.

I froze.

He didn't look away.

"Once," he said, voice low and steady. "It was a pitch I couldn't shake. Stuck in my head. Kept me up at night. The kind that worms under your skin and makes you wish it had been yours first."

My stomach bottomed out.

"Did it work?" someone asked.

He paused. "It landed," he said. "But it wasn't mine to land."

The way he said it, steady and unapologetic, made me wonder what it had cost him to admit that out loud.

The table went quiet.

My pulse didn't. My brain didn't.

But my mouth? Still fully operational.

"Sounds like guilt," I said sweetly. "Wrapped in a confession with zero consequences."

He smiled. "Not guilt. Respect."

Someone at the far end let out a low "damn," and I caught the British guy watching us like it was better than Netflix. The whole table smelled blood in the water, and we'd just fed them chum.

I laughed—low, bitter. "You're plagiarizing my ideas *respectfully* now?"

A fork clinked against a plate. Someone let out a low whistle. Even the frogs shut up.

The host, blissfully oblivious to the emotional war zone at Table 3, clapped again. "Round Four: Mutual Dares! Each pair gets a prompt. Complete it or drink!"

Of course we were paired. It was Dubai all over again—fate or sabotage, hard to tell the difference. The universe had a sick sense of humor when it came to seating charts and stolen work.

Fucking obviously.

Our card: *Slow-dance for one minute. Make it convincing.*

My jaw clicked so hard it echoed in my skull. "Nope." I reached for the tequila like it was a lifeline.

Jerrick caught my wrist before I could toss it back. His grip was featherlight. Barely there—yet I felt it everywhere. "Afraid you'll enjoy it?"

"Afraid I'll impale you with my drink umbrella."

"Try me."

The music shifted. Soft percussion. A sultry bassline. The kind of sound that made dresses feel shorter and corporate ethics feel like a kink.

Someone counted us in.

I stepped into him like I was stepping onto a battlefield—with no armor and questionable instincts.

His hand found the small of my back. Warm. Steady. Professional.

Too professional.

His other hand found mine.

We moved—slow and infuriatingly in sync.

Our bodies didn't touch. Not quite.

But *almost* was worse.

Almost let me feel the heat of his chest.

Almost made me sway closer than I should've.

Almost dragged out a memory I'd buried so deep it still smelled like Dubai spice and sandalwood aftershave.

"This is your fault," I muttered.

"Dancing?" he murmured.

"Existing."

A beat. Heavy; the hairs at my nape lifted.

He leaned in, voice a low whisper against my ear. "You smell like jasmine—dangerous."

I didn't answer. Didn't breathe.

He kept going. "If you're trying to kill me, it's working."

"Good."

Another step. A slow spin.

Our faces—too close now.

"Why didn't you call me out?" he asked, voice barely there. "Back then."

"Because I wasn't about to give you the satisfaction," I whispered.

His hand tightened—barely. "You should've said something."

"You should've known."

Then—mercifully—the song ended.

Scattered applause. One exec actually wolf-whistled. Another muttered, "chemistry," under his breath. They thought it was entertainment. They didn't see the wreckage it left in me.

Lights sparkled. Heat pressed in. And I walked off like I hadn't just slow-danced with the one man on this godforsaken continent I'd happily toss into a volcano—without sunscreen.

I beelined for the open-air bar, because the only thing worse than feelings was having them while sober.

Guests trickled toward their bungalows, tipsy and laughing, already plotting their afterparties. A few disappeared onto private patios and into plunge pools—maybe for a nightcap, maybe to see if jungle sex counts as character growth.

Not me.

I needed ice.

I needed more tequila.

And I needed to be alone with my agitation, my hormones, and whatever the hell *that* dance was.

The fire pit flickered at the edge of the site, embers glowed; the universe had its nerve endings exposed. String lights draped overhead. Somewhere in the trees, a speaker pulsed soft jungle drums. The air smelled like lime, smoke, and something primal.

And of course, he was already there.

Jesus Christ.

Lounging on a carved wooden bench like a panther at peace with its sins. Drink in hand. Eyes locked on me.

"You're stalking me again," I said.

He didn't flinch. "You're predictable."

"I'm volatile."

He sipped. "That too."

I poured a double shot of whatever was closest and dropped into the seat across from him. Not next to him. That would've been fatal.

For someone.

Maybe him.

Probably me.

"You always flirt like it's a full-contact sport?"

"You always get homicidal when you're turned on?"

I choked on my drink. "Excuse me?"

"You heard me."

The flames cracked. Somewhere in the trees, a frog croaked, and I felt that shit in my soul.

I recalled Emme's comment. Don't touch the frogs, Brynn. Don't even look at the fucking frogs.

Pretty sure she meant Jerrick.

"You're seriously sitting there in those tropical fuck-boy slacks with the audacity to—"

"You pushed me into a pool, Wilder. What'd you think that meant?"

"That I hate you."

He grinned. "You hate me with a suspicious amount of thigh contact for someone so morally opposed."

I wanted to throw a coconut at him.

"I don't flirt with men who steal my ideas. Or my thunder."

"And yet you danced with one."

"That was a dare."

"That was a preview."

The air shifted. The fire wasn't the only thing burning.

He leaned in, elbows on knees, gaze locked.

"What's the real reason you didn't say anything back then?"

The question hit—heat lightning.

"You mean when you 'landed' a pitch I spent three months perfecting?"

"Yeah. That."

I stared into the fire. Because saying why it cut so deep meant admitting I gave a shit. And God help me, I'd given too many shits back then. About him. About the way he made me think we were a team—until he walked away with the credit. Enough to lose sleep. About the work. About—

I stopped.

"About me?" he finished.

I didn't answer.

He reached out, fingertips grazing the rim of my cup. Not my skin, but too close. Way too close.

"Tell me," he said, low and lethal, "you haven't thought about that night in Dubai."

"No."

"Liar."

I met his eyes, and it was a car crash of want and war.

"That night meant nothing," I lied. "An almost-kiss."

Except it hadn't been nothing. It had been everything I didn't have words for—the rush, the risk, the raw edge of maybe.

"Funny," he said, eyes dragging over me like déjà vu. "I still remember the color of your dress."

"You remember everything, don't you?"

"Especially the parts I shouldn't."

He leaned in—close enough to count the flecks of silver in his gray eyes. Close enough to feel the hum under my skin.

"You want me to kiss you."

"I want to knock out your teeth."

"Same thing, the way you do it."

The silence stretched.

Neither of us breathed.

And then—because we're idiots—he reached for my face.

Not to touch. Not quite, but the space between us was molten.

Just close enough to feel the heat of it. The edge of maybe.

My lips parted.

But he didn't close the gap.

Thank God.

Because I would've let him.

He leaned back slowly, sipping while my pulse exploded in protest.

I sat frozen—lips parted, throat tight—a starry-eyed idiot caught mid-fantasy.

Bastard.

What was this—some kind of mind-fuck game? Come close, pull back, watch me unravel?

Because it worked.

And fuck me sideways, I wanted him to finish it.

I wanted his mouth on mine. His hands in my hair. His stupid body pressed to every inch of me until I forgot every reason I should hate him.

I *wanted* the man who stole my work and never once looked back.

Wanted him to kiss me as if he had a right to it.

And I hated that.

Hated him.

Hated me more.

For still aching. Still hoping.

For not knowing if he backed off because he respected me—or because I never meant that much.

Then he stood.

"You coming, Wilder?"

I blinked. "Where?"

He smirked. "To bed."

"You're sleeping alone, Thorne."

"I meant back to your room."

"Sure you did."

"Sleep tight," he said. "You'll need it for tomorrow."

I watched him walk away, furious, feral, and painfully aware of every inch of him.

Arrogant prick.

I sat there a long time.

Burning. In every way that mattered.

Chapter 7

This Is Why I Don't Hike

AFTER LAST NIGHT'S NOT-A-DATE, not-a-dare, not-a-damn-chance kiss, I needed a lobotomy. Or a one-way flight. Or a cold plunge in a pool of denial.

Instead, I got a front-row seat to hell in a harness.

"Jungle zipline excursion," the itinerary said, as if that was a normal follow-up to a night filled with too many drinks, too much tension, and exactly zero orgasms.

For me.

What to Bring/Wear:

Lightweight, moisture-wicking clothing
Hiking shoes
Bug spray

Sunscreen

Positive attitude

What I Actually Brought:

A reinforced sports bra engineered by NASA

My steel-toed hiking boots, Helga, who once kicked a Jeep door clean off its hinges (allegedly)

Bug spray, a.k.a. *Back Off, Winged Satan*

SPF 70, because radiance isn't an accident.

Sarcasm. Obviously.

"Great for optics," Summer had said, as if that settled it. "Bonding in nature. Cameras love it."

Good for her. I drafted my will on a banana leaf, wearing a helmet, a harness, and enough monkey gear to guarantee I'd die looking less 'adventure chic' and more tactical piñata.

And then there was Jerrick. Clipped in. Whatever. I didn't give a single horny squirrel fart what outdoorsy thirst-trap outfit he had on today. I was too busy imagining my obituary to drool over his weapons-grade thighs.

And me? I may've looked like a crash test dummy—strapped in, overthinking, sweating through it—but still technically hot. Probably. Not that it mattered. Except, of course, it did. Because suddenly I was thirteen again with a crush on a boy who didn't play fair—and I was reacting to him with all the maturity of a wine-soaked houseplant.

The jungle buzzed with life. Hissing cicadas. Distant birds. A thousand shades of green closing in like nature was trying to cop a feel. Somewhere overhead, howler monkeys screamed their opinions at the sky—loud, guttural, and deeply unbothered by social norms.

They sounded feral.

Yeah. Welcome to my world, monkey.

"Ready, Wilder?" Jerrick called, already clipped into the first line as if he'd just had his way with the rainforest and come back for seconds.

Perfect. Just what I needed—a mental screensaver from hell.

"I'm fine," I snapped, even as the guide adjusted my helmet with a little too much pity.

He smirked. "You sure? You look a little... twitchy."

"I'm plotting your death. That's all."

He laughed—actually laughed—and then launched himself into the abyss with a zip and a whoop that could've been sponsored by REI's after-dark division.

God, I hated him.

And maybe also wanted to lick his stupid neck.

My knees wobbled like drunk flamingos as I launched myself off the edge. Wind tore past. Trees blurred. The zipline screeched with the rage of a banshee on espresso.

By the time I slammed into the next platform—dignity questionable, soul partially detached—Jerrick was already there. Helmet off. Hair damp. Grinning like the wet nightmare of a man I still hadn't figured out how to hate properly.

"See?" he said, all pompous satisfaction. "Told you—easy."

"You say that like you aren't one harness failure from a closed-casket memorial."

He reached over and adjusted my helmet, fingers brushing my cheek, then checked my clip—as if I hadn't already been cleared by the guide.

We moved as a group, guides calling instructions while a handful of VIPs ahead of us shrieked and snapped selfies as if this were a jungle rollercoaster, not a death trap strung together with glorified coat hangers. The lead guide—tall, wiry, with a scar disappearing into his beard—tapped the cable twice before each launch, like a ritual.

But it was him I kept feeling. At my back. At my side. Always too goddamn close.

All heat and homicide vibes, a divine punishment wrapped in abs and a smirk.

Worst of all? He never stopped watching.

Near the end of the course, the drizzle started—light at first, just enough to make the platform slick and my patience thinner.

"Storm's rolling in fast," one of the guides warned. "We'll pause at the next platform."

By the time we crossed, it wasn't a drizzle. It was a full-blown rainforest baptism. Fat drops. Zero visibility. God's own pressure washer set to *repent, bitch*. The air smelled sharp with ozone, green with crushed leaves, the jungle exhaling straight into my lungs.

Okay, fine—I was bitchy. Nature escalated. Message received. Loud and crystal damn clear.

We climbed down the platform and trudged toward the lean-to ahead.

Then—

The wind kicked. Leaves snapped and shivered. Behind us, a crack split the air—sharp and all kinds of wrong.

Not thunder.

Oh fuck. Definitely. Not. Thunder.

I turned just in time to catch Jerrick's eyes locking on mine. And just like that—

Everything went sideways.

A deafening snap. A whoosh of air. A flash of movement.

Followed by *impact*.

Jerrick slammed me to the ground, one arm locked at my waist, the other thrown out to shield us from whatever the hell just hit.

We hit the mud hard. Knees. Elbows. Ribs.

We skidded through it, cartoon idiots on a banana peel.

A massive branch crashed down where I'd just been standing. Splinters. Leaves. The smell of raw, broken wood.

My ears rang.

My heart thrashed.

And Jerrick?

Still on top of me.

Still holding me.

Still breathing as if the jungle had personally filed a hit.

Overhead, a sloth blinked down at me from its branch, slow as sin, like it was unimpressed I hadn't managed to hang on better. Even the wildlife was judging me.

"You okay?" he said, voice low and steady against the chaos still echoing around us.

I blinked up at him, rain dripping off my lashes, breath caught somewhere between a scream and a whimper.

"I—yeah. I think so."

He didn't move.

Didn't flinch.

Didn't crack a joke.

Just stayed where he was, every inch of him broadcasting "don't move" and "try me" at the same time.

My fingers curled instinctively into the fabric of his shirt, slick and clinging to the muscle beneath it.

"You dove," I said, barely above a whisper. "Like—actually dove. In front of me."

His steady gaze held mine. "You were standing where that thing wanted to land. I moved. That's all."

"That's not all," I murmured. For one raw second, I hated how safe I felt. How much I wanted to stay there.

A beat passed. The rain poured on.

"Next time," I said, trying to claw back some dignity, "just yell *duck* like a normal person."

A hint of a smile tugged at the corner of his mouth. "Didn't think you'd listen."

Fair enough.

My heart was still throwing elbows. My pulse had migrated to somewhere between my thighs and my sanity. Everything was wet, muddy, and borderline traumatic—

And yet.

There was something solid in the way he held me.

Which felt like a problem for later.

Much later.

Preferably with tequila. *Again.* And maybe a sanity check-in with Rayann.

A voice crackled through a walkie nearby. One of the guides—probably the one at the rear—sounded breathless but calm. "Rest shelter's just ahead. We're regrouping there."

Right. Other people existed. The world was still turning.

Damn shame.

The rain pelted harder. I heard shouts—somewhere up the trail, a few voices were already rushing back toward us. Jerrick finally shifted, still braced above me, careful in a way that didn't match the chaos. Like I was breakable.

Which was funny, considering I'd been forged in zingers and snark.

"Can you stand?" he asked, voice low but steady.

"I think so."

Total lie. My ankle barked the second I shifted. I winced—didn't mean to, but it slipped out.

His jaw ticked. "Hold on."

He crouched without waiting, one arm wrapping under my shoulders, the other scooping under my knees.

"Absolutely not," I said.

"Too late," he muttered, lifting me like I weighed less than his moral ambiguity.

By the time we reached the rest shelter—a bench, a water station, and enough carved initials to qualify as a hookup hall of fame—everyone else was already there, soaked through and teetering on the edge of a reality show meltdown. Except Bridget from Lüme, who was clearly gunning for screen time, touching up her lipstick in the reflection of her carabiner as if it were a Sephora compact. For half a second, her hands shook before she steadied them, glossing her mouth like war paint.

Jerrick set me down with the kind of care usually reserved for unstable explosives and weepy bridesmaids.

"You're fussing," I said.

"I'm checking."

"You're hovering."

"Still checking."

He knelt in front of me, inspecting my ankle with that infuriating combination of gentleness and laser focus. One of the guides appeared with an ice pack—calm, competent, and just shaken enough to respect the fact we'd nearly been turned into rainforest mulch.

"You'll live," he said finally.

"Excellent. Do I still get a T-shirt that says '*I didn't die today*'"?

He looked up—rain dripping from his hair, eyes locked on mine—and for a second, the whole damn jungle disappeared. "You're not dying on my watch," he said, voice low enough to settle the static in my chest.

I rolled my eyes so hard it probably counted as a head injury. Yet his hands were steady where mine weren't, and the weight of that made my chest ache.

But I didn't move.

Didn't tell him to stop.

Didn't hate how close he still was.

Rain blurred the jungle into watercolor chaos. I peeled off my soaked gloves, hair slicked to my cheeks, shirt glued to my skin.

He was staring.

I ignored it. "Well. This is cozy."

Jerrick nodded, jaw tight, as if wrestling something internal. "Only you could almost get flattened by a tree and still look sexy," he said, voice low.

Lightning flashed—bright and close. Thunder cracked after, sharp enough to shake the ground. I flinched. He leaned forward without hesitation. Not a decision.

A reflex.

We were too close.

Breath and pulse. Skin and steam. His hand grazed my waist—barely there. But definitely there.

"You okay?" he asked. No smirk. Just heat. Concern. Something genuine.

"I'm fine," I whispered.

Total bullshit.

And then we heard it.

Low. Long. Too deep for a monkey. Too wild to belong anywhere near a resort.

A roar.

A real fucking roar—raw and wrong and way too *holy shit* close. The kind that yanks every hair on your body to full alert.

My breath caught. "Tell me that was thunder. Right?"

He didn't answer. Just locked eyes with me.

Because he knew exactly what I knew.

The guide leaned in, voice tight. "*That* was a jaguar."

The sound clung to the air, musky and wild, like damp fur and iron on the tongue.

Another rumble. Closer. Closer than it had any right to be.

I looked at him. "Do they usually get this close?"

He shook his head slowly. "No."

Holy shit, we're jungle hors d'oeuvres.

The air went tight.

Then still.

Tick. Tick. Tick.

No one moved. No one breathed. Somewhere behind me, Bridget let out a sharp gasp. "Oh my God—something touched me!"

"It's your own hair," someone muttered. "Calm your tits, Bridget."

Silence stretched. Leaves dripped. A bird wailed above—somewhere between a horror soundtrack and a Real Housewives confessional.

Twenty excruciating minutes later, the storm eased into a steady drizzle. The guides regrouped us—just one final line to go.

"Think you're up for it?" the guide asked, already wrapping my ankle with jungle-hardened efficiency.

"I'm good," I said.

Which might've been convincing—if I hadn't sucked in a breath my sisters could probably hear from Maris Key.

Jerrick didn't say a word. Just hovered nearby—close enough to catch me if I so much as blinked wrong. And it bugged me how much I didn't hate that.

The trail to the last platform was steep, slick, and absolutely disinterested in my survival. The guide went first, helping me up one slippery step at a time.

Jerrick stayed close behind me. A choice I immediately regretted—because I, unfortunately, have a really nice ass.

"Enjoying the view?" I asked, panting slightly.

"Immensely," he said, not even pretending otherwise.

Jerk.

But—for once—I didn't feel like biting his head off.

Maybe just... nibbling.

We reached the platform. Jerrick zipped first—smooth, fast, and irritatingly graceful.

Of course he did.

The guide clipped me in. "They'll catch you on the other side, okay?"

I nodded. Something tugged in my chest—gratitude, maybe. Guilt, definitely. I hadn't exactly made this easy.

I took a breath, stepped off, and let gravity make the call. The trees blurred. My heart pounded. This time, I let myself appreciate it.

By the time I landed, both the first guide and Jerrick were there—steady hands, calm eyes, catching me as if it was second nature. My mouth betrayed me; a grin broke loose.

"I've got you," Jerrick said, helping me off the line like it was just another day.

No snappy comeback.

Not even a weak one.

Because suddenly, all the attitude I'd been flinging around since I got here felt... loud.

Exhausting.

Maybe even gross.

They were kind. And I'd been auditioning for Worst Guest Ever.

Jerrick just... got under my skin. And I hated that. Almost as much as I hated how steady his hand felt in mine, as if I could lean—for just a second. And for the first time all day... I didn't totally hate holding on.

The thank you hovered on my tongue. One just for him. Right next to seven other things I didn't have the guts to say. Words caught in my throat—real ones. Messy ones. Too much for a girl still covered in mud and adrenaline.

Maybe later. When I can think straight.

Which is exactly when the next guest came in too hot—

Missed the brake.

And plowed straight into Jerrick like a human cannonball.

He took it chest-first and staggered—one hand on the cable, the other catching the human missile by the harness. Guides shouted. Metal clacked.

I moved without thinking—fingers lifting toward his jaw—then stopped an inch shy. Heat. Rain. Breath. He glanced at my hand; I glanced at his mouth. We withdrew at the same time—him tightening a carabiner that didn't need it, me fussing a helmet strap that wasn't crooked.

"You good?" he asked, voice even.

"Peachy," I lied.

The moment hung—thin as a line between trees—until the guide waved us on and the jungle took the answer for us.

Not yet.

Chapter 8

Don't Make It Weird

I DIDN'T CRY. I *didn't*.

Even if mud had infiltrated places it shouldn't, and my ankle had swollen into something that belonged behind a bakery glass. Even after the shuttle ride sucker-punched me with an adrenaline crash. And even though Jerrick still haunted the backs of my eyelids—damp curls and jungle-slick heroics I absolutely did not request.

Still. No tears. Only vibes. And maybe a quiet little meltdown with an ice pack.

Which is why I ghosted social hour with the efficiency of a feral introvert.

I needed a break. A breather. A full-system reboot after nearly becoming jaguar chow, ziplining straight into a human-sized death sack, and getting scooped up by my mortal enemy mid–Tarzan-scented delirium.

Negative. I was one humid breeze away from losing it completely.

I told myself it was about the ankle. The swelling. The bruising. The undeniable truth that I'd spontaneously combust if forced into anything other than a tank top and sleep shorts. But really? It was everything. One-way ticket to Emotional Hot Mess Island.

The near-death brush. The way Jerrick looked at me—like maybe he hadn't always hated me. Maybe he doesn't. The way his hand closed over mine with a weight that suggested it meant something.

And the worst part?

He was being nice. Genuinely nice. No jabs. No smirks. No casual sabotage. Disarmingly considerate, maddeningly helpful, and... *gentlemanly*. I didn't know what to do with it. And I sure as hell didn't trust it.

So I scrubbed my face raw, stood under a scalding shower until every trace of jungle muck circled the drain, and yanked my hair into a real-life messy bun. No Instagram filters. No cutesy captions. Just me. I was bare-faced, barefoot, and radiating the unstable grace of a Florida thunderstorm.

And I was *alone*. Blissfully, fucking alone. Exactly how I wanted it.

Or so I told myself.

I sprawled across the villa's private terrace, tucked between lush greenery and a stone firepit that flickered with nosy little secrets. One leg propped on a pillow, a glass of wine sweating nervously on the table, clearly panicked on both our behalves. I picked up my phone to call Rayann. And then—the knock.

Nope. Nope-nope-nope. Absolutely not.

Three taps. Not a request—a statement.

I should've ignored it. Let whoever it was bother someone less inclined to greet company with murder eyes.

But I didn't.

Because I can't even commit to un-peopling properly.

I dragged myself to the door on pure spite and one functioning nerve. Somehow, that was enough to summon the complication I'd been trying to outrun. The one man I'd sell my sanity *not* to be hot for—because apparently I collect red flags like souvenirs. And there I was, trapped in tank-top purgatory, sleep shorts, and hair that screamed *send help*. No makeup. No bra. Just skin, sweat, and the lingering aroma of stress and meltdown musk.

My stomach dropped. My soul tried to climb out through my hairline. I should've cared. I should've panicked. I should've turned around and sprinted for concealer.

But I didn't.

I stood there like a dumbass, dangerously close to losing my entire goddamn mind. And for one awful, fluttery second, I wasn't even fucking embarrassed.

I was undone.

Fuck. I was so fucked.

And somehow—some *goddamn* how—he was still looking at me like I was the whole point of the trip.

Jesus Christ. He was going to ruin me—and I was standing there in my sluttiest sleep shorts like it was a goddamn meet-cute.

Jerrick Tarzan Thorne. Armed with two takeout containers, a bottle of something bougie, and the same infuriating grin he'd flaunted while ziplining through mayhem—devilish bastard Indiana Jones–on-vacation energy.

"I brought dinner," he said, shrugging one shoulder. "And backup wine. I figured near-death experiences pair best with carbs."

I blinked.

What fresh hell is this, and why is he suddenly speaking fluent love language?

Then blinked again.

Because holy hell, he looked edible. Casual tee. Damp, messy hair with a tousle that practically begged for fingers.

"You didn't have to come," I said, trying not to sound impressed.

"You're right," he said, already stepping past me toward the terrace like it was familiar territory. "I absolutely didn't."

The firelight caught his jaw as he set the food down beside the fire pit and took a seat across from me—close enough to rattle me. Not close enough to catch me falling for it. Smart man.

"Ankle?" he asked.

"Still there. Rude as hell."

He nodded. "And your pride?"

I shrugged. "Mostly intact. Light bruising. Standard issue."

"Resilient, that pride. Almost as stubborn as its owner."

I glanced down, fiddling with the edge of my top like it might answer for me. "My dad used to say I came out of the womb negotiating with the doctor, but that didn't mean I always believed the shine wasn't hiding cracks. Some of us need a little extra breaking in."

His expression flickered—just for a second. Like maybe he wasn't expecting me to admit that.

"Are you hungry?"

My stomach growled before I could lie. *Traitor*.

"Starved."

We ate in surprisingly comfortable silence for a few minutes. Rice. Curry. Something spicy barely registered over the mental sirens wailing: Abort. Back away. You're catching feelings. *Gooey, terrifying* feelings.

"So," he said finally, "did I officially earn my jungle bodyguard badge, or...?"

I looked up. "I'm still pulling leaf bits out of unholy places. You get partial credit. Maybe a gold star if I stop finding foliage where it doesn't belong."

He smirked. "Is that your way of saying thank you, or are you stalling until I demand a merit badge ceremony with a drum circle and awkward eye contact?"

"Neither," I said, grabbing my wine. "Though now I *do* need to know what your ceremonial outfit entails."

He grinned, slow and knowing. "Nothing but the badge."

I choked on my sip and set the glass down hard. "You're disgusting."

He leaned in—close enough to short-circuit common sense. "And yet... you opened the door."

Touché.

I narrowed my eyes. "So you dragged your cocky self here just to barter for imaginary jungle credentials?"

"Nope." He held my gaze. "I came because I wanted to."

My stomach launched into a full Olympic floor routine and stuck the landing right in my throat—with bonus points for emotional damage.

Cool it, Wilder. You are a professional. You give keynote speeches and manage million-dollar accounts. You do not make big dumb swoony eyes at your corporate nemesis over curry and candlelight.

"That's stupid," I deadpanned.

"Extremely."

A beat passed.

"You know," he said, gaze lingering just long enough to make my skin warm, "didn't expect this version of you." He paused. "Looks good on you."

Perfect. Compliment the one version of me I don't let anyone see and expect coherent thought afterward.

I let out a quiet, suspicious laugh. "You're not supposed to be sweet. It messes with the narrative."

"I know." He sipped his wine. "I suck at staying in character."

The air shifted, warmer now, tight with his restraint and my reckless need to test it. The firelight kissed his jaw, all crush and no self-control. Traitorous little flames.

His gaze dropped to my leg—still propped, still a nuisance—then slowly climbed back up. Not gross. Just... *present*. He noticed something I hadn't exactly offered.

"Want me to elevate that more for you?" he asked—casual, composed. "Promise I'll be a gentleman. Ish."

"Ugh. You almost sounded respectable."

He smirked. "Didn't hear a no."

I rolled my eyes, groaned internally, and gave in to the worst idea I'd had all day. His fingers brushed my ankle, lifting it a little higher to tuck another pillow beneath. Gentle. Slow. Unapologetic. My lungs noped out completely.

"Still swelling," he murmured. "Should ice it again later." His fingers pressed along the side of my ankle. Efficient. Skilled. Weirdly precise.

"Wow," I said. "Charming *and* medically responsible. You're basically a walking red flag."

He laughed. The bastard.

I didn't.

Because my pulse was pounding, my brain was glitching, and he looked at me as if figuring me out had officially become his new hobby. "You okay?" he asked, voice soft enough to make me want to cry.

I nodded.

Yeah, sure you are.

One more touch and I'd melt straight into this damn cushion, no questions asked. His thumb skimmed the bone beneath the swelling, warm and assured. "You do this a lot?" I asked, shooting for normal. Unbothered. Totally not unraveling over a glorified ankle check.

"What, rescue damsels and recommend ice packs? My services are in high demand."

"Focus, Tarzan. I meant the ankle thing."

He chuckled. "Jiu jitsu. Long time now." He nodded toward my leg. "You learn a lot about injuries when you're the one constantly getting thrown."

"Hold up. You do martial arts?"

He chuckled, low and modest. "Yeah. Black belt. Started as a hobby. Turned into something I couldn't walk away from."

I took a long sip of wine to drown out the part of my brain screaming, *Ask him what kind of holds. Ask how tight. ASK EVERYTHING.*

I squinted at him. "Seriously? That's not hobby-level."

He shrugged. "Didn't say I was casual about it."

Every cell in my body voted yes, please. *My brain, the lone dissenting voice, was losing fast.*

"Two truths and a scar," I said, pointing my glass at him. "Your belt earns you first blood."

He huffed a laugh. "That a game or a trap?"

"Both."

He tipped his head, then set his wine down like he was setting intent. "Truth one: I lost a regional final my second year. Decision match. I held back—too focused on control, not enough on the win." His smile was slow, deliberate. "That's not how I play anymore."

I took a sip to hide the fact that every word he said was doing inappropriate things to my bloodstream.

"And the scar?"

He traced the inside of his forearm with his thumb, not quite touching. "Caught in an armbar in a different tournament. I could've tapped earlier. I didn't. Spent six months rehabbing a ligament and a lesson." He looked up. "I don't leave things undecided anymore." His jaw tightened like the memory still lived under his skin. Losing control—of a match, of a moment—wasn't something he forgave easily. Maybe not at all.

The air between us went a shade quieter. The fire popped. My ankle throbbed in agreement.

"Truth two," he added, voice even softer. "I don't like watching people I care about take hits they don't see coming."

The way he said it wasn't casual. It sounded like a vow he'd already failed once. Something in his eyes made me wonder who hadn't been spared, and what it cost him to say it now.

His gaze flicked to my ankle, then back to my face. No smirk. No angle. "Your turn."

I should've picked something easy—favorite city, favorite sin. Instead, my mouth went rogue.

"Truth one," I said. "I'm terrified of being the Wilder who's all fireworks and no foundation."

His brow pulled, the way it does when he's reading a market trend and it surprises him. "Explain."

"My dad built Wilder Horizons on intention," I said, picking at the label on my glass. "Summer is steel in a blazer. Juliette can turn a timeline into scripture. I'm the spectacle. The spark. The show. Some days I worry I'm... shine. Not structure."

He didn't jump in. Didn't fix it. Just listened—too carefully.

"And the scar?" he asked.

I tapped my sternum. "Right there. Every time I chase the big swing, I hear him asking if the bones underneath can hold it. I don't want to be the daughter who sells wonder and drops the standard."

For a breath, the terrace held both of us steady.

"The fireworks get them to look up," he said finally, quiet and sure. "The foundation is how you think. You didn't build your pitch on glitter, Brynn. You built it on nerve."

"Careful," I said, aiming for flippant and landing closer to grateful. "You're ruining our rivalry."

"Temporary lapse." The corner of his mouth kicked. "Don't quote me."

I wouldn't. I would, absolutely.

I stared. Not because of the black belt—though *Jesus*, that was a dangerous mental image—but because it was the first time he didn't lead with ego. No flex. No humblebrag. Just... him.

Just... fact. And somehow, that rattled me more than the actual touching. "That explains the smooth takedown earlier," I muttered. "And the casual hero complex."

"That wasn't a takedown," he said, voice dipped low enough to stir every hormone I'd locked in a vault labeled *not now, Satan*. "That was a save."

And then, because he's *the worst*, he winked.

I rolled my eyes, but my ankle betrayed me, settling deeper into his lap with the shameless instincts of a sunbathing housecat. His thumb kept moving—slow, steady, and way too gentle for my mental health.

"Don't make it weird," I said.

"I'm not," he replied smoothly. "You are."

I opened my mouth, fully prepared to sass him straight off the terrace—

But then he looked up.

Met my eyes and held on.

I opened my mouth—probably to insult him—but something in his expression shifted. "You know, you don't have to spar with every emotion that tries to land a hit."

Easy for him to say. He didn't grow up in a house where weakness was like blood in the water—where one slip meant three sisters covering for you before the sharks circled.

My chest cinched. "Says the guy with a twelve-foot wall and emotional booby traps."

"Touché," he murmured. "But I still meant it."

"You're trained to fight," I snapped.

"You hold your own." He paused, eyes steady. "Better than most."

Ooh, if you only knew. But that secret was mine—for now.

My brain flatlined. My pulse clawed its way up my spine.

He gave my foot one last squeeze. Firm. Final. Then leaned back and reached for his wine. The absence hit harder than I expected. We both stared at the fire, pretending it could talk us down. The flames snapped and hissed, each pop a reminder of how much heat could live in silence, how much weight could hang in everything unsaid.

Then he stood. "I should go," he said—except his feet weren't cooperating.

I tilted my head. "Because now it feels suspiciously like a truce?"

"No." He dragged a hand through his hair, jaw tight. "Because if I stay, I'm going to kiss you."

The words hit fast. Hot. No takebacks. Everything in me shorted out. Skin flushed, breath shot to hell, and every rational thought I'd ever had bolted for the fire exit. I wasn't even sure who I was mad at anymore—him, me, the gravitational pull between us that refused to back off.

Enemies? Please. My hormones had burned that memo hours ago. He didn't move. Didn't close the space. Just let the heat hang—thick, electric, one breath away from something reckless.

"I'll see you tomorrow," he said, voice low and measured. "Get some sleep."

Not a threat or tease. Just calm, devastating certainty.

I didn't move. Couldn't. Because under all that control, all that maddening quiet—

He meant it. That if he stayed, he'd kiss me—and nothing would be the same after. And I could see it in his eyes—he hated that he meant it.

He lingered a second longer. "Sleep well, Wilder," he said, stepping back toward the door. His voice dropped. "You're gonna need it."

"For what?" I asked, already annoyed in how shaky I sounded.

He smirked, persona back on. Cocky enough to trademark it. "Tomorrow's the first round."

I narrowed my eyes. "Of what?"

"The pitch-off, remember?" he grinned, already too pleased with himself. "I'm going to wipe the floor with you."

I snorted. "Big talk from a man who just played footsie with the competition."

His grin widened, but he didn't bite. Just gave me one last look and walked out, leaving the room smoldering behind him.

The second the door clicked shut, I collapsed into the cushions. Wine glass limp. Ankle throbbing. Heartbeat punching holes in the ceiling. The quiet hit harder than the heat ever did. It settled in, slow and deliberate, the kind of quiet that made you realize how much noise you'd been carrying just to keep from noticing the ache underneath.

I was fully planning to finish that curry. Drink my wine. Process like a responsible adult.

But then Jerrick Thorne lit the room on fire and walked out.

Now?

The curry's cold. I'm not.

Because Jerrick—infuriating bastard that he is—might've just shown me something real.

Again.

I was ready for a fight. A flirt. Maybe a snark-off. Not... this. Not feelings, for fuck's sake.

Damn him for rewriting the story I'd already decided on. Fucking plot twist in expensive cologne.

Tonight he rattled me.

Tomorrow? I return the favor.

Not for those eyes. Not for those hands. And *absolutely not* for whatever slow-burn striptease he thought counted as strategy.

Round one was coming.

And I planned to make him *beg* for round two.

Chapter 9

Talk Dirty—Then Pitch It

S UNLIGHT FILTERED THROUGH PALM fronds like liquid gold—artful, innocent, and lying through its teeth. Meanwhile, I was already sweating through my game face.

Under the canopy, the event pavilion buzzed—an open-air lounge turned battleground Branded banners snapped between ceiling fans while too many VIPs sipped citrus cocktails and pretended to be impartial. Beyond the open sides, the jungle pressed close, humidity thick with wet earth and the occasional birdcall sharp enough to slice through the playlist. Out there was wild. In here, spectacle pretending to be control.

Tropical notes—passionfruit, maybe rum—hung in the air, sweet enough to seduce your better judgment.

Tech crews weaved through the seating, photographers clicked, and the so-called jungle soundtrack tried for chill but landed closer to haunted spa with bongos.

And Jerrick?

He was in full strategist mode. Calm. Crisp. Already working the judges with an ease that made my stomach twist.

"...not just high-end travel," he said. "The right kind of fear activates something primal. It sharpens focus. Heightens connection. Reminds people what it means to be fully present."

The pavilion had been transformed into a sleek showcase—teak tables arranged in a wide circle, each company's station prepped for its scheduled turn. Right now it was his. Behind him, a slim digital screen on a teak stand looped drone footage and luxury touchpoints—canopy trails, cliff-edge yoga decks, champagne at altitude. A few concentric rows of cushioned benches and folding chairs ringed the floor; guests and potential partners watched, rapt. He didn't rush. Didn't overplay. He held them with that quiet, dialed-in certainty that made people lean in.

I wanted to smack him. Or kiss him. Maybe both. Hard to say with adrenaline buzzing in my veins.

He wrapped with a single, clipped phrase that landed like a signature: "Risk is the new luxury."

Classic Jerrick—still chasing the high, the edge, the thing that left you raw. Same man who once turned a harmless strategy session into a full-blown sparring match in Dubai, who'd baited me into a debate just to watch me burn hot. He always played close to the fire—and worse, he usually won.

Then, casually—*too* casually—he added, "And for the record? Some of us find risk pretty damn irresistible."

A beat of silence. Then applause. Polite at first. Then louder.

I rolled my eyes so hard I nearly saw yesterday. Bastard actually pulled it off. *Cooler than cucumber-fucking gin.*

The lead judge lifted a hand. "Mr. Thorne, just a couple of questions from our panel?"

He gave a tight nod, professional as ever.

"Your proposal leans heavily into isolation and challenge. What makes you so confident these high-level clients actually want that?"

Jerrick didn't hesitate. "Because they're bored. The real elite? They've done the yachts. The safaris. The private chefs in private jets. What they haven't done is confront their own limits in a curated wild.

"Controlled danger is an aphrodisiac. The right kind of fear? Makes you feel alive. Makes you reach for the nearest... support system." He let his gaze skim toward me.

"That's what we give them—edge, safely delivered."

The woman in the middle—silver-haired, sharp-eyed, with a notepad and calculation in her smile—tilted her head. "And how do you quantify impact? Is this sustainable excitement, or just adrenaline tourism in disguise?"

He smiled, just slightly. "Adrenaline fades. Identity sticks. We measure impact by what the client does next—what they change, what they chase, who they become. That's what lasts."

That landed. Hard.

A beat of applause, then a few murmurs of approval.

The lead judge gestured to the next row of stations—agency reps queued for lightning-round pitches—the so-called friendly competition before Saturday's co-hosted event. But everyone knew the real showdown was already underway.

Truthfully, this wasn't really about showcasing ideas. This was about who would win the client's confidence—and the long-term contracts that came with it.

And to keep things sporting, a literal scoreboard: three judges, three categories—clarity, innovation, audience engagement—each scored out of ten. No smoke, no mirrors. Just numbers in black and white.

Still, it was hard to ignore the barefoot man now pacing across the teak floor—white linen suit, headset mic.

"HELLO, BEAUTIFUL CAPITALISTS!" he boomed, sweeping his arms wide. "I'm Axel with Ferox Experiences—where we strip life down to its rawest truths and build you back better. Stronger. Feraller."

Someone coughed.

"Ask yourself," he continued, eyes blazing, "when was the last time you truly *earned* your espresso? At Ferox, our clients forage for theirs. Barefoot. At altitude."

A beat of silence.

"We begin with a ceremonial phone burial. You will cry. That is expected. Then we drop you—gently—into a remote jungle basin with a pack of protein bars, a vintage machete, and your deepest unresolved childhood wound."

A few VIPs leaned forward.

Seriously—what peyote-powered vision board birthed this crew?

"Our platinum-tier immersion includes ego-disassembly therapy, a guided confrontation ritual we call *Scream Into the Void—But Make It Strategic,* and our signature climax: an identity-resetting firewalk led by

Lars, our resident goat shaman and executive recalibration coach."

Axel pointed to an image of a goat in aviator goggles projected behind him.

"Lars holds space. Lars demands respect. Lars is why Jeff Bezos keeps texting us."

If the scoreboard had gone live right then, Lars the Goat Shaman would've raked in a perfect ten for *unintentional comedy*. Zeroes for clarity, innovation debatable, audience engagement... fine, maybe a reluctant five.

My laugh stuck halfway up my throat. Because next up? Me. No goats. No gimmicks. Just sweat, a blazer welded to my skin, and the weight of every stare waiting for me to prove I belonged center stage.

A smattering of confused claps followed, something halfway between a laugh and a wheeze. Jerrick made a sound. Could've been either. Beside me, he calmly flipped open his leather journal and jotted something down.

I glanced once.

He didn't look up.

Just kept writing—focused, composed, maddeningly unreadable.

Whatever it was, it wasn't for me to see. Once, years ago, I'd watched him do the same thing—head bent, jaw set, as if putting ink to paper could cage chaos. I never got to read those notes either. And maybe that's what drove me nuts: he kept the best parts locked away.

I rolled my shoulders back. My turn was next.

My blazer clung to my arms, sweat-sealed and clingy, every movement tugging like a second skin.

Axel passed off the mic to the lead judge and strutted back to his seat, beaming like he'd just cured world hunger. A gust rattled palm fronds, sunlight flashing in through the slats as if the jungle wanted in on the contest too.

"You're up," Jerrick said, voice low enough that only I could hear. "Try not to make me regret going first."

His voice slid down my spine like cool marble. I didn't respond. Just stood. Smoothed my blazer. Took the damn mic. My station—Wilder Horizons, polished to within an inch of its life—waited across the pavilion. Looping footage, branded signage, the works. I crossed the teak floor, heels steady, pulse anything but.

"My name's Brynn Wilder," I began, forcing my breath to cooperate. "And I don't sell travel. I sell the stories people tell about themselves after the trip ends."

The slide at my station popped up—an image of a woman cliff-diving in Santorini. Her arms spread wide. No filter. No crowd.

"The clients we're pitching today don't want another private yacht. They don't want bragging rights. They want proof they're still alive. They want stories that rattle them—in the best way. We craft experiences that rewrite the bio."

"And if we're being honest, most bios could use a litt le... rewriting. Fewer credentials. More adrenaline. More *heat*."

I saw a few heads nod. One guy murmured *that's good* into his recorder.

And just like that, I was in it.

I led them through the pitch—tight itinerary, customized adventure arc, luxury-to-wildness contrast. This isn't just itinerary and logistics—it's heartbeat stuff. The kind that grabs you by the collar and yells, *this is your life*.

Not because I wanted to beat Jerrick.

Because I needed to. Every look, every scorecard, every whisper from the crowd pressed in, reminding me that this wasn't just about numbers—it was about proving I wasn't the Wilder sister playing dress-up in someone else's arena.

"Ms. Wilder?" The lead judge lifted a hand. "One question from our judges before we move on."

Showtime.

A woman in a flowing caftan, probably old money with a new podcast, leaned forward. "How do you balance luxury and authenticity when exclusivity often strips a place of its cultural integrity?"

I nodded once. "By leading with respect and partnership. We work directly with local communities to co-design every experience. No prefab resort excursions. If we can't elevate both the client *and* the culture, it doesn't make the cut."

Another judge chimed in. "You're pitching high-adrenaline experiences. What about risk mitigation?"

"Client profiles determine thresholds. Some want the edge. Some want the illusion of danger with the security of a net. We tailor accordingly." I smiled, sharp and steady. "We bring them to the edge—but never over it. Danger that flirts, not wounds. Thrill that leaves a mark, not a scar."

A slow exhale rippled through the room—interest sharpened, posture shifted, a few jaws slack with curiosity or something darker.

"And for our more adventurous clients? Some stories are meant to get a little reckless. The kind that make you blush the next day... and book the next trip."

A few snickers in the crowd.

And then came the curveball.

From the back: an older man in a crisp linen suit—one of the legacy investors Summer warned me about. "Wilder Horizons has a reputation for flair. But is all that branding sustainable in the long-term—or just... noise?"

My pulse spiked. I caught Jerrick glance over—just once. I leaned into the mic. "We don't do noise. We do signal. Everything we create is rooted in story, strategy, and soul. The aesthetic is just the vehicle. The impact is what lasts."

A brief pause. Then someone clapped. Another followed.

And just like that, Q&A was over.

When it was done, I sat back down and willed my heart rate back to human. The cushion beneath me felt too warm, too soft, like it was absorbing every ounce of my restraint. I resisted the urge to stab Jerrick with my pen.

I leaned closer. "You're still sweating."

"You're still staring."

We both blinked. Neither denied it.

"Nicely done," he said, not smiling. "Didn't even flinch."

"I don't flinch," I muttered. "I recalibrate."

His mouth twitched. Not a smile—just a flicker of acknowledgment.

Around us, the next team started setting up, but apparently we were still the entertainment. Two rows back, someone whispered, not even bothering to lower her voice: 'Those two have insane chemistry. Are they a thing?'

Another voice chimed in, hushed but grinning: "I don't know, but if they don't rip each other's clothes off by lunch, I'm suing."

I stiffened. He didn't move, didn't turn. But I swear I felt it—the slow curl of satisfaction rolling off him.

I braced for the score announcement, already rehearsing how to clap politely while plotting my revenge. Everyone here knew the real showdown was between Wilder Horizons and Adventura Luxe—the rest were just garnish with cocktails.

And even if he won this round—and he would—I'd win the next.

One way or another, Jerrick Thorne was going down.

The lead judge stepped forward, smiling with the barely disguised glee of someone who *lived* for drama.

"Thank you to all presenters. Our judges have submitted their first round scores," she said, flipping a branded notecard with theatrical flair. "Results are in."

A flask clicked open nearby. Spiced rum cut through the room—warm, biting, and not exactly discreet.

A hush rippled through the pavilion.

"In third place," she announced, "with twenty-six points... Bridget from Lüme Travel."

Polite applause. Bridget beamed, waving with the poise of someone who once trained for a pageant and never fully let it go.

The lead judge continued. "In second place..."

My spine straightened.

"Brynn Wilder, Wilder Horizons with 31 points."

I smiled. Nodded. Clapped politely. My jaw only cracked a little.

"And in first place, edging ahead with 32 points... Jerrick Thorne, Adventura Luxe."

More applause. A few murmurs of *well played*. No gloat. No glance. Just that maddeningly neutral nod—the kind that said everything and nothing. The LED scoreboard—slim and unromantic—blinked the numbers: 31, then 32.

One single fucking point.

The shift in his eyes said it all—quiet victory, neatly folded. The internal scoreboard being updated. The quiet, superior little checkmark.

It wasn't gloating. It was fuel.

"Round Two after lunch," the moderator added. "Same location. New prompt. Fresh fire."

I stood, pretending not to feel the heat of his gaze tracking my every move.

He didn't say a word.

Neither did I.

But our eyes locked for half a second too long.

The fans overhead churned the air, lazy and useless. My cheeks, my chest, my pride—already lit.

In that half second, the pitch-off turned personal.

Round one: his.

Round Two?

Let's raise the damn stakes.

On my way past him, I forced the kind of professional smile that could double as dental torture. "Congratulations," I said, smooth as I could manage.

"Appreciate it," he murmured, low and even—and it landed like a hand at the small of my back. Not a touch. Worse. The *idea* of one.

I kept walking. Because if I didn't, I might not.

Chapter 10

Rinse Cycle

V ICTORY TASTED LIKE ADRENALINE and petty vindication. But mostly? Confusion.

Because I won.

Final round: mine. By one point. A mirror to his win from earlier.

It felt deliberate. The judges split the win on purpose, caught between two tightly wound contenders too evenly matched to crown outright. So they handed each of us a round and called it balance.

But I still won.

And I should've felt cocky. Hell, I *wanted* to feel cocky. I had a whole speech queued up in my head. A flawless closer. All bite, no apology.

But when they announced the score, Jerrick didn't flinch. He simply stood there, calm and steady, unreadable as ever, and shook my hand as if he'd expected it. As if I hadn't surprised him at all.

No snark. No smug little dig.

Just a low, smooth "Congratulations" that made my skin prickle.

I muttered a vaguely polished reply and turned away before my brain could start filling in blanks it had no business exploring.

Then I walked out, past the applause, the camera flashes, and the kind of peanut gallery commentary that branded itself into my skull.

"You could cut the sexual tension with a machete."

"Oh my God, are they fighting or flirting?!"

I didn't stick around to clarify.

I rounded the corner, pressed against the wall, and finally let go of the breath I'd been hoarding since Round One.

Victory was weird. Especially when it came with a side of him—every look, every tease, every innuendo—still zinging through my body, all heat and static with nowhere to go.

I won.

And somehow, I was still losing my goddamn mind.

After the post-panel debrief, I needed time.

Time to think.

Time to breathe.

Time to call my sisters and scream into the void while pretending to be a functional human.

I found a hammock tucked between two palm trees near the far end of the pool, partially hidden by thick tropical leaves and isolated enough to pretend I wasn't spiraling. The heat was fading with the sun, a soft breeze rustling through the canopy overhead.

Perfect.

I peeled off my blazer down to my fitted tank and tied a knot in the side of my skirt to let my thighs breathe.

I dialed Summer first. She picked up on the first ring.

"I saw it." Her voice was smooth, proud, and terrifyingly even. "Well done."

A pause.

"You were watching live?"

"Of course." Another pause. "Your deck was strong. Delivery was sharp. You and Jerrick clearly found your rhythm."

I waited for more—for the snark, the commentary, the barely veiled big-sister side-eye about the sexual tension I *knew* she picked up on.

It never came.

Instead, she added, "The whole thing felt tight. Balanced. Looked like real collaboration. Keep that momentum through Saturday, and we'll be fielding offers
before the credits roll."

A pause. Then, slightly softer, "Nice work, Brynn."
In the background, I caught the faint clink of a wine
glass and what sounded like Juliette's laugh. Even on a
weeknight, Summer was never off-duty—but she wasn't
alone either.

Then she hung up.

Zero   drama.   Zero   mention   of   any
are-they-or-aren't-they side commentary. Nothing more
than strategic praise and expectations for fol-
low-through.

God, I hated how much I loved her for that.

I flopped back into the hammock and stared at
the leaves above me. They swayed gently, mocking-
ly—oblivious to the fact that one more breeze might
push me off the cliff of sanity.

I tapped Rayann's name. She answered mid-laugh.

"Please tell me you watched the summit panel," I said.

"Oh honey. I didn't need to. You two broke my group
chat." Voices spilled behind her—Max, her boyfriend,
probably making some dry remark that set her giggling

again. My sister's chaos was always threaded with something steadier, and I envied her for it in that moment.

Rayann paused. "You okay?"

"No. I think I might be insane. Or clinically dehydrated. Or both."

"Talk to me."

I laid it all out—the win that felt off, the unexpected restraint, and the voice that still tangled in my ribcage. The innuendos. The glances. The way my heart lost all rhythm the moment he entered my airspace.

Rayann, after a long silence, cleared her throat.

"So... hate-fuck him."

"What?"

"You heard me."

"I'm not—That's not—I can't just—"

"Brynn. You are a grown woman with a deeply punchable attraction to a man who clearly wants to crawl inside your brain and redecorate it. Sleep with him. Hate-fuck him. Love-fuck him. I don't care. But *do something* before you combust."

I hung up on her mid-giggle.

Mostly because she was right.

And I hated it.

I took the scenic path back to my suite, winding past the spa where soft music drifted from hidden speakers and the air smelled like eucalyptus and indulgence.

The path curved toward the edge of the property, where bamboo walls loosely shielded a few outdoor rinse stations meant for hikers and sweaty tourists. It wasn't clearly marked—a simple stone archway and the soft sound of splashing water beyond.

I paused. My ankle ached faintly—a dull reminder of yesterday's zipline disaster. A quick rinse sounded kind of amazing. Maybe it'd clear my head.

I stepped around the corner—

And froze.

Oh.

Oh, no.

Oh. Holy. Hell.

It wasn't just a rinse station.

It was *him*.

His back was turned. Water flowed over broad shoulders and golden skin, trailing in slow, criminally perfect rivulets down the length of his spine. The hint of a tattoo on his side.

He was naked.

Of course he was.

And I was staring.

Of course I was.

My brain attempted a reboot.

Turn around. Run. Apologize. Black out. *Anything*.

I opened my mouth.

Nothing came out.

He turned his head slightly but didn't look over his shoulder.

"You know," he said, voice low, casual, maddening, "most people knock before they trespass on someone's rinse ritual."

I choked. "I thought this was the spa rinse station!"

"It is," he said, still not facing me. "You caught the deluxe package."

"I didn't see anything," I blurted.

A pause. Then—

"Shame." His voice was light, but the corner of his mouth twitched like he was fighting a real grin. He reached for a towel and finally turned, wrapping it around his waist with obnoxiously smooth efficiency.

But not before I caught a glimpse of his half-grin—the one designed to test my sanity.

And the trail of water running down his chest.

And the way his eyes dragged over me with zero apology.

"Or maybe..." he added, stepping forward enough to close some of the space between us, "...lucky you."

I made a strangled noise. Somewhere between a cough and a confession.

He didn't laugh. Just gave me that exasperating almost-smile and turned away again.

"Enjoy your walk, Wilder."

I spun on my heel so fast I nearly sprained the other ankle.

Dinner was supposed to be casual. Low-key. No panels. No name tags. No ten-slide pitches. Only flickering lanterns, an open-air buffet, and a playlist that sounded like a rich person's idea of jungle ambiance—equal parts steel drum, lo-fi hip hop, and bird sounds that I'm ninety percent sure were piped in.

I sat with the Montreal marketing crew and a woman from Iceland who was *very* passionate about VR immersion rates. There weren't enough tables, so everyone ended up scattered across long teak benches, plates balanced on knees, conversation layered in a dozen different accents. Cutlery clinked in uneven rhythm, an accidental percussion under the chatter that made the whole pavilion hum like it had its own soundtrack.

Jerrick didn't sit with us.

He didn't have to.

I could feel him.

Not in a woo-woo soulmate way. In the painfully specific *I saw him naked and now my brain's running low on bandwidth* kind of way that made focusing on my mahi tacos a full-time job.

The teak bench was still warm from the day's heat, sticky against the back of my thighs, anchoring me in a body I barely trusted to stay still. We didn't talk. Barely even looked at each other. But every time he laughed—low and rich and effortless—it hooked straight into the base of my spine like some kind of Pavlovian punishment.

He wasn't ignoring me. He was busy, the way people in our world always were—always engaged, always accessible, never still.

Even so. It bugged me.

Which was *so* stupid. I'd won. I should've been riding high on strategic dominance and grilled pineapple. I stabbed at my plate, half expecting the grilled pineapple to apologize for my entire mental collapse.

Because that was what started it. The damn water.

The way it slid down his back. The casual confidence. That voice. That smirk. The way he didn't scramble for a towel, didn't flinch, didn't *care*. He owned it. Owned *me*, for a breathless second I couldn't unlive.

I needed a lobotomy. Or a cold drink. Or maybe to fling myself into the ocean and let the waves sort me out.

After the plates were cleared and the drinks slowed to a trickle, the crowd finally began to thin. A few guests trickled out toward fire pits and hammocks. Lantern light caught on the rims of cocktail glasses, flaring like tiny suns before they disappeared into the dark.

I'd just stood to sneak away and grab dessert when I felt him behind me—heat and presence, subtle and intentional.

"You've been on that foot all day," he said quietly, over my shoulder. "You good?"

I turned, startled. He wasn't arrogant. Wasn't teasing. No smirk, no edge—just a steady focus that said he'd been tracking every step, even the ones I thought I'd hidden.

"It's fine," I said, a little too fast. "Honestly. Feels way better after all the ice and... creative pillow elevation last night."

His brow lifted. "Creative?"

"Structurally unsound," I admitted. "But effective."

He didn't smile, but his face softened.

"Glad to hear it," he said, and started to turn away.

I stopped him. "Why didn't you say anything?"

He blinked. "About what?"

"The panel. Dinner. Me winning. You *existing in my direct line of sight while being objectively offensive to the laws of physics.*"

That one got him. His mouth curved. Barely.

"I figured you needed space." He looked at me for a second longer. "And I didn't want to interrupt your dinner with a crowd."

Oh.

Well, shit.

He gave me a final nod and slipped back into another conversation as if I hadn't short-circuited in his presence.

"Okay, I have to ask. Was that tension part of the pitch, or are you two actually fucking?"

Jerrick's hand tightened almost imperceptibly on the glass, a blink-and-miss tell under the mask of composure.

The voice came from the other side of me—Lucinda Marsh, a legend in the luxury travel circuit and the only person on this continent who could say *fucking* with that much casual authority. She swirled her wine and raised a brow, equal parts amused and unbothered.

I blinked.

"Because if that wasn't foreplay," she added, "you two missed a real opportunity."

Someone laughed. Another person choked on their cocktail. Jerrick didn't flinch. He took a calm sip of his drink, as if she'd asked about his preferred brand of rum.

I, on the other hand, was actively trying to astral-project into the nearest volcano. I opened my mouth. Closed it. Then stabbed another piece of mahi-mahi and pretended to find it *very* interesting.

Don't react. Don't engage.

Don't picture the damn water again.

But a switch had flipped, and there was no turning it off.

And my brain was still waterlogged from watching it drip down his abs.

I got back to my suite and tossed my shoes halfway across the room. I didn't bother with music or lights. Just flopped onto the bed, fully clothed, and stared at the ceiling waiting for divine wisdom—or a ceiling tile to fall on me.

Neither happened.

I picked up my phone. Put it down. Picked it up again. My thumb hovered—ten seconds, maybe more—before I finally gave in.

BRYNN:

You awake?

Three dots appeared. Then vanished. Then appeared again.

JERRICK:

Should I be concerned?

BRYNN:

Nope. But I've booked us gym time tomorrow morning. Figured we could work out a little... tension.

JERRICK:

That sounds dangerous. Planning a rematch?

BRYNN:

Something like that. Be there at 6:00.

No winks. No smiley faces. No training wheels of foreplay.

But I turned off the screen with a grin anyway.

Let him wonder.

Chapter 11

Tap Out or Give In

T HE GYM WAS QUIET. Dim light. Cool air. Early morning mist clung to the glass walls, curling at the edges like the gym was auditioning for drama. Only the soft hiss of the air vents and the muted thud of bare feet broke the silence.

I was already stretching when Jerrick walked in. I wrapped my ankle as a precaution. Hair twisted into a tight bun.

My tank clung like a second skin, cool fabric against my warming back. Yoga pants. Form-fitting in the deadliest of ways. Weaponized spandex. I'd take every tactical edge I could get.

Jerrick took one look at me and cocked a brow.

Fitted tee. Athletic shorts. Damp hair that made my brain unspool faster than I could stop it.

Honestly, it's getting rude. The man even makes sweat look expensive.

He looked rested. Sharp. Slightly amused.

Too amused.

"Let me guess," he said as he approached. "Mobility and breathwork? You strike me as a core-and-cardio girl."

"Oh, you've noticed my abs?" I smirked.

His response was a rough sound that belonged nowhere near a gym mat.

I smiled without looking at him.

"Stretch however you want, Thorne. I'll be on the mat."

He blinked.

Then looked—really registered—and zeroed in on the jiu jitsu mats set up at the center of the gym. His mouth parted for half a second. That was all I needed.

Gotcha, sucker. Checkmate. Yoga pants win again.

"You brought mats?"

"Reserved them last night." I stood, rolled my neck, and met his eyes. "We've been building tension for days. Thought it was time we worked some of it out."

He stepped closer. Slower this time.

"You want to spar."

"Unless you're afraid."

He watched me longer now. Posture shifting. Shoulders squared. Chin lifted slightly as if running a silent calculation.

"I didn't pack a gi."

"I didn't ask you to."

"What exactly is this, Wilder?"

I stepped onto the mat. Calm. Controlled. Everything I hadn't been since he walked into my damn life again. "You've been underestimating me since day one," I said. "Figured it was time you learned how that usually ends."

And maybe I needed a space where all this tension had set rules.

Where I could close the distance without actually caving.

One more beat passed.

Then he smiled. Real. Slow. A touch feral.

"This is a mistake," he murmured, stepping onto the mat. "I don't pull punches."

"Good," I said, pulse already kicking. "I'm done playing it safe."

He hesitated. "Brynn, I'm a black belt. I'm not reminding you of that to brag. I've trained a really long time." His tone was steady, but the faint crease between his brows said he wasn't just bragging. He was worried about hurting me.

Great. A gentleman ninja. And also very, very turned on.

"I know. I can hold my own."

He nodded once. "Then rules."

"No striking," I said. "Grappling only. Tap means release—immediately. If my hands are trapped, I'll say *red*."

"Copy," he said, eyes on mine. "*Red* ends it. Want a *yellow* for ease up?"

"Yeah. *Yellow* if I need space."

His gaze dropped to my wrapped ankle. "Permission to check range?"

Heat skittered up my spine. "Permission granted."

He crouched, fingers gentle at the wrap, testing carefully—no pressure, just contact. "Pain scale?"

"Two," I said. "If it hits four, we pause. At five, we stop."

He repeated it back, quiet and precise. "Two now. Pause at four. Stop at five." His thumb brushed feather-light. "You good?"

"Good," I breathed.

He rose into my space without touching more than he'd asked for. "One more. You sure?"

"Positive."

The corner of his mouth ticked up. "Then let's work it out."

We circled.

I dropped my center of gravity and kept my elbows in. This wasn't about strength—it was about pressure and timing.

He moved with ease. Precise, disciplined, with that masterful training in every step. I mirrored him. Calm. Focused. Not here to match him. Here to rattle him.

I feinted left. He held position.

I pivoted, dipped low, baited him forward. He responded with a light sweep attempt, meant to test me, not drop me.

I dropped into base, hooked my right leg behind his, and used his forward momentum to take him down with a simple inside trip.

His breath hitched.

Mine didn't.

For one beautiful moment, I had Jerrick Thorne off balance.

Not down. Not yet.

But close.

He caught my forearm to steady himself. His knee hit the mat—then mine. A shift of weight. A collision of limbs. Breath against breath. Hands slipped into holds.

His skin burned where our arms tangled, but the mat stayed cool and slick with condensation. The heat between us had nothing to do with exertion.

I could feel him adjusting.

Not just to the fight.

To me.

His grip tightened on my forearm.

"You've trained," he said, low and even.

"Obviously."

"No, I mean—really trained."

I shifted to rebalance, sweeping my knee around as he adjusted with me, our centers still locked.

"You going to try to guess?"

His mouth ticked upward, focused. "Purple? Maybe brown."

"Not bad," I said, sitting on my heels. "I earned my brown belt two weeks ago."

I leaned into the next move, weightless for half a breath, then twisted through and broke his balance again. His back hit the mat with a thud that vibrated through both of us.

His breath hitched, eyes locked on mine. "Yellow?" he murmured.

"Green," I shot back, steady. "Keep going."

Something shifted in his expression then, no longer testing my defense but my resolve.

I want this on a t-shirt. Or better yet—stitched into his memory. Whispered in his ear while I ride him into next week.

He exhaled—just once—and it felt half like admiration, half like a reckoning.

"No wonder I'm getting my ass handed to me."

I stood and offered a hand. He took it, his look a mix of unfinished business and temptation.

We circled once more. This time closer.

"So," he said, breath still controlled, "was this all part of the plan? Humiliate me in front of the dumbbells and ghosts of CrossFit past?"

I didn't answer. Not right away. Instead, I grabbed his wrist, twisted, and threw him again.

His back hit the mat harder this time.

I didn't let go.

"That's for the campaign you stole in Dubai," I said, voice sharper now. "The one you rebranded and pitched like it came straight from your own brilliant brain."

I snapped into a hip throw—tight, practiced, meaner than necessary.

His eyes locked on mine. "That's what this is about?"

I dropped my weight onto his chest, not a straddle, not quite a pin. Just contact. Intentional. Unforgiving.

"You knew it was mine. My concept. My market research. My budget notes. And you never even blinked. You just took it."

"It wasn't that simple."

"It never fucking is."

He moved to sit, but I shifted my hips to block him.

"You think I haven't had to fight to be taken seriously? You think I haven't seen men take credit for my work and call it 'collaboration'?"

"Bryn—"

I hip-tossed him, a tight, practiced movement that hit the mat with authority.

"And then you had the nerve to flirt with me. To look at me in Dubai like maybe there was more. And the minute I let myself believe that—" I broke off, chest heaving. "You went cold."

His voice lowered. Not defensive. Just wrecked.

"I didn't mean to."

"You didn't *have* to. That's the point."

He reversed into side control with fluid ease, pinning me beneath him before I could react.

"I was engaged."

Wait. Wait wait wait. Back the fuck up. There was a fiancée?

The word hit like a heel to the solar plexus.

Fiancée. As in: cozy Sunday mornings, naked IKEA battles, and shared dental insurance. The picture hit me harder than the admission—like a glimpse of the life he'd almost had, the one I'd never been invited to, and suddenly I was furious at myself for even caring. He'd been somebody's forever plan—and I was out there catching feelings like a damn rookie?

The air shifted.

I stared up at him.

"Excuse me?"

He swallowed. Hard.

"I was engaged. Four years. I don't know. We were always too busy to set a date. I came home a week before Dubai and found her with someone else." His voice dipped on the word engaged, like even now it still scraped raw on the way out.

His grip loosened.

"She said I was never around. Always working. Always chasing something bigger. She didn't want to marry a man married to his job."

He pushed up farther, one hand brushing his hair back, fingers shaking just enough to betray it.

"I was a wreck in Dubai. I shouldn't have even been there. But I had this campaign to land, a million-dollar client on the line, and a father who didn't believe in recovery time."

I was still frozen, still staring. Still locked underneath him.

"And yeah, I saw your campaign," he added. "I knew it was good. I was drowning. And I used it. Not in spite of you—but because I knew it was brilliant. I knew *you* were. You were always the smartest one in the room, and I hated that I admired you more than I could admit."

Silence.

Breathing.

Just the soft sound of mat under skin and the unspoken truth humming between us.

I shifted my hips and threaded one leg across his shoulders—baiting a triangle setup to make him react.

"You should've said something."

"I know."

"You still should. You've been flirty with me all week. Fucking with my head."

He nodded. Slowly.

I stared at him. "Why, Jerrick?"

He stared right back. No armor. No game face.

Just sweat. Guilt. Raw honesty.

And the kind of tension you can't train your way out of.

I created just enough space to reset my base.

He was still half-sitting, half-crouched on the mat, watching me with that wrecked, open face I didn't know what to do with.

"Because you make me forget I'm supposed to be careful," he said, voice low, like it cost him something. "I've spent my whole life playing a role—CEO's son, star employee, picture-perfect fiancé. I even fucking learned golf. All of it curated. Expected. And I hate golf with every fiber of my soul."

His gaze didn't waver. "And then you show up. You challenge me. You don't give a damn about my last name or what it looks like on a business card. You push back. You call me out. You make me feel like I can actually *breathe.*"

He dragged a hand through his hair, frustration breaking through. His knee bounced once, fast, like the words were leaking faster than he wanted them to. "And damn it, you make me laugh when I don't want to. You make me *feel* when I'm better off numb. I've never let anyone see me, Brynn. Not really. Not the mess. Not the man who's not sure he wants any of this anymore."

I should've let that confession sit. Let it breathe. Instead, pressure built in my chest until it pressed against every rib, begging me to do something reckless with it.

A beat passed.

"But you see me. And it scares the shit out of me... because I think I want you to."

My heart thudded, traitorous and loud.

"You sure you want me to see you?" I asked, eyes locking with his. "Because I don't play pretend. I don't chase headlines. And I don't run from the truth."

My chest clenched. My brain fuzzed. My body hummed in all the wrong frequencies. I stood. "I'm not done with you yet."

He raised a brow.

I dropped into position. "We're not finished."

"You sure?" His voice was low, cautious, even as his eyes tracked every breath I took.

"I need time to process all that. But right now, I need this more." I lunged for side control, shifted my hips, and tried a scissor sweep. He blocked it. Fast. Clean.

Good.

"Don't hold back," I said, voice sharp, sweat starting to sting at the edges of my vision. "I mean it. Give me everything you've got."

That flipped something in him.

The hesitation was gone.

He came at me with full finesse—no ego, no show-boating. Just skill. His footwork cut the space between us clean. His grip caught my wrist. I countered, twisting away, only to find him behind me, arm around my middle, using my own momentum against me.

I hit the mat with a hard thud.

But I rolled.

Reversed.

Mounted. My knees locked under his arms, weight centered. One forearm pressed firm against his chest.

"You've done this before," I said, panting.

He grinned. "Regularly."

I stared down at him. Then shifted.

"That sweep you did earlier?" I asked. "Show me again."

His brow furrowed. "Now?"

"Now."

He sat up. Slower this time. And showed me. Step by step. I mirrored it.

"Again," I said.

He did it again. This time faster.

I tried to counter. Failed.

"Again."

"Brynn—"

"I said again."

We rolled. Hit. Countered. Moved. Collided.

I lost track of how many times he pinned me. How many times I slipped out. We weren't sparring anymore. We were exorcising demons neither of us had named.

Everything.

My breath turned ragged. My arms shook. He blocked another move and I finally collapsed, arms braced over his chest, sweat dripping from my hair.

"I didn't choose this either," I said, voice nearly gone. "This job. This company. My life."

He stilled beneath me.

"My dad built it. Then he fucking died. Cancer. I still can't believe how fast it hit—how brutal it was."

He said nothing. Just listened. Eyes on mine.

"In his will, he handed it over to all six of us—his daughters. But only if we were all in. Or all out. No in between. No choice. If one of us backed out, we all lost it."

His hand brushed my shoulder lightly. Not to comfort. Just to say I'm here.

"I love them. I love what we do. But some mornings, I wake up and wonder if this life ever belonged to me... or if I'm just the obliging daughter keeping my dad's ghost happy."

"You're not stuck in his story, Brynn. You're rewriting it—with your name at the top."

I stared at him.

And that's when he flipped me.

Fast.

His legs slid under mine. His hips pressed against my thighs. My wrists pinned over my head in one fluid motion. His breath—hot and sharp—met mine in the space between.

"You're relentless," he said.

Jesus, don't say things like that.

"So are you."

He caught my eye, breath short. "Yellow?" he asked, voice low.

"Green," I shot back, steady. "Keep going."

Something changed in his expression, the test no longer about defense but about how much I'd give.

He still had my wrists.

But I wasn't losing.

Not yet.

It was tap out... or give in. And God help me, I wasn't doing either.

And then—

No warning. No slow slide. No testing the heat.

He kissed me.

Correction: he claimed me. Mouth hot and hungry, tongue coaxing mine open, one hand still gripping my wrist, the other dragging me closer like he was starving and finally allowed to eat.

Lips. Tongue. Heat. A groan that tore through both of us. My legs locked around his hips. His hands slid from my wrists to my waist like he needed to memorize every inch before we exploded.

We stayed tangled. Not moving. Not talking. His breath still ghosted across my mouth. And I wasn't sure which one of us was going to lose it first.

Then—

The door creaked.

"Shit," Jerrick muttered, pulling back just as a voice called out.

"Whoa—damn. Sorry! Didn't know the mat was booked for... uh... "

I whipped my head toward the entrance.

It was that goat guy with Ferox. Axel Something. Holding a smoothie and looking *way* too delighted with himself.

He raised both hands, grinning. "Don't mind me. Just gonna squeeze in a little cardio before the gossip mill explodes."

Jerrick straightened and ran a hand down his face. "It's not—"

"Sure, sure. Nothing to see here." Axel smirked and backed out of the gym, calling over his shoulder. "You two need towels, or privacy? I can run interference."

The door clicked shut.

I sat up.

Jerrick stayed on his knees, his chest still rising and falling, his lips red and kiss-bruised.

"That's going to make the rounds."

"Yeah," I said, not even pretending to be sorry.

Fantastic. Nothing screams take me seriously, I'm a professional *like being caught in a full-mount makeout by a guy slurping kale.*

"Let them talk."

Chapter 12

My Spirit Animal Has Questions

I PUSHED HIM OFF me the second I heard the door open.

Thirty seconds.

That's all it was.

Maybe less. But long enough to drown. Long enough for Goat Guy to round the corner and find me flat on my back—ankle bandaged, shirt rucked so high it could've joined a choir—while Jerrick Thorne rounded second in the middle of the damn fitness room.

I didn't wait for commentary. Or clarification. Or divine intervention.

"See you on the trail, Thorne," I grumbled, heat flaming up my neck like I'd licked a blowtorch. Then I bolted—ankle screaming, ego bleeding—straight to my suite.

Now I was hiding behind plantation blinds, pacing in damp underwear, and trying not to hurl into a complimentary fruit basket. Because by the time I peeled off my yoga pants and found a granola bar that hadn't collapsed into a sticky blob, the Coconut Telegraph—basically tropics code for gossip on speed—was already firing off like a goddamn emergency flare.

What the rumor mill is definitely saying (according to my spiraling internal monologue):

"Oh, we all saw this coming. The tension? Off the charts."

"Bet they've been banging for weeks. That kind of chemistry doesn't just happen."

"Did you hear they were grappling? On the mat? In public? Like, sweaty-face-to-crotch grappling?"

"Listen, if my enemies kissed me like that, I'd tattoo their company logo on my ass and call it brand loyalty."

I dragged a hand down my face. What the hell was I thinking?

Oh wait—I wasn't. The second he kissed me, rational thought nosedived into a coma. I went full hormone with zero brain backup.

In a resort full of clients.

During a branding retreat.

On a sparring mat.

In front of the weird livestock guy.

Jesus Christ.

I had one fucking job. *Represent Wilder Horizons. Be composed. Be untouchable.* Instead, I let a man crawl over me in my sports bra, full soft-core Gladiator mode—minus the sandals.

Deep breath, Brynn. You got this.

No tears. No texts. No throwing myself into a ravine.

Strategy time.

Step one: pants.

Step two: bra without visible paw prints.

Step three: own it.

If anyone says a word, I laugh. I deflect. I redirect. I become so aggressively unbothered they question their own memory.

And if Jerrick dares bring it up?

I'll smile. Tilt my head. And tell him he must've imagined it.

After all, he hit his head on the mat.

Hard.

Probably concussed.

No kiss. No scandal. No history.

Brynn Wilder?

Totally fine.

Totally chill.

Totally not about to see him again and melt into a puddle of cortisol and bad decisions.

I grabbed a fresh shirt, squared my shoulders, and reminded myself of one important truth: This is not my first humiliation rodeo.

And if I could survive the Waffle House bachelorette incident of 2019, I could survive a little public floorplay.

Probably.

Creative clarity through nature.

That's what the itinerary claimed.

I was still relearning basic motor function after kissing Jerrick.

Correction: after he kissed me—and I kissed him back—hard enough to forget my name and nearly my job title.

And now, here we were. Mid-morning. Mid-hike. Full denial spiral.

God, I needed a reset. And possibly adult supervision.

Instead, we got a half-mile uphill slog, ninety-nine percent humidity, and a branding exercise featuring river rocks and whispered affirmations.

There better be a goddamn shaman waiting at the end of this ritual nonsense.

I stepped over a vine that may or may not have pulsed and glanced back at Lucinda—still monologuing about her spirit animal, still throwing side-eye.

I hadn't said a word to Jerrick at the trailhead.

Mostly because I wasn't sure what version of myself would show up if I did—the pissed-off professional who'd just gone viral on the Coconut Telegraph, or the feral wreck who'd been one growl away from asking if the gym had condoms in the first aid kit.

And he?

Was fine.

Like... freshly showered, emotionally unbothered, casually unfazed fine.

As if he hadn't short-circuited my nervous system and smiled about it.

Dick.

His smile barely moved, but his eyes kept skimming my mouth like they hadn't forgotten anything. But his jaw ticked when Lucinda cracked another spirit-animal joke. Like maybe he wasn't as unbothered as he wanted me to believe.

"Remind me why we didn't fake food poisoning," I muttered, trying to keep my voice neutral.

"I offered," Jerrick said—cool as ever. As if he hadn't kissed me senseless two hours ago. "But someone insisted we be team players."

His shoulder nudged mine. Too casual. Happening too often.

He was playing it cool. Which was infuriating.

I was over here auditing every moan-adjacent sound I'd made on that mat while he auditioned for Jungle Ken.

"Yeah, well, that was before the bugs turned my inner thighs into an all-you-can-eat buffet."

He chuckled—low and lethal. God, that sound. I pretended it didn't detonate somewhere deeply inconvenient.

Pelvic floor? Times Square on New Year's.

We kept going—or stumbling, in my case. The incline steepened, same as my resolve. My ankle? One step from a full-blown protest. We rounded a bend and found the others clustered near a thatched pavilion—one good gust from total collapse. A woven sign flapped in the breeze: *Align. Ground. Create.*

Oh, hell no.

Lucinda gasped as if we'd unearthed the lost city of Atlantis. "Is this where we do the energy map journaling?"

Kill me. Actually, kill her first, then circle back.

A wiry guide in head-to-toe hemp waved us over. "Welcome, seekers. Please remove your shoes and select the stone that speaks to your creative essence."

I blinked. "My *what* now?"

Jerrick covered a snort with a cough. Didn't work. Bastard.

The guide gestured to a carved wooden bowl overflowing with smooth river rocks. "Let your intuition guide you."

I grabbed the first rock I touched. My intuition said: *wrap it up—we've got bugs to swat and scraps of dignity circling the drain.*

Jerrick held his stone aloft with mock reverence. "Mine says I'm destined for greatness."

I squinted at his rock. "Yours looks like a testicle," I snickered.

"It's symmetrical," he said, totally unfazed. "Rare. Powerful. Possibly magic."

My skin still buzzed from every place he'd touched me.

Jesus. The man had a *touch highlight reel* and didn't even know it.

Or worse—he *did*.

We sat cross-legged on yoga mats while the guide droned about "creative wind" and "soul grounding." Halfway through, my foot went numb—and then his pinkie brushed mine on the mat.

He left it there.

So did I.

By the time the guide told us to whisper our stone's message into the earth, my foot was numb, my patience shredded, and I was one breath away from screaming my truth into the sun just to get it over with.

I muttered something vaguely spiritual and stood too fast. My ankle rage-quit without warning. Jerrick caught my elbow.

But his fingers didn't let go.

Neither did the heat crawling up my neck.

Eventually, the group splintered. Lucinda floated ahead with Goat Guy, still deep in her one-woman show. The trail narrowed. Trees thickened around us.

And just like that, it was down to the two of us.

Alone.

Great.

Time for that inevitable, awkward post-makeout debrief I absolutely did not want but would overthink for the next decade.

I should've said something. A joke. A jab. Anything to cut the tension strung tight enough to slice steel. But my brain was short-circuiting—trapped somewhere between *That kiss was incredible, what does it mean?* and *Why the hell hasn't he mentioned it?*

I opened my mouth. No plan. No filter. "So... about earlier—when you, um... got on top of me."

His head turned slightly. Enough to let me know he was listening. And clearly enjoying it.

"You mean on the mat?"

"Obviously," I muttered, already regretting this entire conversation.

Cool. I sounded like I was grading his hip action for the Olympic finals.

I powered through, because stopping would only make it worse. "I meant—you were, you know. Assertive. And... firm."

"Firm?" he echoed, voice curling around the word like it had an aftertaste.

"Tactically," I lied. "Your grip. And that thing with your—uh—*hip* placement?"

His smirk deepened. "Hip placement?"

Jesus. Send a snake. End me now.

"You've clearly practiced," I muttered.

"So have you." His voice dropped half an octave. "Your guard was tight. Real tight."

My entire nervous system short-circuited.

We were alone.

In the jungle.

Fresh off a kiss so hot I could still taste want and sweat and the salt of his skin.

I was gearing up to say anything to claw back the last thread of sanity when my foot hit a patch of moss and slipped.

Jerrick's hand snapped to my waist.

Not just caught. *Claimed.*

And everyone probably thought we were deep into the enemies-with-benefits saga. That we'd been sneaking off between panels to fuck like it was a sport.

And yet here I was—still tingling from his grip on my waist. His thumb pressed just beneath my ribs, and breathing? Suddenly not my strong suit.

"You good?" His voice was low. Closer than it should've been.

"Perfect."

Liar. My brain was soup. My body? Full traitor.

My hand latched onto his forearm—firm, solid, unfairly sculpted—and I wasn't exactly in a rush to let go. Maybe I was holding on for more than balance.

His eyes dropped to my mouth. Again. As if he was remembering how it tasted.

Like he'd do it again if I didn't stop him.

Every nerve I owned stood up and saluted.

"Don't," I whispered.

I knew exactly what I meant.

Don't make me want this again.

Don't make it worse.

Don't turn this into another tabloid-worthy headline for the rest of the group to snicker about.

And for the love of God—don't look at me like I'm still the only thing lighting up your radar.

"Why not?"

I exhaled, already unraveling. "Because. People. Gossip. Slack threads. Group chats."

His brow arched up, but I plowed ahead.

"Pretty sure at least three departments think we've been fucking since check-in. I've been sweating since sunrise, there's a leaf in my bra, and this was supposed to be about branding enlightenment—not a goddamn Jungle Sex Scandal."

He didn't laugh.

He just looked at me.

Steady. Unshaken. Eyes locked on mine as if the chaos didn't faze him.

"I don't care what they think, Brynn." His voice was steady, but his hand twitched like the words cost him something to say out loud.

I froze.

"I used to," he said, voice low. "Every move. Every word. Had to be calculated. Scripted. Approved." He stepped in—closer, slower—one heartbeat at a time. "But I'm done letting other people decide who I can want."

The space between us snapped tight.

"You already branded me," he added. "Back on the mat this morning."

His hands flexed at my waist, a small betrayal of everything he was trying not to do.

I blinked. "Branded you? What the actual stupid fuck does that mean? You gonna whip out your branding iron or just drop your pants and let me inspect the placement?"

The second it left my mouth, I wanted to choke on a bug and disintegrate.

Jerrick smirked. "You offering to inspect the goods, Wilder?"

I made a noise that might've been a laugh or a warning siren and shoved past him—before I could admit that yes, I absolutely was. Because now I was picturing the pants dropping. And the merch.

And holy hell, I needed help.

He didn't move. Didn't even blink.

Which made it worse. Of course.

Because now I couldn't stop picturing where I'd put the merch.

And just how long I'd make him earn it.

A mosquito dive-bombed my ear. I slapped at it—somewhere between a ninja move and a full-body panic. "Serious question—if one of these bastards lays eggs in my sweat glands, you still down to make out again?"

He smirked. "If you think mosquito eggs are a deal-breaker, you seriously underestimate how badly I want to kiss you again."

He looked down. I looked up. The air locked between us—thick, electric. Even the jungle had gone quiet.

Was he going to kiss me again?

Was I going to let him?

Then—

Something plopped onto his shoulder.

We both screamed.

"Is it a snake?" I shrieked. "Tell me it's not a snake!"

Jerrick flicked it off—some squishy fruit. Or a tropical bitch slap in pulp form.

Panic launched me backward, pure reflex—fangs, poison, doomsday vibes.

Bad move.

My ankle buckled the second I landed, pain zipping up my leg like a taser. I hissed as Jerrick turned fast.

"False alarm," he said, eyes scanning me now. "Just Mother Nature, out here cockblocking."

"She's already blocked us," I muttered, trying not to cry. "Right on the mat. In front of Goat Guy."

Honestly, I deserved a medal for not combusting. Or crying. Or both.

I took another step—just to prove I could—and nearly toppled again.

"You okay?" Jerrick's brow pulled tight.

"Define okay."

"You're limping."

"It's called jungle swagger. Not everyone can pull it off."

He gave me that look—the one that said I was completely ridiculous, and he liked it.

"Okay, hear me out," I said. "We fake a branding emergency—urgent, spiritual, possibly mystical—and backtrack to civilization."

"You want to lie to the group?"

"No," I said quickly. "I want to hobble nobly back to the resort while you pretend to argue and fail spectacularly."

He raised a brow. "Or..."

I narrowed my eyes. "Don't say it."

"We tell them you twisted your bad ankle again."

I scowled. "Fine. But only if you still act like you hate me a little."

He held out a hand. "So I get to play the chivalrous escort and score snacks sooner?"

Of course he made *jungle escort* sound hot.

The man was literally glowing—shirt dry and not a single bead of sweat in sight.

"Sit," Jerrick said firmly, steering me toward a half-decent rock with the authority of a man training a golden retriever with boundary issues.

I *shouldn't* have liked that. The tone. The touch. The take-charge confidence. But apparently, my body had decided to imprint on the most inconvenient man alive. I dropped onto the rock with a wince. "Are you *serious* right now?"

"You're done walking on that ankle," he said, already moving back up the trail. "I'll let them know we're turning back. Five minutes."

I scowled. "You're seriously leaving me? In the murder jungle? Alone?"

"It's Costa Rica," he said. "Not Jurassic Park."

"You say that now. But if I get eaten by a wild cat or abducted by a cult leader with a coconut crown, that's on you."

He just shook his head and ran off—annoyingly competent, infuriatingly sexy. He glanced back once—fast, like he didn't mean to—and the flicker in his eyes wasn't annoyance. It was calculation. And something protective he'd never admit.

Which left me alone.

In the jungle.

With one good ankle and anxiety boiling in my ear canals.

I was being *reasonable*. Also possibly overdramatic. But mostly reasonable.

The first minute was fine. Peaceful, even. Birds chirped. Leaves rustled. My sweat had *sweat*.

By minute three, I was cataloging potential crime scene details. Just in case someone needed to CSI my last known location.

And if I did get eaten by a wild animal, I could already picture the headlines:

Local Branding Expert Dies in Jungle, Leaves Behind Scandal, Lip Gloss, and Broken NDA.

Minute five? The trees got suspiciously quiet.

I froze.

"Oh no. No-no-no-no-no. Why did it go silent? That's horror movie rules. Something's stalking me. I *am* being stalked."

A twig snapped behind me.

I launched off the rock. Scalded. Scorched. "FUCK THIS."

I hauled ass down the trail. Adrenaline steamrolled my ankle, my pride, and every rational thought I'd ever owned.

A vine snapped against my leg. Then a bug dive-bombed into my mouth, wings and panic everywhere. And when the brush thrashed beside me—heavy-footed, hellbent, too close—I stopped being human and became pure flight.

"THIS IS HOW I DIE," I shrieked, crashing through ferns, full feral panic unlocked.

And then—

Jerrick.

Chapter 13

Namaste Out of My Pants

I BARRELED INTO HIM at full speed, nearly taking us both out.

His arms snapped around me, solid and hot and so damn safe I almost sobbed.

"Whoa," he breathed, steadying us. "What the hell—"

"I heard a noise," I gasped. "Then another. Then silence. Way worse. And I swallowed a bug. I'm either being hunted by a monkey or Latin Satan."

He blinked.

"Also? My dignity. Left it somewhere back there. Possibly bleeding out."

He didn't answer. Just stared—mouth parted, breathing hard.

As if we hadn't already done this today. As if doing it again was inevitable.

His hands gripped my waist. His chest rose sharp against mine.

Could've been the impact—or the fact that I was clinging to him, treating him as my last ride out of the apocalypse.

He looked down. I looked up. And I knew exactly what was coming.

But all I could do was hold on and burn.

We weren't even supposed to be kissing. We were supposed to be stretching—breathing, aligning, whatever new-age brochure bullshit Lucinda was selling. But the second his hand skimmed my hip, the whole idea of inner peace went up in smoke. My pulse raced harder than the drums on Lucinda's "soul playlist."

I shifted closer, close enough that his breath feathered my cheek, close enough that one tilt would've ended me. His eyes darkened, locked on mine, the jungle falling away until it was just this—heat, want, and the worst possible timing.

And that was it.

His mouth found mine, certain and hungry—hot, and absolutely done pretending. One second I trembled. The next, I melted into him.

His grip tightened. One hand clamped my waist, the other slid into my hair, tilting my face as the kiss deepened.

A low, desperate sound slipped out before I could stop it.

He swallowed it whole, tongue sweeping in—hot, wild, relentless. This wasn't a kiss.

It was a goddamn reckoning.

A terrible idea. A career nightmare. A scandal with tongue.

And God help me, I craved every second of it.

Lips. Teeth. Gasps. Growls.

It all erupted. Months of tension, wound tight and waiting, finally snapping free.

We should've stopped. Lucinda's chakra circle was practically within chanting distance.

But stopping wasn't in my toolbox anymore.

He kissed me with the force of surrender—whatever he'd been holding back, gone.

Breathing? Optional.

Caring? Not even on the radar.

I hooked my arms around his neck, yanked him closer, and pushed up on my toes, half-hopping on the one foot that hadn't betrayed me. He groaned, low and guttural, and lifted me as if his body had already decided.

His body moved on instinct, as if this was already written in muscle memory.

I should've been terrified.

But all I felt was heat, everywhere.

I locked my legs around him, tight and trembling.

My fingers clutched his shoulders, then threaded into his hair, pulling until that growl returned.

He pinned me to the nearest tree, hips grinding, breath wrecked.

Holy shit, I was seconds from combustion.

And I didn't stop.

Not unless the tree snapped in half or Lucinda summoned us with a spirit gong.

Everything blurred—heat, pressure, friction.

Bruising kisses. Frantic hands.

I yanked at his shirt, desperate for skin. Heat. Him.

"Tell me to stop," he rasped, forehead pressed to mine, breath coming hard. "Say the word, or I swear..."

I kissed him harder.

That was my answer.

That was *all* he needed.

He kissed me with the urgency of lost time clawing to catch up.

I arched into him. No hesitation. No thought. Every nerve begged for pressure and contact. My fingers slipped beneath his shirt, tracing the heat of taut skin. His abs flexed beneath my palms.

I had no idea if I wanted to ruin him or write him a thank-you note.

Maybe both.

Maybe *right now.*

I needed more.

All of it.

"Jesus, Brynn," he groaned, breaking the kiss just long enough to stare. Eyes wide. Wrecked. Ravenous. "You're gonna kill me." He looked at me like I was both salvation and sabotage, and he couldn't decide which was worse.

"Shut up and kiss me," I breathed, gripping his jaw and dragging him back down.

And he did.

His mouth moved with purpose—claiming, marking, *owning.*

Tongue, teeth, lips—down my throat, across the spot that unraveled me.

And yeah, I felt every inch of him. Hard. Relentless. Perfect.

One hand caught the back of my thigh and lifted. The other slipped beneath my shirt, his palm hot over bare skin.

I was panting.

Sweating.

Drenched in him.

One wrong breath from letting him fuck me against a tree. Broad daylight. Terrible decisions. Full chaos-goddess mode.

Wait. A voice. I'm hearing a fucking voice.

"Jerrick?" someone called from the trail. High-pitched. Perky. *Hydrated.* "Hey! Wait up—I think I'm gonna head back too!"

My blood froze. "Down," I hissed, shoving at his shoulders. "Drop. Fake an ankle wrap. Now."

"What—"

"Move!"

He dropped fast, hands fumbling for my calf while I yanked my shirt straight and wrestled my underwear back into a location that vaguely qualified as *on*. My hair was a disaster, his face was wrecked, and my mouth? Swollen, like I'd deep-throated a ghost pepper.

"Shit," he muttered, yanking his pack around. "Where's the damn wrap—where is it—ah. Okay. Faking it. I'm faking it."

"Less narration. More nurse roleplay."

I dropped back against the tree, wincing dramatically while he secured a bandage that didn't need securing.

By the time she rounded the bend, I had both hands on my cheeks and a wince dramatic enough to pass for pain. Maybe. Hopefully.

"Oh no," she said, eyes wide. "Is your ankle worse?"

It was Bridget. Of course it was Bridget.

Tiny matching workout set, pink reflector shades, and a Lume-branded water bottle in one hand.

Please let there be a yoni crystal wedged somewhere in her top.

Just for the symmetry.

"Little bit," I breathed, cheeks blazing. "Stepped wrong. Again."

Jerrick looked up, all business, like he was prepping me for surgery. "She needs to stay off it completely," he said. "Group knows we're heading back. I texted the resort—clinic's expecting us."

"What?" I whisper-coughed. "You did *what*?"

"Medical check. Standard procedure."

"Oh my God, it's a *minor twist*, not a battlefield wound."

"You were limping. Sweating. Clutching a tree like your life depended on it."

"Because *you were the one making me see stars!*" I growled under my breath.

She nodded, glancing between us. "Mind if I join? I'm kind of over the heat and I think my spiritual aura's fully hydrated."

I forced a smile. "Of course. Safety in numbers."

He glanced at Bridget, completely unbothered. "Someone should be there when we arrive."

She nodded, visibly impressed. "That's so smart. We carry healing packs at Lume, but nothing with, like... *real* medicine."

I blinked. "Do you have a chakra kit in your pack?"

She tapped her chest. "No, silly. That's in my bra. Closest to the heart chakra. Balance matters." And she said it like anyone with half a brain should've known.

Oh. My. God.

"But I do have something else that might help."

She turned to dig in her bag, and that's when I saw him shift. Subtle. Then again. And again.

Oh no.

His shorts were useless. That man had a situation.

A very *vertical*, very *prominent* situation.

His eyes locked on mine: *Help.*

Mine answered: *Fix it.*

He glanced down, panic rising fast. Yanked his drawstring tighter. Tugged his waistband up an inch. Lowered one knee, reverent and tense, like prayer might tame the beast.

Which, frankly, might be needed.

But no. *It moved.*

A twitch.

A pulse.

A full lurch toward freedom.

I slapped a hand over my mouth, biting back a laugh. He was losing a full-scale battle with his own dick. There was an uprising in those cargo shorts.

He leaned toward me, jaw tight. "If she asks, you're crying from the pain."

"Why would I be *crying*?"

"Because your face is red as hell and I'm visibly pitching a tent in breathable nylon."

"Think harder!" I whispered. "Adjust your bandana or distract the dick—do something!"

He ripped the sweat towel from his bag and tucked it into his waistband, folding his hands like he was about to pray. "Better?" he muttered.

"You look like a camp counselor with a secret."

Bridget turned around, still blissfully unaware. "Ready when you are," she chirped.

"Let's go," Jerrick said, voice strangled with restraint.

He offered me a hand, and I took it—limping harder than I meant to, avoiding eye contact, trying not to combust from the heat still crackling between us.

"Hmm, that's not happening."

"What?"

"You. Walking. Get on."

"What the hell—"

He stepped forward. "Too late."

And suddenly, I was airborne. Legs hooked around his waist, arms gripping tight, chin smushed into his shoulder as he adjusted me higher without breaking a sweat.

"I'm not piggy-backing you down this trail."

"You're injured."

"I'm fine."

"You're lying."

"You've got a raging boner and an audience."

"Correction. Had a boner. It died the second I made eye contact with Bridget's hydration aura."

Behind us, she called out, "You guys are so cute. Seriously. This is, like, sacred masculine energy."

I buried my face in Jerrick's neck. "I need a crystal for my sacred energy," I whispered. "Preferably one I can shove up your ass after this. "

He choked on a laugh. "That's not how they work."

"It's how I work."

We thudded down the trail, me bouncing like a bobblehead in heat, trying to rearrange my face into something less post-orgasmic.

"We are not done," he growled.

I didn't look at him. "You are absolutely done if that towel falls off."

We reached the main path, Bridget trailing behind—a glittery emotional support animal with zero shame. "I'm gonna peel off here," she chirped, veering toward a cluster of bungalows. "Need to realign my root chakra before dinner."

"Godspeed," I called, still draped on Jerrick like a resentful koala.

She threw us a peace sign and vanished into the foliage.

The second she was gone, I dropped my head against his shoulder. "This is humiliating."

"You could walk," he offered.

"Nope. Already committed to the drama."

"Good," he said. "Because we're going straight to the clinic."

I stiffened. "You're kidding."

"Not even a little."

"I don't need—"

"Professional confirmation that you're stubborn and mildly concussed from *orgasm-adjacent* activity?"

I groaned. "I *told* you I was fine."

"And I told you I plan to spar again. That requires functioning ankles."

That shut me up. Because... Jesus. *Spar* wasn't safe in his mouth. Not with that low promise tucked inside it. Not after last time, when I'd nearly blacked out from friction. Not when I was still throbbing.

By the time we reached the clinic near the spa, I was flushed all over again—and it had nothing to do with the tropical air.

Jerrick carried me straight through the doors, ignoring my protests and the nurse's lifted brow, like I didn't weigh a damn thing.

"Twisted ankle," he said. "She needs to be checked out."

"Sure," she said slowly. "We can take a look."

He set me on the exam table, careful as if I were spun sugar, then crouched beside it and brushed my calf. "You okay?"

I glared. "Stop being sexy while you're fussing over me. It's confusing."

"Confusing for you or for me?" he murmured, thumb tracing the edge of the wrap.

A tall man in scrubs entered, flipping through a clipboard. "Alright. I'm Dr. Miguel. What's going on here?"

"Possible ankle strain. Want to rule out worse," Jerrick said, standing tall.

"Complete overreaction," I added.

Dr. Miguel looked between us—my tousled hair, flushed face, and Jerrick's towel still covering a very suspicious region—then blinked twice and sighed. "I see."

"Nothing wild," Jerrick said quickly.

"Uh-huh," said the doctor. "So how did this happen?"

"Tree root," I said.

"Lust spiral," Jerrick said at the same time.

Dr. Miguel blinked. "So... tree root via lust spiral. Noted."

He started prodding my ankle while I tried not to whimper—or moan—because Jerrick's hand hadn't moved from my thigh. I swatted at him. "Stop touching me."

"You love when I touch you."

"You've scrambled every fuse in my body and you know it."

"That's on *you*," he whispered. "I'm being a gentleman."

"Your boner says otherwise."

Dr. Miguel cleared his throat sharply. "Still here," he said. "Still medically licensed."

"Sorry," I muttered. "We're working through some... workplace tension."

"I'm sure."

Ten minutes later, I was cleared. Mild strain. No permanent damage. Just a note to rest, ice, and maybe avoid getting railed against a tree without stretching first—okay, he didn't say that last part, but the look said it all.

Jerrick thanked the staff and grabbed the release papers, hand sliding to the small of my back like he already owned it.

I didn't stop him.

He turned to me. "My suite's closer than yours."

"Convenient," I said.

"Think of it as a tactical decision."

I shrugged. "Lead the way, soldier."

And I followed. Because whatever was about to happen in Jerrick Thorne's suite?

Wouldn't need a crystal.

Just a headboard with reinforced bolts.

Chapter 14

Team Building

WE MADE IT TO his suite. I stepped inside, and my sanity promptly ghosted.

Rational thought? Evaporated.

Restraint? Urban legend.

I wasn't leaving this room unmarked.

He took my mouth as if it belonged to him. His hands locked me down. Heat barreled through me, full-contact, marrow-deep. He pinned me to the door, thigh driving between mine, kissing me with the hunger of all the time we hadn't touched.

Not gentle.

Not hesitant.

Just relief, finally allowed to feast.

My back hit the door. I didn't even flinch. All I felt was him—his mouth, his hands—igniting every nerve until my skin forgot how to behave.

"Say no, Brynn," he said, knuckles brushing my jaw. "I'll stop."

He meant it. Even now. But I'd burn this whole damn resort to ash before I let him stop. So I kissed him back, ruin screaming through every nerve.

There were already rumors. Let 'em spread. If we were going down, we were going down scorched-earth.

His control broke—and I had a VIP seat for the implosion. His kiss turned punishing. Possessive. Each stroke deliberate, heat inked across my skin like his signature.

I shifted, baiting him.

He didn't fall for it.

Well shit. Guess we're skipping foreplay and going straight to consequences.

Instead, his hands locked around my wrists, pinning them to the door above my head. "Try that again," he murmured, lips grazing my ear, "and I'll make you beg to come before I let you come."

I squeaked. A full-body shiver cracked through me. *Who the hell was this man?*

That smirk? Pure fucking sin. "You've been running your mouth for months, Wilder. Let's see if you can take what you've been dishing out."

Then his hands were back—gripping my hips tight, unrelenting, holding me in place as if I was already his. His tongue swept over mine, slow and possessive, a *promise* of what was coming. Each touch was deliberate—palms branding, thumbs grazing, fingers digging in enough to make my pulse stutter.

I didn't just let him.

I *offered* myself up.

"You drive me fucking insane," he growled into my neck, his teeth dragging across skin already wired to explode. His fingers slid under my waistband, knuckles skimming lower, teasing and testing. "And right now?" His voice dropped, each word rougher than the last. "You're mine."

Yes, daddy.

There it was—control, rerouted. Not lost. *Focused*.

He hadn't unraveled. He'd snapped into place. All of it zeroed in on *me*.

He yanked my shorts down—no hesitation, no warning, no fucking mercy. *Starvation in motion.*

"Bed. Now."

It wasn't a bark. It was a *prophecy*.

My knees? Already giving in.

He stripped like a man on a mission—precise and practiced, no time for hesitation. Too much waiting.

Not enough skin. That chest? An *actual* crime against my sanity.

When the shirt came off, my sanity took another hit. Five tattoos—deliberate, secret, hidden in places only someone like me would ever see. A circle at his rib. A wave at his side. A lotus by his hip. A mountain on his oblique. And the last—black feather inked low, sharp and dangerous. Not trophies for the world. Private victories etched on skin, each one tied to the belt progression of jiu-jitsu, every rank earned the hard way. Every mark screamed discipline, control—until now. And fuck me, it turned me feral.

Every tattoo told a story of restraint. His hands? They said he'd been dying for permission to finally let go. I wanted my mouth on every line, wanted to trace his journey with my tongue until he broke. Sexy didn't even cover it. They were lethal, and I wanted to worship every inch.

I yanked off my top. My bra—lace, decorative at best—hung on by a thread, same as my dignity.

He looked once. Only *once*. And I knew—he wasn't here to take.

He was going to *feast*.

My shoes weren't even off before he was on me again—waist locked in, hand sliding beneath my thong.

He paused. Knuckles brushed damp fabric. My breath caught, thighs tensing.

"Fuck," he muttered, low and dark. "You're soaked already. Just from my hands."

A filthy little sound spilled out—because fuck, he wasn't wrong.

"This what you wanted, Brynn? All those meetings—snarking off, crossing your legs like you didn't know exactly what you were doing? You want my fingers buried in you while you bite that smart little mouth?"

His thumb circled, cruel and steady, each stroke a power play. I arched, but his other hand clamped down on my hip, pinning me exactly where he wanted. "Uh-uh. You don't get to rush this."

He peeled my thong away, slow, merciless, fire sparking with every drag. His gaze stayed fixed on me, watching every small tremor with unnerving focus.

Then his mouth was at my ear, breath hot. "You enjoy testing me? Good. Now let's see how well you take orders."

My body arched into him, shameless and ready, completely ruined for anyone else.

His mouth crashed into mine before the fabric even hit the floor.

Not a kiss. A fucking reckoning.

He didn't savor. He *consumed*. His lips claimed and devoured, no softness left between us. His need inked into the way he touched me.

I wasn't being worshipped.

I was being taken.

Fuck me. I'd unleashed a dragon—and handed him the leash.

This wasn't the Jerrick the world saw. This was the man who'd waited. Who'd let me play power games. Then wrecked me the second he got close enough.

His teeth caught my lower lip, firm and deliberate. Not punishment. "That's right—bite me back if you don't like it."

"I don't want you gentle. I want you destroying me."

"Christ, the sounds you make," he growled against my mouth, his grip tightening on my throat just enough to make my pulse kick. "This pulse is mine. Your breath is mine. Use your words if you want something different."

Then his hand twisted in my hair, angling me exactly how he wanted—no hesitation, no uncertainty. He didn't guess. He commanded.

He didn't need to say it. Every kiss said *mine*.

He groaned into the kiss—raw, ragged—and I felt it, all of it, pressed hard and unforgiving against my stomach. "Tell me you want this. Now."

My legs wrapped around him on instinct—needy, greedy, starved.

"Words, baby."

"I want everything, Jerrick. Every fucking second."

His hand slid down my spine. Both palms gripped my ass, rough and possessive. He lifted me like I weighed nothing, walking us backward until the mattress hit my calves. Then he rolled his hips—slow, deep. Not teasing. Promising.

"You want more? Ask for it."

I ignited, all nerves and no brakes. "More."

"You feel that?" he growled, lips dragging over mine. "That's what you fucking do to me. Any time you give me that look—as if you're daring me to lose control."

His kiss turned brutal. Dominant. Unapologetic.

I sank my nails into his shoulders, clawing down his unforgiving body, inch by inch.

"Mmm... that's what I've been waiting for."

Each pull of his lips marked me.

Each nip? A sealed contract.

If this wasn't sex, I didn't want the real thing. This was destruction, and I wanted the whole brutal ride.

When he pulled back for air, it wasn't surrender.

It was *calculated*.

"Still so fucking loud. I wonder what it'll take to shut you up." His mouth found my throat, teeth closing over the pulse he'd summoned. "Mine," he growled—etched into my skin with teeth and heat. "And you'll feel it tomorrow."

Then he was on me again—mouth demanding, kiss deeper, darker.

Rewriting me cell by cell.

His hand slid up my ribs and sternum, pausing right beneath the weight of my next breath.

Then—

Jesus.

His palm cupped my breast. Rough. Certain. His thumb sweeping across my nipple in a slow, punishing drag.

A wrecked sound cracked loose from my throat.

He didn't stop. Didn't flinch. Both hands found me—teasing, pinching, *claiming*—until my knees straight-up surrendered. "So fucking soft." His voice was a dark scrape against my ear. "And you feel—Christ, Brynn—you feel unreal."

Then he latched on—tongue flicking, lips sealing, desperate and reverent.

I arched into him and let his name fall from my lips like a prayer too dirty for church. "Jerrick... holy fucking hell..."

He groaned low and shifted—teeth scraping across the other breast, tongue chasing after, again and again, until I shook with it. Every kiss, every stroke, every breath-stealing pull of his mouth was worship—wicked, filthy worship—and I craved it like breath.

But he wasn't done, each inch he took sending the heat deeper, threading through muscle and marrow.

"Jesus fucking Christ, who even are you?" That smirk—fuck. He didn't just know how to ruin me; he'd designed the whole damn blueprint.

Then his tongue—no teasing, no testing. Just taking. One slow, devastating lick—

Every nerve lit up. Salt on my skin, sweat mingling with the faint bite of his cologne as he breathed me in—dark, sharp, impossible to ignore. My back bowed. "Fuuuck—"

He hummed—deep, satisfied—as though I'd passed some filthy fucking test. His grip tightened on my thighs, holding me open, holding me still.

"That's it," he murmured against me, voice thick with approval. "Let me hear how much you love it."

His tongue was relentless.

Greedy.

Unforgiving.

God help me—I'd let him feast on me forever and call it a fucking meal plan.

His tongue circled—slow and cruel. Then he dragged it through me in one long, devastating stroke.

"Jerrick—fuck—"

My thighs tensed. My hands fisted the sheets. I was already teetering, seconds from breaking—

And he knew it.

He smirked against me. "Tell me what you need." A command, not a question.

"You," I gasped. "Only you. Always you."

He growled—low and pleased. "That's pretty." Then he blew a hot breath over my clit. "Now tell me what you want me to *do.*"

His teeth grazed my inner thigh—a warning, a promise—and my hips jerked.

"Yes," I choked out. "Yes—don't you fucking dare stop."

"Good girl." Then he dove back in—deeper, dirtier, ruin delivered by mouth. I trembled, straining, clinging to the edge, and he held me there. *Made me feel it.*

He dragged his tongue up—unhurried, merciless—then sucked. Hard. I shattered, screaming as the world split open. My hips bucked, but he didn't budge—just locked one firm hand on my stomach, pinning me with unshakable grip.

"Stay still." His voice was rough, commanding. "We do this my way, remember?"

His tongue kept going—merciless, reverent—driving me through the wreckage, worshipping every pulse, every quake, every twitch until I was shaking, boneless, and gone.

Only then did he lift his head—lips wrecked, eyes pure sin. "Still think we came back here to ice your ankle?" He licked his lips, slow and satisfied, every inch the smug bastard who knew exactly what he'd done.

I gasped, still shaking. "If your cock isn't in me in thirty seconds, I swear—"

He cut me off with a grip that warned, *careful, baby.* I'm still in charge.

"You'll what, Brynn?" His smirk was lethal. "Gonna punish me? Try."

Then he laughed—low and dirty—that growl hitting my nerves like a lit match. He reached into his bag, pulled out a condom, and rolled it on with slow, deliberate strokes, his eyes locked on mine the entire time. "Tell me you want it."

He gripped my chin, forcing my gaze to his. "Words, Brynn. Or I stop."

I swallowed. "Yes."

"Yes, what?"

"I want it. I want *you*. All of you. Don't make me wait another second."

He pushed my thighs apart and looked—didn't glance, didn't hesitate. He devoured me with his eyes, hungry, focused, already planning his next masterpiece of destruction.

"Oh, I know you've been waiting, Thorne," I breathed.

His grin was all teeth. "Longer than you fucking know."

Then he leaned in—voice low, possessive, carved from hunger.

"You're mine tonight, Brynn. Your breath. That tremble. Mine. And I'm going to take exactly what I want."

He sank into me—slow, deep, ruin etched into the stretch of him.

I arched, gasping, nails dragging down his shoulders until he caught my wrists in one hand and pinned them high above my head. "Uh-uh. You don't get to hide."

And when he moved? It wasn't fucking. It was a possession. He didn't ease up. He drove into me, the impact rough enough to shake reason clean out of me. His free hand locked on my hip as if he was daring it to bruise.

"You take me so fucking deep, baby," he growled, dragging his teeth over my pulse point. "That's how much I've wanted you. How much I still want you."

I was unraveling—moans turning to pleas—but he didn't let up.

"Come on, Brynn. Let me hear all of it."

I broke—loud, sharp, gone—but he didn't stop. He drove me higher, harder, until I shattered a second time, shaking so violently I couldn't breathe.

"That's it," he snarled against my ear. "Take it. All of it."

He came with a strangled groan, his whole frame braced over me, trembling with release.

Then we collapsed—tangled, slick, wrecked.

The silence that followed?

Decadence.

"You officially win the 'shock the hell outta a girl' award for that performance, Thorne."

"Didn't hear you complaining."

"Nope. Just—wow. Never saw that coming."

Then, without a word, he lifted me. Carried me to the shower as though I was breakable. Sacred. We both knew better. I was a wrecked mess. And he looked at me like I was the prize.

The water was warm. His hands? So hot they made the steam feel shy. He lathered soap onto a cloth and washed me with slow, deliberate care.

My arms. My collarbone. Then—between my thighs, where I was tender, ruined, and still pulsing.

He moved with care, each pass a quiet kind of worship. Like he knew I'd given him everything—and he was going to honor every goddamn second of it.

He rinsed me gently. Lifted my chin. "You okay?" His voice was low. His eyes—wrecked. He'd felt it too.

I nodded, unable to speak. My body was obliterated, my heart stupid and split wide open. Then he dropped to his knees—in the water, between my thighs—like a prayer.

"Jerrick—fuck—"

"Hush." His mouth was already on me, tongue firm, hot, merciless.

"Told you," he murmured against me. "I wasn't done."

"Jesus, Jerrick."

And that—that was it. The moment I knew we were in this, neck-deep, with no coming out clean.

The spray hit my back. His mouth hit my soul. And I didn't even try to pretend it was only sex anymore.

Steam still clung to my skin when we fell onto the bed, the afternoon light slipping through the blinds in slow stripes. The world outside kept spinning—emails, deadlines, expectations—but for that brief, stolen hour, none of it mattered.

Chapter 15

Nothing to See Here

I WOKE TO THE weight of his leg thrown over mine, his hand already mapping the territory of my hip in the half-light. Late-afternoon sun leaked through the blinds, soft and gold. We must've actually fallen asleep.

Great. I nap like I trust people now.

The sheet was a tangled mess between us, and the air still smelled of us—sweat and skin and the lingering charge of the night before.

His mouth found my shoulder, a slow, open-mouthed kiss that was more claim than question. No "good morning." No words at all. Just the rough scratch of his stubble and the heat of his breath as he moved up the line of my throat.

I arched into him, a silent answer, my hand fisting in his hair. It was all the permission he needed.

He reached for the nightstand, tearing open a foil packet without taking his eyes off me. The sound alone made my pulse stutter. Then he rolled over me, his body a familiar, welcome weight. The look in his eyes was pure, undiluted hunger—the same focused intensity he used to dismantle a business rival, now aimed entirely at me. It should have been terrifying. It was the biggest turn-on of my life.

Note to self: never underestimate the power of bad ideas.

He entered me in one smooth, devastating stroke, and my gasp was swallowed by the crush of his mouth on mine. This wasn't the desperate, exploratory sex of last night. This was raw. Needy. A frantic, wordless conversation with our bodies.

My nails dug into the hard muscle of his back, urging him on, closer, deeper. The world narrowed to the slick, driving rhythm, the sound of our ragged breathing, the creak of the bedsprings keeping time.

"Look at me," he growled against my lips, his voice rough with sleep and want.

I forced my eyes open, meeting that searing gaze. He was watching me come undone, studying every flicker of pleasure across my face like it was the most critical data he'd ever seen.

"Jerrick," I choked out, a warning and a plea all in one.

His pace turned ruthless, purposeful, chasing his own release and determined to take me with him. The coil in my belly tightened, snapped, and I shattered with a broken cry, my body clenching around his. He followed a moment later, his groan a hot vibration against my neck, his entire frame shuddering as release overtook him.

For a long moment, there was only the sound of our panting breaths slowly returning to normal. The breeze coasted over my skin, warm and salt-heavy, lifting the edge of the sheet still wrapped around my hips. But nothing cooled the flush still clinging to my chest—or the way he was looking at me as if I'd just rewritten gravity.

I stared at the ceiling fan above the bed, motionless in its decorative uselessness. "I think we broke Costa Rica."

Jerrick didn't answer. He was too busy watching me as if I might vanish if he blinked.

So naturally, I panicked.

"I mean, I think I lost a contact. Not that I wear contacts. But I might need some now, since I apparently blacked out and saw God."

He huffed a laugh. "Is this your version of pillow talk?"

I rolled onto my side, dragging the sheet with me, a flimsy shield after such total surrender. "No. My version of pillow talk involves post-coital scheduling and a debrief PowerPoint."

His hand settled low on my back, thumb moving in slow, absent circles. "Is that a thing you've actually done?"

"I'll never tell."

"You're unbelievable."

"Thank you."

He didn't laugh this time. Instead, he leaned in and swept a strand of hair away from my face, slow and deliberate, without asking. "You throw all this fire and control, like a facade. But underneath it..."

I didn't move. Didn't blink.

His gaze lingered—measured, not invasive.

"You rattle me," he said simply.

My throat threatened mutiny.

Nope. Not today, vulnerability. Not when I was still sticky with sex and stupid with oxytocin.

"You should see me during tax season," I said. "Real menace to society."

Still, he didn't let go. His hand stayed at the small of my back, not rough or possessive—just steady. Anchoring. And suddenly, I couldn't seem to pull a full breath.

I exhaled. "We have to rehearse for the panel tomorrow night."

He nodded. "Yeah."

"And shower."

Another nod. "Definitely."

"We'll be late."

"Let's be late."

I slipped out of bed and wrapped the sheet around me, twisted tight at the shoulder in my best imitation of a toga. "I call first shower."

"You don't even have shampoo in there."

"I have optimism and hotel samples. I'll survive."

But I didn't head to the bathroom.

Instead, I bent to collect my bra from the floor—snagged on the corner of the chaise, half-draped and shameless, surrendering on my behalf. My shirt was balled under the edge of the bed. Helga, my hikers, kicked off at opposite corners of the suite, casualties of a particularly dramatic breakup.

Jerrick propped himself up on one elbow, all quiet calculation and indulgent heat. The edge of the sheet dipped scandalously low across his hips. "You sneaking out on me?"

"Not sneaking. Strategic retreat. Big difference."

"You're walking back to your suite in the same clothes."

"It's early afternoon. No one will blink. For all anyone knows, I've been out running strategy drills and charming billionaires since we left the trail."

He grinned. "You're not even going to pretend this was a one-time thing?"

"Oh, honey. I stopped pretending with you days ago."

I pulled my shirt over my head and gave the hem a sharp tug to smooth the wrinkles. My lipstick was long gone, and my hair looked like I'd wrestled a palm frond and lost. But I'd take that shower, swap into a clean dress, and by the time we met again to go over our slides, I'd be a new woman.

Or at least one who didn't smell like sex and sandalwood.

He didn't say a word. Just tracked every movement, cool and unreadable, that strategist's brain still spinning. That same relentless precision he used with clients now stripped me bare.

His eyes held calculation, yes, but also something softer—like he was testing whether I'd bolt if he let me see it. It rattled me more than I wanted to admit.

I crossed to the door, bare feet silent against the warm wood floor. My hand hovered over the handle—then paused.

Don't look back.

I looked anyway.

He hadn't moved. The intensity in his gaze had deepened—sharper now. Unmasked.

You rattle me.

Goddammit.

I forced a smile. "Give me an hour."

Don't do it. Don't crawl back in. Don't let it all keep unraveling.

Then I opened the door and slipped into the hallway, clutching Helga, my ankle wrap, and what was left of my composure—because of course I was going to walk out like a goddamn professional.

The door clicked shut. I exhaled—cool in theory, disaster in execution.

The hallway lay quiet and still. No staff. No guests. No witnesses to my strategic withdrawal. I padded across the tile barefoot, Helga swinging from one hand—part accessory, part evidence in an emotional crime scene.

What the hell was that?

I knew what it wasn't: casual. Or forgettable. And definitely not smart.

My skin buzzed in the places he'd touched. My thighs ached in a way that made me want to text my chiropractor—and maybe my therapist. My mouth? Bruised—in the best kind of way.

And my heart?

Nope. Not going there.

I rounded the corner toward my suite, already plotting the emotional rinse cycle I'd need before seeing him again. Hair with bounce. Voice steady. Not a trace of the girl who'd practically begged him not to stop.

Rehearsal first. Breakdown later.

My suite greeted me with cool air and the faint, lemony scent of housekeeping sorcery. I tossed Helga into the corner, peeled off my shirt, and beelined for the bathroom. That place had explaining to do.

The shower blasted to life with a hiss, steam fogging the mirror before I could finish unhooking my bra. I stepped in and let the water burn. I needed a scrubdown of epic proportions—tropical sins and sandalwood soaked straight into my pores.

The heat worked its way into my muscles, loosening all the places that still held him. His hands. His mouth.

The slow, ruinous way he said *mine*—stating it as fact, not fantasy.

I lathered twice and conditioned with all the focus of a woman preparing for battle.

Then I wrapped myself in a towel, padded across the room, and opened the closet. A color-coded wardrobe stared back in passive-aggressive judgment.

I pulled on a white button-front cami that dipped low enough to be interesting but still said *I'm here to work, not seduce you again... probably.* The olive green paperbag shorts cinched at the waist with a self-tie belt and made my legs look like they'd been professionally sculpted by sunshine. Leopard slides—Claudia. Gold hoops. A few stacked bracelets. And the tiny woven crossbody bag that couldn't hold anything useful but made me feel adorable anyway.

Outfit: casual with a strategic edge—flirty-adjacent.

Ankle: re-wrapped.

Game face: loading.

By the time I looked in the mirror again, she was back: Brynn Wilder. Collected. Brilliant. Absolutely not spiraling.

I opened my laptop anyway.

Rayann answered on the second ring, already suspicious. "Oh, no. That face? That's a feelings face."

"It's not a feelings face."

"It is a feelings face. You look like you're about to cry or commit a hostile merger. Possibly both."

I plopped onto the edge of the bed and crossed my legs. Claudia flopped to the floor with a satisfying slap. "I had sex."

Rayann blinked. "With?"

"Jerrick."

She blinked once, then again. "Was it... good?"

Was it good? My soul left my body for a minute. I'm still sore in places I didn't know could be sore.

"It was so good I need to reorganize my entire personality."

"Ah," she said, leaning back and lacing her fingers behind her head. "So, spiral prevention mode. Got it."

I let out a breath. "It wasn't supposed to mean anything. But now I can't stop thinking about what he said. How he looked at me. The way I almost stayed."

Rayann tilted her head. "Do you want to stay?"

"I don't know," I snapped. "He's the enemy. But also... not. He's a competitive, annoyingly attractive chaos enabler. And he told me I rattle him."

Rayann's laugh crackled through the speaker. "That's practically foreplay in your language."

"Rivalry wasn't a hobby with us—it was oxygen. Cut the supply, and we'd both be gasping like amateurs."

"Did you rattle him with your mouth or your emotional availability?"

"Both. I hate it here."

"Maybe you do need to be clear with yourself—what are you hoping this becomes?"

I didn't answer. Couldn't. Because saying I wanted more than sex meant accepting the fallout when it inevitably exploded.

"Nothing," I said. "It becomes nothing."

"Right," Rayann said, dry as the Sahara. "That's why you called me in a full outfit that has its own agenda."

I arched a brow. "My outfit is not the problem."

Her smile widened. "Go work on your presentation. Be brilliant. Try not to fall in love until the PowerPoint's done."

"Maybe too late," I muttered, then hung up.

The screen went black. My reflection stared back at me—equal parts calculated charm and slow-brewing crisis.

I flopped backward onto the bed.

Okay, maybe not love. Maybe lust spiked with emotional confusion. Or post-orgasmic delusion. That's a thing, right? It had to be. Because the alternative was that

I'd fallen for the one man I was absolutely not supposed to fall for. The competition. The rival. Smug forearms and weaponized strategy.

And yet... he hadn't played me. Not really. He'd touched me like I mattered. Looked at me and actually *seen* me. Told me I rattled him—and meant it.

Which is exactly why I should've left it at sex and silence.

But nooo...I called my twin. Talked about it. Named it. Like some neurotic feelings archaeologist digging through layers I'd buried for a reason.

I blew out a breath and sat up, brushing a wrinkle out of my shorts. One leg crossed over the other. Spine straight. Mask back on.

Time to see if we could be civil in the light of day. Time to find out if we still made sense outside the bedroom. I grabbed my phone, stared at it for a second too long, then thumbed out a quick text.

ME: You ready to meet? I need a drink and a few slides that don't end in mutual undressing.

ME (again, seconds later): Tiki bar. Ten minutes. Don't wear that smug face. I'll bring flashcards.

Send.

I watched the message deliver, then closed my eyes.

Let's see what happens when the sex haze lifts.

Let's see if I still like him when he's not inside me.

I barely had time to toss my phone onto the bed before a knock rattled the door. Three sharp raps—confident, impatient.

Of course.

I opened it anyway—and there he was. Shirtless. Damp hair. That strategist's gaze gone molten.

Neither of us moved for a beat. The air between us was thick enough to drink.

"You said ten minutes," he murmured. "It's been eight."

I should've laughed. Should've shoved him back into the hall. Instead, I let him step inside. The door clicked shut behind us, the sound final. Heavy.

He leaned down, his mouth a whisper from mine. "Still want that drink?"

My pulse stuttered. My answer would've been dangerous. So I didn't give one.

Not with words.

Not yet. The lock slid. So did my restraint.

Chapter 16

Mistakes Worth Making

THE TIKI BAR WAS mercifully empty.

I didn't expect a crowd mid-afternoon, but it still felt like we were getting away with something. Maybe it was the way his hand brushed mine when he handed me the pineapple-thing I didn't order. Or the scrape of his stool as he dragged it closer.

I'd told him I needed a drink.

What I really needed was insulation. Something to stop me from crawling onto his lap in broad daylight and turning this strategy session into a rehydration break of an entirely different kind.

"So," I said, propping my laptop between us and angling it toward him. "Let's talk about client archetypes instead of orgasms."

He smirked. Took a slow sip of his iced black coffee—of course he did. Then leaned in. "Shame. I was ready to graph the overlap."

God help me, I smiled. "Focus, Thorne. We've got fifteen minutes before your smugness becomes a choking hazard."

We started with the bones. Hook, flow, timing. Slide transitions. Stats. All the sexy metrics that kept consultants up at night. His notes were sharp and smart—exactly what I'd expect from a man who probably bullet-pointed his grocery lists in Roman numerals.

But every time our fingers brushed, I forgot what language was.

My body remembered too much. His mouth. His voice. The way he looked at me like I was a challenge and a reward all at once. But this wasn't about that. Not now. Not when his ideas synced with mine so neatly they left my stomach flipping.

"So we hit them with the impact numbers first," he said, scrolling through the deck, "then layer in your story example—what was the one about the boutique brand with the coastal cleanup collab?"

"Salt & Stone," I said. "They were one of our first clients. They underestimated their environmental messaging until we showed them the return-client metrics."

He nodded. "Use that. It's strong. I'll build the lead-in."

I stared at him.

Not because of the compliment—but because it was so... normal. Easy. Like we'd been doing this for years. As if earlier hadn't happened. Or had—and this was what came after.

"You're really good at this," I said before I could stop myself.

His brows lifted, surprised. "You sound shocked."

"I'm not. I mean, I am—but not in a way that insults you. More in a *'this shouldn't be working but somehow it is'* kind of way."

His smirk faded.

Not in a bad way—more like the moment caught him off guard. He looked down, tapping his pen once against the edge of the notebook. Then his voice dropped.

For a second, I swore I could see the fight in him—shoulders held too straight, jaw clenched like he was biting back something truer. He didn't let much slip, but that flash of tension said more than any smirk ever could.

"This wasn't what I thought it'd be," he said. "Coming here."

I leaned back. "What did you think it'd be?"

He went still. Then let out a long, measured breath. "Painful. Awkward. A week of you avoiding me, or worse—pretending I didn't exist."

I laughed, but it snagged on something sharp. "You're lucky I didn't launch a cocktail umbrella at your jugular on day one."

"I would've deserved it," he said simply. "And I wouldn't have blamed you."

Silence settled between us—not sharp or uncomfortable. Just... open. Curious. I nudged the edge of his glass. "What happened in Dubai?"

He didn't answer right away—just closed the notebook, pushed it aside, and folded his hands.

"My father called three times while I was there," he said. "Each time with a reminder of what I was risking. My reputation. His legacy. The image he spent decades curating."

My stomach tightened. It wasn't just pressure—it was ownership, the way he said it. Like his father still had a hand on the wheel.

"He's never cared that I have my own plans. He wanted me in golf tournaments, boardrooms, country clubs. I chose martial arts instead. Chose teaching, discipline, focus—things that never made sense to him. If I had it my way, I'd walk away tomorrow, open a studio, spend my days teaching kids how to fight without breaking. But to him, that's wasting potential."

The problem was, it wasn't just about his father anymore. The pitch, the clients, Wilder Horizons—if either of us stumbled now, there'd be more than family pride on the line. Our reputations, our futures, the whole damn week hinged on keeping this partnership together. And sitting across from him, I wasn't sure if I wanted to win the account more—or him.

I stayed quiet.

"He knew I'd seen you. That I'd considered staying a few extra days." He glanced away, tension flicking across his features. "He didn't say her name, but he didn't have to. The implication was clear—don't make another mistake."

A mistake. My chest went tight. *Dad used to say the only mistake worth making was falling in love. He'd know—he only got one shot before Mom died.*

I snapped alert. "Wait—he considered me a mistake?"

Jerrick looked at me then. Not defensive. Not pitying. Just honest. "He considers anything that doesn't serve him a threat. You? You terrify him."

I wanted to ask if his fiancée ever terrified him too—but I doubted it. More likely, she was exactly the kind of woman Charles approved of, the kind who checked every square he valued. Four years promised to her while I was left wondering if the almosts between us had meant anything. But dredging that up now would be like reopening Dubai itself, and I wasn't sure either of us could survive the fallout twice.

The idea made me laugh—but it landed low. Right in that part of me that had always been *too much* for someone.

"You didn't kiss me," I said.

"No," he agreed. "I didn't."

"But you wanted to."

He nodded once. "More than I wanted to breathe."

No games. No flourish. Brutal truth.

I swallowed. "Did she hurt you?"

"My ex?" He paused. "Yes. But not the way people think. It wasn't betrayal—it was priority. I didn't show up. Not for the small things, not when it counted. She waited for me to choose her. I didn't realize she was keeping score until she was gone."

I reached for my drink. Took a sip I didn't need.

I hesitated. "Do you ever talk to her?"

He shook his head. "No. She's married now. Two kids—twins, I think. I heard through some mutuals."

"You okay with that?"

"Yeah," he said, calm. "I'm happy for her. It worked out the way it was supposed to."

"And now?"

His eyes met mine. "Now I know better. Or at least I'm trying to."

The way he said it cracked something open in me. Not pity. Not softness. Just... clarity.

I tapped the side of my glass. "My dad used to sing show tunes while he grilled."

That startled a laugh out of him. "What?"

"Yep. Full Broadway medleys. Always in a ridiculous Scottish accent—said it gave him more range."

I smiled, remembering.

"He was loud. Giant-hearted. Somehow raised six daughters and made each of us feel like his favorite. He used to sneak me out for milkshakes after long days. Just me. Said even chaos needed its own reset button. I'd sit there in a sugar haze, convinced I was secretly the chosen one. Of course, he probably did the same with all my sisters—but he made it feel like mine."

Jerrick leaned forward. "Sounds like a hell of a guy."

"He was," I said, the smile already slipping. "Lost him five years ago."

"I'm sorry."

"Me too." I rubbed a hand down my arm. "It still hits weird sometimes. Weddings. Big stuff I wish I could call him about. He would've loved this place—thrived on meeting new people, getting lost in other cultures."

Jerrick's hand slid across the bar, slow and sure, until his fingers found mine.

"I can see that."

"My mom died when my youngest sister was born. I was six. I only remember flashes—her laugh, the smell of oranges. Dad met her while traveling. Said he fell hard on day two. That she was the chaos before I was."

He didn't speak. Just reached out and brushed my hair back, slow and gentle, like I might disappear.

"She'd be proud," he said finally. "No doubt in my mind."

I smiled faintly. "He raised us on his own after that. Six girls and no clue what he was doing—but he never made us feel like we were missing anything. Except her."

I traced the rim of my glass, the condensation cool against my fingertips. "Rayann and I are identical, but she always craved steady. We're both chaos—I just happened to light the match more often. That's the job when you're the 'older' twin."

He exhaled, low. "I don't know how he did it. Your dad. But I can see he raised a hell of a woman."

I pulled my hand back. Not because I didn't want the contact, but because I felt too much already. And this was starting to feel like something I couldn't control.

"I'm not good at this part," I admitted. "The soft, open stuff."

"You're doing fine."

"You're not exactly known for oversharing either."

"No," he agreed. "But with you, it's different."

I arched a brow. "Different how?"

His expression didn't change, but his voice dropped. "Because you see the parts I don't show anyone. And you don't flinch. You don't look at me like I'm failing if I want something different. You make it feel... possible."

Goddamn him.

Goddamn the way he made that sound like reverence.

My phone buzzed across the table. A reminder ping. "Shit," I said, grabbing it. "I've got to check in with the audio team. They're finalizing mic setups for tomorrow."

He stood with me. Didn't crowd. Didn't reach. But his energy clung, close as a second skin.

I hesitated, then looked up at him. "This was... good," I said. "Surprisingly."

He tilted his head. "You sure you don't want to graph it?"

I smiled despite myself.

He reached for the bill without ceremony, signed, and slid a generous tip under the glass. Of course he paid. Of course he didn't say a word about it. "Mind if I tag along?" he asked. "Figure I should hear how many times I'll need to say 'pivot' into a microphone tomorrow."

I fell into step beside him.

"Try not to undress me in front of the audio guy," I muttered.

He didn't miss a beat. "No promises. But I'll keep my hands off your mic pack."

And just like that, I was back in trouble.

Chapter 17

Click to Advance

THE ROOFTOP CONFERENCE PAVILION was all coastal breeze and expensive calm—teak flooring, gauzy curtains shifting in the wind, and the steady hum of surf in the distance. It should've felt serene. Somewhere below, steel drums drifted up from the pool deck, clashing with the boardroom vibe.

But Jerrick Thorne adjusting his collar beside me didn't scream *peaceful*. He radiated composed menace—impeccably groomed and terrifyingly focused. If intimidation had a scent, it would be sandalwood and quiet judgment.

I flashed my best PR smile as the AV tech approached. "Good afternoon! We're here to run our audio for tomorrow's presentation."

He gave a polite nod, adjusting the strap of the gear bag slung across his chest. "Name's Toby. I'll be handling sound for the panel."

He had the easy grin of someone who'd been bribed with too many resort cocktails already, his shirt half untucked like he lived on island time.

"Brynn Wilder," I said, extending a hand. "And this is Jerrick Thorne."

Jerrick offered a firm shake. "Appreciate you, Toby."

Toby gestured toward the mic station. "Lapel mics and packs. I'll show you how to mute yourselves in case you need a sidebar—or want to avoid broadcasting any accidental shit-talk."

I grinned. "Oh, we save that for the Q&A."

Jerrick aimed a look at me that could've doubled as a warning label. "Or a tactical break from personal attacks."

I smiled sweetly. "No promises. I work best with a live audience." The wire was cool against my skin as Toby clipped the mic, sliding it down my blouse. Jerrick's gaze never wavered—one brow lifted, his mouth curving like he was already mapping other ways to take it off.

Do not blush. Do not adjust your thighs. Do not give him the satisfaction.

Once Toby handed us the mute clickers and signed off, I grabbed my laptop and dropped into a sun-warmed chair. "All right, let's get into the slides."

He followed, rolled sleeves and all, carrying his stupidly sexy leather journal like it held nuclear codes. When he set it on the table, it smelled faintly of leather and ink—authority dressed up in stationery. "Not gonna lie, it's nice to have the deck locked. First time I haven't been tweaking things at midnight."

I nodded, pulling up the file. "Yeah. Super locked."

He dropped into the chair beside me, completely unsuspecting.

I, meanwhile, was trying not to vibrate out of my damn chair.

I tapped through the opening slides—title, agenda, company logos, the crowd-pleaser case study—and waited, pretending not to hold my breath.

Slide twelve.

And there it was. Exactly where I buried it.

He leaned in, blinked once, then sat back. "Is that... a *fake app*?"

"*ManSplainer: Now with Less Interrupting,*" I said casually, as if it belonged in a professional panel deck. I bit back a grin so wide it threatened to split my face. God, I lived for this moment.

He turned his full attention to me. "We finished this an hour ago," he said, locking eyes with me. "This wasn't in it."

"Nope."

"Brynn."

I winced. "Okay, fine. I may have pre-loaded it earlier in the week. It was... hanging out. Waiting for its moment."

"Jesus." He narrowed his eyes. "You planned this?"

"Strategically. Also recreationally. And—fine—because I was trying not to obsess about... everything else."

He looked back at the screen. "We're presenting to investors."

"I know. That's why it's funny."

"This is not funny."

"Oh, it's educational. Think of it as educational satire. Infographics meet therapy."

"You animated the logo."

"Professionally. I used Canva."

He didn't speak, but his jaw flexed hard enough to make my ovaries stupid.

"Relax," I said. "It auto-advances. Six seconds. Eight, tops. Unless they laugh—then we milk it."

"You're actually insane."

"Technically. But with a strategy. Obviously."

He leaned over the table—one hand braced beside my touchpad, the other gripping his journal like he was about to take notes on my descent into madness. "You buried a fake pitch slide inside a co-branded presentation."

I pointed at the screen. "It ties in. I swear. The panel's about emotional connection, right? This is what *not* listening looks like."

He didn't move.

I tapped the screen again. The app mockup zoomed slightly, showcasing a sleek coral-and-black interface with glowing buttons and a pop-up alert mid-sentence: *You've interrupted the conversation 3 times in 90 seconds. Take a breath and reconsider.*

"Clients aren't buying plunge pools or thread counts anymore," I said. "They're buying ease. Anticipation. The feeling that they don't have to repeat themselves or fight to be heard."

His brow lifted. "So this is a... satire-slash-case study?"

"Exactly. It's a red flag with a glossy finish. A tongue-in-cheek reminder that the luxury experience starts with shutting up and listening."

Another tooltip appeared onscreen: *"Mute Yourself for Once — Your opinion may be valuable, but not right now."*

A glowing badge at the bottom: *"Beta-Tested by Real Women with Better Ideas."*

Jerrick stared at it. "And the glitter?"

His jaw ticked, the kind of micro-flinch that told me he was calculating risk versus reward. I could practically see the Roman numerals lining up in his head.

"Branding."

Below the badge, three fake testimonials flickered into view like a smug little slideshow:

"I thought I was just 'passionate about ideas.' Turns out I was a nightmare. This app saved my marriage." – Josh, Former Think Piece Addict

"It buzzed every time I said 'not to be devil's advocate, but...' Honestly? Life-changing." – Travis, Now a Feminist Probably. Working on it.

"ManSplainer made me realize my 'helpful advice' was actually condescending noise. Five stars." – Ethan, Still in Therapy

I grinned. "We've all worked with a Travis. Let's not make our clients feel like Travis."

He exhaled. Closed his eyes. And then—annoyingly—laughed.

"I hate that it's good," he muttered.

"I know," I said, barely resisting the urge to curtsy, flipping to the next slide.

Slide thirteen appeared. Minimal. Sleek. *Wilder Horizons and Adventura Luxe*.

He glanced sideways at me, then back at the screen. His tone sharpened, slipping into that professional cadence.

"And this is where we come in. At Wilder Horizons and Adventura Luxe, we design experiences that anticipate needs, eliminate friction, and—most importantly—listen. Whether it's a private jet itinerary or a secluded wellness retreat, we stay in zero-interruption mode."

He didn't smile. Didn't break.

But then: "We are not affiliated with *ManSplainer*™, but we do support its mission."

If I'd had a drink, it would've gone flying.

He closed his eyes. Exhaled. Then—annoyingly—laughed. "It shouldn't work, but it does," he muttered.

"I know," I said, pompous as hell, and blew him a kiss like I'd won a damn award.

We moved through the rest of the slides, double-checking transitions, polishing timing. The audio pacing was solid. The rest flew by—slides synced, transitions smooth, delivery locked in.

He tapped his pen against the table. "We need a stronger CTA."

"We need fewer buzzwords and a bolder close." I turned to face him fully. "You want to impress people? Ditch the buzzwords. Show them what we are."

He dropped the polish. Something more dangerous surfaced.

"And what exactly are we?"

Oh no.

Abort. Abort.

"Collaborators," I rattled off. "Complementary strengths. Mutually aligned." Every word too clipped, too defensive.

He didn't blink. "That all?"

I swallowed, shoulders tensing. "You want more?"

His voice was low. Even. "I want honesty."

The air thinned, my pulse doing that traitorous stutter again. This wasn't about slides anymore, and my body knew it. "You want raw vulnerability in a pitch deck?"

"I want it from *you.*"

I stared at him—my former almost-something turned current co-presenter and dangerously viable rebound fantasy—and realized I was seconds from either kissing him or smashing my laptop.

To buy time, I leaned over the screen. "Let's make a deal."

One eyebrow lifted. Classic.

"If tomorrow goes well—and I mean standing ovation, champagne-cart level success—we each plan the other a fantasy weekend."

His smirk deepened. "Define fantasy."

"You pick the destination. I plan the rest. Full control. And vice versa. Strictly motivational."

"And if it tanks?"

"Then we pretend it never happened."

He extended his hand. "Shake on it?"

I slipped mine into his. His grip was warm. Infuriatingly steady. Exactly like everything else about him. I noticed the faint scar near his knuckle, the one from sparring, and hated that I knew exactly how it felt against my hip. He didn't let go. Not quickly. Not casually. Definitely not safely.

The hold wasn't just about pressure—it was his way of memorizing, cataloging, daring me to pull first. "Deal," I said—once my brain caught up.

The pads of his fingers brushed the base of my thumb, sparking heat in a place that had no business tingling. "Good," he murmured. "Because I already know your dream weekend includes a vintage convertible, a rooftop villa, and at least one professional fire-dancer."

I blinked. "How the hell—?"

He tapped his journal.

"You took notes?"

He leaned in. "You told me. Last summer. Milan."

Shit. I did.

He stepped back, utterly smug. "I listen, Wilder. Even when I shouldn't."

I stared at him—stunned. And maybe a little wrecked. Not because he remembered. But because I didn't think he would.

"Okay," I said, recovering fast. "Your turn. What's *your* dream weekend?"

He didn't answer right away. Just looked at me like I'd asked something loaded.

When he finally answered, it wasn't flirty. Not even cheeky.

"Somewhere no one knows who I am," he said softly. "No meetings. No flights. No image to manage."

I blinked. The way he said it sounded less like a fantasy and more like a plea, and something in my chest tightened—dangerously sympathetic.

That wasn't a fantasy. It was an escape plan.

"Okay..." I said, drawing it out. "So... remote mountain cabin vibes?"

He shook his head. "I still want hot water. A real bed. And you."

My stomach flipped so hard I had to cover it with a snort. "Wow. Bold move, Thorne—sliding that in like a bullet point."

He held my gaze. "Wasn't a slide. It was the headline."

I hated how fast my heart flipped.

I folded my arms, mostly to contain the chaos happening south of my elbows. "So you want me to plan a fantasy weekend where no one talks to you, you get to sleep in, and I... what? Keep you company in silence?"

"You'd break it within ten minutes."

I grinned. "Please. Five. Tops."

His smile turned crooked. "Exactly."

And just like that, I was back in dangerous territory—with a man who remembered the color of my dream car and the shape of my silence.

I clicked the laptop closed before I launched myself at him. "Great," I said. "Then listen to this. If you even *breathe* on the slide transitions, I'm swapping your outro with a stock photo of a sloth in a bathrobe."

He didn't flinch. "I'd make it work."

I narrowed my eyes. "Pure villain energy."

"You love it."

Unfortunately, I really fucking do.

"So," I said, shifting my weight. "What now?"

Jerrick glanced toward the steps leading down to the pool deck, where the tiki bar buzzed with early-evening energy—laughter, steel drums, the tang of grilled fruit in the air. "You want to make a quick appearance?"

I hesitated, already picturing Lucinda's hawk eyes zeroing in.

He tilted his head. "Just enough to show face," he said, a little too casually. "And show off that bandage."

My eyes narrowed. "Lucinda."

He didn't deny it. "She's subtle as a brick."

"She asked me point-blank if we were fucking."

His mouth twitched. "You tell her yes?"

I gave him a look. "We make a loop around the bar. Arrive together, leave separately. One drink. Nothing suggestive."

"Right. Just two professionals... casually ignoring the very obvious tension."

"Thank you."

We headed down to the tiki bar. Warm light slanted through the palm fronds. The sun drifted lower toward the ocean. The sharp tang of grilled pineapple and rum syrup curled in the air. I took the lead, the wrap on my ankle angled just right—minor injury, but enough to justify bailing on the hike. Subtle messaging, but critical.

A few heads turned as we walked in. Familiar faces. Panel judges. A competitor or two who pretended not to be watching. Axel lounged at a corner table, sunglasses still on indoors, drumming his fingers loud enough to be heard over steel drums. Subtle as a marching band. Lucinda was posted up at the bar in a crisp linen jumpsuit, sipping something citrusy and eyeing us like she'd been assigned surveillance duty. The woman could've weaponized a raised brow—her version of a dossier thicker than the bar menu.

"Two drinks," I murmured. "One strategically timed laugh."

Jerrick smirked. "I like when you set boundaries," he said, low and amused.

We claimed a pair of barstools. "Margarita," I told the bartender. "Make it with Fortaleza if you've got it. Otherwise—surprise me."

"And a Clase Azul," Jerrick added, nodding toward the top shelf. "Neat."

The salted rim bit into my lip, tart and bracing. His tequila smelled smooth and smoky, unfairly adult next to my citrus bomb. The bartender set them down with a wink. "Special occasion?"

Lucinda's voice floated over from two stools down. "Or recovering?"

Before I could reply, another voice cut in—one of the older panel organizers with a clipboard and an excellent poker face. "Are you two ready for tomorrow?"

Jerrick straightened, shifting toward the organizer with smooth, professional ease. "As a matter of fact, we just wrapped a session with the audio tech. Slides are finalized."

I lifted my glass. "And color-coded."

Lucinda raised an eyebrow, sipping slowly. "Good to know."

We clinked glasses. Mine was chilled and sweet. His, smooth and golden. We settled in for just long enough to look relaxed—but competent. I laughed at something vague. He said something charming. I flexed my wrapped ankle with theatrical timing.

Ten minutes of timed laughs, careful sips, and pretending not to notice his thigh pressed close to mine. Then I brushed his knee, casual as possible. "I'm starving."

He turned, eyes steady. "Want to grab dinner? Somewhere... not here?"

My stomach flipped, but I kept it breezy. "Sure. I've got wine and snacks in my suite. Might even let you see the color-coded pitch deck again." My tone was breezy, but my pulse was anything but. Every step toward my suite felt like walking a balance beam in heels.

He tossed back the rest of his tequila, then stood. "Now you're just showing off."

Chapter 18

Toucan Play That Game

THE MOONLIGHT TURNED THE terrace silver, the kind of night that felt scripted for romance, thick with the scent of salt air, hibiscus, and damp earth. Dinner had been incredible, cocktails lethal, which explained why the hammock outside my suite suddenly looked like the sexiest idea on earth.

"Romantic," I announced, kicking it with my toe. "We'll be like one of those glossy travel ads—except with more tequila and less stability."

Jerrick eyed it. "That thing is not built for two."

"Neither is this dress," I said, tugging the straps off my shoulders.

He swore under his breath, a low growl that sent a shiver across my skin, and climbed in after me. The hammock dipped violently, nearly spilling us both. His shin slammed into the wooden post.

"Romance is pain," I whispered, trying not to laugh.

And a potential medic visit if we keep this up. Again.

The first touch was a spark, the second a full-body arson. The world narrowed to the space between our mouths—aka ground zero of my impending bad decisions. My lips parted, not in invitation but in pure feral demand. He answered with a growl so deep it rattled my sternum.

This wasn't a kiss. It was a takeover. Borderline hostile acquisition.

His mouth was hot and desperate, all messy chaos barely disguised as control. He didn't just kiss me—he consumed me. And some reckless part of me wanted it. Wanted to disappear into him so fast I wouldn't have to ask what came after. That was the terrifying part—not the kiss, but the risk of wanting more.

Congratulations, sir. You passed Kissing 401 with honors.

His teeth caught my bottom lip, tugging until I whimpered, then releasing only to soothe the sting with his tongue.

And then the invasion began. His tongue swept in like he meant to claim every corner of me, thorough and greedy, tasting me like I was the only thing that mattered.

His growl deepened, but underneath it I caught something else—restraint. Every move he made had an edge of discipline, like he was holding back more than he gave. Like letting go scared him worse than falling.

His tongue swept in like it paid rent, not asking, just taking. Thorough, greedy, tasting me like I was a five-course meal and he'd skipped lunch. I met him thrust for thrust, our tongues tangling in a wet, obscene slap fight that somehow counted as kissing. The sound of it was *so loud* in the tiny, swaying hammock.

My breath hitched, became his breath. He tasted of tequila, night air, and pure male menace. Addictive. Infuriating. I could drown in this taste, in this feeling. One of his hands fisted in my hair, anchoring me like I might float off, while the other slid up my thigh, thumb making a slow, deliberate circle on my hip.

I gasped into his mouth, and he swallowed it whole, stealing even my oxygen. I was dizzy, drunk on tequila, lack of air, and the sheer sensory overload. My fingers clutched his hair—not guiding, just clinging for dear life—as the hammock pitched beneath us, creaking like it was about to file a noise complaint.

He broke away for a ragged breath, foreheads pressed, and lips swollen. His eyes were black, his pupils blown wide with a need that mirrored the frantic, throbbing pulse between my own legs. Then he was on me again, teeth grazing my jaw, finding the hammering beat in my throat and nipping there.

His teeth grazed my throat—sharp, possessive—and my laugh cracked into a gasp. Then he stilled, breath hot at my ear. "Condom's in my pocket."

His voice was steady, but his hand brushed his thigh once before digging into his pocket—a flicker of nerves that didn't match the lethal smirk. For a man built on preparation, this felt less like habit and more like hope.

"Wait—you brought one to dinner?"

"Prepared." His smirk was lethal as he dug for it.

He kissed me again, foil packet flashing in his hand, his body pressed hard against mine. I was seconds from tearing it open with my teeth when the hammock jerked. Hard.

"Shit," he hissed, body stiffening.

My giggles broke out instantly. "Don't tell me—"

"My dick's caught."

"Your dick is caught?"

"In the hammock."

I wheezed so hard I nearly fell out. "Oh my God. We'll have to call security. 'Hi, my rival's cock is tangled in the hammock—send maintenance.'"

"Brynn." His laugh rumbled into my chest, shaking the net harder. "Do *not* make me laugh."

Too late. We were both convulsing, the hammock swaying until the strap snapped with a deafening *crack*. We landed on the terrace in a heap, mosquito net draped over us like a crime scene.

At that very moment, a toucan landed on the railing above, tilting its head. Judging. Startling me.

"Don't," Jerrick warned.

"Don't what?"

"Say Fruit Loops."

The bird squawked like it had rehearsed. I broke, laughing so hard I could barely breathe. "You're a Fruit Loops guy."

His ears flushed. "It's nostalgic."

I kissed him mid-laugh, laughter melting into something hungrier. "God, you're ridiculous. And I want you so much it terrifies me."

The word *terrified* clung in my chest. Because want was easy. Need was dangerous. And the line between them was vanishing by the second. The words hung between us.

Serious. Too raw.

Well, shit. That came out louder than intended.

His gaze sharpened, thumb brushing my cheek. "Then be scared with me."

The foil tore with a snap, his movements calm even as his body vibrated with restraint. He rolled the condom on with steady hands, then pressed me flat against the warm deck boards, his weight caging me in. The wood dug into my shoulder blades, humid air plastering sweat to my skin. No hammock this time. No straps. Just him in full control.

"Spread your legs," he murmured. I obeyed without thinking. His mouth curved into a wolfish grin. "Good girl."

Oh, hello full-body kink activation.

Heat shot straight through me, my entire body clenching at those two words.

He slid into me slow at first, deliberate, making me feel every inch. Then his hips snapped forward, deep and unyielding, until the laughter in my throat broke into a gasp.

"Eyes on me," he ordered, catching my chin when I tried to squeeze them shut. "I want to watch you take it."

Every thrust was relentless, purposeful, the kind of rhythm that left no room for escape.

Don't stop. Don't you dare stop.

My nails raked down his back, but he only groaned, grinding harder, his voice rough against my ear. "That's it. Hold me tighter. Let me hear you."

The hammock net twisted around us like a fallen banner of defeat, creaking under our chaos. Somewhere above, the toucan shrieked once, indignant, before flapping off like it had seen too much.

But Jerrick didn't break rhythm. He fucked me through it, every stroke deeper, dragging me higher until my thoughts shattered into white-hot static. My cries dissolved against his mouth, swallowed by his kiss.

Fuck, he's going to ruin me.

And yes, please.

"Come for me," he commanded, voice like gravel, and I obeyed, breaking apart beneath him with a strangled cry.

He followed with a curse, burying himself deep, his body locking against mine as he groaned into my neck, raw and undone.

We collapsed together, breathless, sweat-slick, the deck boards warm and rough against my back, the humid night clinging to our skin, the busted hammock net draped across us like a flag of victory.

For approximately ten seconds, I was boneless bliss.

Then I tried to move.

"Um." My voice was muffled against his chest. "So, funny story. I think my hair is actually...yep. Tangled in the crime scene netting."

Jerrick lifted his head, still panting, and looked down at the mess. "Christ."

He shifted carefully, peeling strands away from the frayed rope. His brows pulled together in fierce concentration, like this was some kind of bomb defusal.

"You're taking this very seriously," I said, wincing as another strand pulled. "Should I start saying my goodbyes? 'Tell my sisters I died how I lived — chaotically horny in a hammock?'"

"Hold still," he muttered, mouth twitching like he was trying not to smile.

The toucan screeched from the railing, louder this time. I jerked, and a few more strands yanked free.

"Goddamn it."

I aimed a glare at the bird. "I don't come to your tree and heckle your sex life."

It tilted its head. Judging. Again.

Jerrick finally freed me with a victorious tug, smoothing a sweaty curl off my forehead. "Got it."

"Bless you," I said dramatically, rubbing the sore spot. "My scalp thanks you, my dignity does not."

He chuckled low, leaning in to press a kiss against my temple. The shift in him was subtle but seismic — from smug chaos co-conspirator to something softer, more dangerous.

"Good girl," he murmured again, this time gentle, reverent.

My stomach dropped straight through the deck.

"I... " The words slipped before I could stop them. "You scare me more than the jaguar did."

His hand stilled on my hair. "Brynn."

I tried to laugh it off, waving weakly at the shredded hammock above us. "You know. Because you're obviously out to murder hammocks. And maybe my pelvic floor."

"Brynn." His voice was quiet steel. "I would never hurt you."

My chest constricted so hard it felt like I couldn't breathe. Which was why I yanked the mosquito net over myself like a blanket and rolled half off his chest.

"Well, this has been fun," I forced out. "But if that toucan brings backup, I'm checking into a Marriott."

He let me have the escape, even though I could feel his eyes on me. Burning. Knowing.

And for once, I couldn't think of a single joke sharp enough to cut the truth of it: I was already in far deeper than I should be.

Chapter 19

The Cost of Winning

T HE RESORT WOKE UP slow, but my nerves didn't. My ankle ached like it was auditioning for a soap opera, my brain was running hostile takeovers of our pitch slides, and my stomach had vetoed breakfast entirely.

So I did what any totally-stable, highly-professional woman would do: I snuck off to the terrace to call my twin while Jerrick still slept.

Rayann answered on the second ring. "Why do you sound like someone about to hide a body?"

"Because I might," I whispered. "If Jerrick tries to pull another font-change ambush—"

"Cute deflection. What's actually going on?"

I groaned, pacing a rut into the flagstones. "He's impossible. He's infuriating. He—"

"Uh-huh." Her tone sharpened. "You're spiraling. Is this pitch impossible or heart impossible?"

"Ray!" Heat shot up my neck.

"Don't Ray me. You already told me you two hooked up. So why do you sound like you're about to hyperventilate into a paper bag?"

I pressed a hand to my forehead. "Because it wasn't just a one-off, okay? It's not just sex anymore. Every time we're in the same room, it's like my body and brain sign different contracts. He drives me insane one second and then—" My voice caught. "And then he'll look at me, and I swear to God, it feels like he's the only one who's ever really seen me."

Rayann went quiet. Too quiet. Which meant she was sharpening her words like knives.

Finally: "Love and ambition are combustible, Brynn. And you're the genius who parked herself in the middle of a fireworks warehouse with a blowtorch."

I squeezed my eyes shut. "I know. I can't lose the pitch. I can't lose myself. And I really, really can't lose to him. But the more time I spend with him, the less sure I am what 'winning' even means anymore."

"And yet you want him," she said softly. "Even after all this time."

The truth I'd been ducking all week cracked me open. "Yeah. I do. And it terrifies me."

"Terrifies you how?" Rayann pressed. "Like scared-he'll-break-your-heart terrified, or scared-be-cause-you-actually-want-him-in-it-for-real terrified?"

My throat tightened. "Both. He's not supposed to be the guy I want, Ray. He's the guy I'm supposed to beat. But when I'm with him... it's like the noise shuts off. Like I don't have to fight so hard to be heard, because he already gets it. Gets *me.*"

"Brynn." Her voice softened, the way it only did when she knew I was dangling over a ledge. "That's not lust. That's intimacy. That's the part you can't fake."

I pressed a fist against my stomach, trying to hold the ache down. "And that's exactly why it's dangerous. Because I can't trust it. What if he's playing the long game? What if I'm the idiot who lets her guard down while he sharpens the knife?"

"Then you'll do what you've always done," she said matter-of-factly. "You'll survive. You'll rebuild. But don't pretend you're not already halfway gone, sis. You don't call me whispering in the corner over some guy's slide fonts."

A shaky laugh slipped out, even though my eyes stung. "You're infuriating."

"And I'm right," she shot back. "So you'd better figure out if you're more afraid of losing *to* him... or losing *him*."

"Yeah," I said quietly. "I've gotta go."

Rayann started to protest, but I wasn't listening anymore. My gaze had already snagged on the man sitting on the side of the bed, and the look on his face cut deeper than anything he could've said.

The sliding door clicked behind me as I stepped in from the terrace, the sound small and definitive, phone still warm in my palm.

The look on his face gutted me—like I'd cracked something open he wasn't ready to show.

***

JERRICK

I ended the call harder than I meant to. The crack of plastic in my hand was too close to the sound of something breaking. My mouth tasted like sleep and metal; a thin animal part of me was already braced for another blow.

My father's voice was a bruise: polite, sure, and impossible to ignore: *"I've ensured the right people will see things."* The words landed like a verdict.

He never said the words outright, but he didn't have to. His favors always came stamped with a receipt—a dinner, a handshake, a price no one admitted out loud. For him, business was never business. It was a blood sport dressed in Armani. Every deal had to echo his name, every outcome had to prove his control. He didn't just want me to win—he needed me to, because anything less would mean admitting he couldn't shape the world into his image.

A memory slammed in before I could shove it down: I was fifteen, sweating through my gi at a local martial arts tournament, finally about to face the kid who'd beaten me the year before. I'd trained for months, bruises layered on bruises, ready for a clean fight.

Then Dad leaned down in the locker room, suit crisp, cologne sharp. *You'll win today,* he'd said flatly. *I've spoken to the organizers. No surprises this time.*

I remember staring at him, gut twisting, realizing he didn't care about my discipline or hours on the mat—only the photo op. The trophy on his shelf. Proof that his son was unbeatable, even if it wasn't real.

When I pinned my opponent that afternoon, the victory was hollow. I'd never hated winning more.

And here I was again, a grown man with his own career, feeling fifteen all over with my father's hand already in the picture, arranging the pieces.

For the first time in years, I hated him for it—because this wasn't just business. This wasn't golf trophies or corporate handshakes. This was Brynn.

I glanced up and caught her watching me from the terrace—and for a second I forgot the static in my bones. Her eyes were sharp, searching, like she already suspected something had shifted. The wall I threw up between us was instinct, survival. If she read what was boiling in my chest, it would ruin everything before I had a chance to fight for it.

Brynn Wilder terrified my father. He never said it outright, but I heard it in the way he spat her name like rot—too unpredictable, too independent. Not the kind of woman who could be owned or silenced. Her company kept surfacing in circles he thought he controlled, proof Wilder Horizons could outshine Adventura Luxe without his blessing. Untouchable. Unclaimable. And that made her a target.

And maybe that's why I couldn't stop thinking about her.

The thought of him putting his thumb on this scale—on *our* fight—made my stomach twist. Did he really think I needed help to beat her? Or worse, did he want me to win so badly he'd destroy her to make it happen?

I wanted this win clean. Earned. Head-to-head, fair. If Brynn beat me, at least I'd know it was real. But if my father's shadow touched this, the whole thing would be tainted.

And if Brynn ever found out?

She'd never believe I wasn't part of it. She'd never forgive me.

The phone was heavy in my hand—a weapon I hadn't meant to pick up. For the first time all week, I wished I could climb into her head, just for a second, and show her the truth: I wasn't the enemy she thought. Not here. Not with her.

Her eyes swept over me where I sat on the edge of the bed, phone gripped too tight, pulse still running hot from my father's voice.

"Everything okay?" she asked, cautious but steady.

I wanted to tell her yes. Wanted to tell her no. Wanted to tell her everything. But my father's voice didn't belong here, not with her hair still mussed from sleep and the faint crease of a pillow on her cheek.

"Yeah," I said finally, though the word came out rough. "I should probably get dressed. Coffee might make me less of an ass before we dive back in."

Her brow pulled tight, but she didn't push. Just nodded, letting me have the space I didn't deserve.

I stood, got dressed, pocketed my phone, and lingered a beat too long before heading for the door. The soft click behind me felt like more than wood and hinges—it felt like I'd shut her out.

I spent the next hour pretending to work in my own space, though each slide blurred into his line—*ensured the right people*—like a fly trapped under glass. By the time the sun climbed high enough to warm the terrace, I gave up. I needed air. Noise. Something to drown out the static.

The infinity pool stretched like glass toward the horizon, bright and merciless. Palm fronds rattled overhead, scattering shadows across the deck. Laughter from the swim-up bar drifted over the water, punctuated by the clink of bottles dropped into ice. Half the resort had already claimed loungers, staff weaving through with trays of fruit and drinks. I should've kept walking. Instead I saw Brynn's sunhat, her ankle propped on a towel, and something in my chest pulled tight.

Her laugh carried across the water. Sharp. Deflecting. Armor aimed at whatever ridiculous story Axel was telling from the lounger beside hers.

Of course Axel was here. Shirt off, sunglasses crooked, probably drunk before noon. He was gesturing wildly, nearly tipping his piña colada onto Brynn's arm, and she let him. She actually let him.

I slipped into the pool, just cool enough to feel refreshing, and forced myself to swim a steady length. Discipline. Control. Don't let her see the mess under your skin. Don't let anyone see it.

But when I surfaced, Brynn's gaze found me anyway. Just for a second. Long enough that the static dropped out, replaced by something far more dangerous—her.

By the time I came up again, Axel was already climbing out of his chair with all the grace of a newborn gazelle. "Gotta find the goat," he announced to no one in particular, sloshing the last of his drink onto the tile before stumbling toward the resort path.

Brynn blinked after him. "The goat?"

He waved a hand over his head like it was explanation enough.

I hauled myself out of the pool, dripping, and crossed to the empty lounger before anyone else could claim it. She tracked me with those wary eyes, the ones that saw too damn much.

"Mind if I sit?" I asked, already lowering myself onto the cushion.

"Go ahead," she said, shifting her ankle on the towel like it suddenly needed her full attention.

I leaned forward, elbows on my knees, water dripping down my forearms. "About earlier... I wasn't at my best."

Her lips pressed into a line, but she didn't look away.

"My father has a talent for putting me on edge," I admitted. The words scraped out before I could second-guess them.

Her brow softened. "Still pressuring you about the company?"

"Something like that." It was easier than telling her the truth. Easier than admitting I suspected he'd poisoned the well we were both drinking from.

Silence stretched. She tipped her head, studying me like she could pry the truth straight out of my chest. "You're handling it better than I would," she said finally.

I huffed a laugh. "Don't give me too much credit. You're the one sitting here in the sun, ankle swollen, still giving Axel your best fake laugh. I've seen CEOs with less grit than you."

Her mouth twitched, almost a smile, but not quite.

I sat back, forcing my shoulders to loosen, trying to look less like a man unraveling. Compliment her. Keep it light. Cover the guilt until I figured out how to deal with it.

Because one thing was clear: if my father had tilted this game, I wasn't going to let him play me like a pawn again. Not with Brynn in the crosshairs.

I'd take matters into my own hands.

Chapter 20

Stacked Deck

JERRICK

BY THE TIME I ducked back to my room, the pool water had barely dried on my skin, and the tension clung like a second shirt. Brynn's wary eyes. Her careful question. My half-truth about my father. It wasn't enough to sit on my hands and hope this storm passed. If my father had greased palms, I needed to know before the pitch tonight.

I toweled off, changed, and thumbed through my contacts. Old colleagues. Clients. Judges I'd shaken hands with at past events. Names blurred past until one landed—Arturo Rojas. A consultant-turned-judge who'd once owed me a favor.

I hesitated before pressing call. If Dad's fingers were already on this, even asking questions could set off alarms. But if I didn't ask... I'd walk into that pitch blind, Brynn beside me, and I'd never forgive myself for it.

The line rang twice. Three times.

"Jerrick?" Arturo's voice came in, surprised and rough like I'd woken him. "Haven't heard from you in a while."

"Yeah. Sorry to hit you out of nowhere." I tried to keep my tone light, casual. "You're on-site for the Wilder pitch competition, right?"

A pause. "I am."

I pinched the bridge of my nose. "Off the record—have there been... changes? To the panel? Anything I should know?"

Another pause, longer this time. Too long.

"Jerrick," he said carefully, "you know I can't—"

"I'm not asking for an advantage," I cut in. "I just want to know if this is a fair fight."

He exhaled, the sound sharp through the speaker. "Then I'll give you the only answer I can. Watch closely tonight. Don't assume the scorecards will tell the whole story."

The line clicked dead. My grip tightened until the case creaked. I wanted to hurl it across the room, but the thought of shattering another thing I couldn't replace kept my hand pinned to my side.

I stared at the phone, bile rising. Not confirmation. Not denial. But the meaning was clear: my father had moved something into place—and if Brynn ever found out, she'd never believe I wasn't part of it.

I paced the room, phone in my hand. Arturo's warning rattled around my skull, clanging louder with each step.

Watch closely tonight. Don't assume the scorecards will tell the whole story.

I scrolled again, thumb hesitating over another name. Marco—one of the coordinators I'd worked with in Dubai. Sharp, discreet, owed me a favor or two. He wasn't here, but he had system access if I asked the right way.

He picked up on the first ring. "Thorne? Didn't expect to hear from you outside the Gulf."

"Keeping busy," I said, forcing casual. "Listen, I won't waste your time. Can you pull today's pitch schedule for Costa Rica?"

A pause, then the sound of keys clattering. "Give me a minute... Alright, I've got it. What am I looking for?"

"I need to know if there've been... additions. Substitutions. Anyone new on the judges' list."

Keys clattered faintly through the line. "Funny you ask. One of the panel had a last-minute change flagged in the system—flew in last night with an extra guest. Not on the original roster. Their suite's already coded as comped. High-level override."

My stomach sank. "Name?"

"Not in the notes. Confidential tag. But let's just say the guest didn't route through standard channels. Came from higher up the food chain."

I scrubbed a hand over my face. Higher up. Dad. It had his fingerprints all over it.

"Appreciate the info, Marco."

"Anytime. But Jerrick," he lowered his voice, "if your name's tied to this, watch your back."

The line went dead, leaving the weight squarely in my hands. I stood too fast, the chair legs scraping sharp against the tile. My pulse kicked like I was back in the ring, but there was no opponent to strike—only shadows I couldn't land a punch on.

So my father had a judge in his pocket. The fight wasn't clean. And I had two choices: sit on this and let Brynn step straight into the crossfire, or take control before the ground shifted beneath us both.

I set the phone facedown and leaned hard on the desk. My arms shook from the strain, but it was the only thing keeping me from unraveling. Marco's words buzzed in my head like hornets: *an extra guest... higher up.*

My father's fingerprints. I could smell them a mile away.

I pulled on a clean shirt and headed for the dining patio. Maybe I needed food. Maybe I needed proof the world was still normal—grilled fish, chatter, the clink of glasses, nothing rigged.

Sunlight spilled through the palm-thatched roof and caught on pitchers of sangria and half-empty plates. Guests lingered over long lunches, and at the far end of the patio three of the judges sat together. A man in a navy suit slid into the empty chair beside one of them—too polished for the tropics, cufflinks flashing like a signal. Their handshake was quick. The envelope between them was quicker, hidden in plain sight like it belonged there.

I grabbed a plate of empanadas I didn't plan to eat and forced my jaw to unclench. My father had stacked the deck. If Brynn went into that pitch unarmed, she'd pay for his greed while I stood complicit. The idea of her finding out through whispers instead of me telling her first made my chest lock tight.

My gaze hunted the edge tables for her sunhat. Empty. The bile rose. No. Not this time.

I set the untouched plate down and left before I did something I'd regret.

The midday sun pressed down hard, scorching the stone path as I headed back toward the suites. Every step I took was a vow. If my father thought he could buy my victory, he was wrong. If the judges thought their scorecards were safe, they weren't. *I'd find the paper trail. I'd trace every late booking, every comped suite, and I'd make the math undeniable.*

And God help me, if this rigged game cost her a clean shot at winning, I'd torch the whole board before I let her believe I was part of it.

When I passed the patio again, the man in the navy suit was still with them. Not eating. Not laughing. Just listening, polished cufflinks flashing each time he steepled his hands.

One judge noticed me watching. His shoulders went stiff, conversation halting mid-sentence. The suited man leaned in, murmured something, and the whole table shifted—forced laughter, too bright, like they'd been caught red-handed.

I turned away before I could see more. It looked ordinary. But the air around that table carried the weight of his kind of deal—quiet, polished, poisonous.

The suited man didn't linger long. By the time I circled back from the buffet with a glass of water I didn't want, he was already slipping out the far side of the patio, judges scattering like gulls behind him.

I wasn't the only one who noticed.

"Who's Captain Cufflinks?" Axel slurred from two tables over, sunglasses crooked on his nose. He lounged sideways across a chair, shirt hanging open, a new drink sweating in his hand. "Looks like he wandered out of a hedge fund convention and into our little luau."

I kept my tone even. "You know him?"

"Me?" Axel grinned. "I know everybody. Or I pretend to until they buy me a drink." He leaned in conspiratorially, breath heavy with rum. "But that guy? Not on the guest list. Not unless I missed the memo about *Resort Chic: Wall Street Edition*."

He cackled at his own joke, then nearly toppled off the chair as he reached for his sunglasses case.

Useless. Not wrong.

I scanned the path where the man had gone, jaw tight. An outsider. A shadow. And Brynn nowhere near to see it.

Which meant this was mine to carry.

I dropped the water on an empty tray and headed back toward the suites. My pulse wouldn't steady. The more I turned it over in my head, the clearer it became: I couldn't control my father, couldn't root out every whispered favor or slipped envelope.

But I could control the pitch. We were building one deck together, yes, but the judges weren't scoring the slides—they were scoring the people. Each section would be judged on who owned it.

If the deck was flawless, airtight, undeniable—if Brynn and I stood shoulder to shoulder and delivered a performance no judge could dismiss—then even my father's shadow couldn't smother it.

The thought steadied me. Barely.

I pulled out my phone again, thumb hovering over her contact. I'd make it simple: regroup in an hour. Go over the slides, polish every word, rehearse until it was muscle memory. We needed to rehearse not just to make the deck sing, but because the judges would score our sections separately—if one of us stumbled, the other could still walk out with the win.

And maybe—God willing—if we made it undeniable, she'd know the only thing I wanted fixed tonight was our chance. Together. Unstoppable. I pictured her laugh at the pool, the way it cut sharp and bright through the noise. That was what I wanted to carry into the pitch—her chaos, my control, welded into something even my father couldn't break.

Chapter 21

Borrowed Glory

BRYNN

THE BALLROOM LIGHTS DROPPED to that flattering, cinematic glow that hides sins and heightens cheekbones, and every nerve snapped to showtime. Rows of white-clothed tables sat sweating with glasses of water no one touched, the judges perched in the front row with notepads angled like weapons. The air smelled faintly of citrus polish and nerves.

I smoothed the front of my tailored wrap dress—Wilder pink with a slit sharp enough to make HR nervous—and clocked Jerrick beside me in slate-gray, jacket off, sleeves rolled to just the right degree of menace.

The screen behind us hummed awake. The Wilder logo pulsed pink and gold, a heartbeat on the canvas that lit pride straight through me—my family's work, alive and undeniable. Beside it, Adventura Luxe's mark glowed in sleek silver and indigo, all sharp lines and modern minimalism—a logo that looked just as at home on a skyscraper as it did on a resort brochure. Beside me, Jerrick's shoulder brushed mine—barely there, just a steadier—like we were about to run into a burning building and call it a date.

The touch lit a fuse in me, memory colliding with the present. The last time he stole a win, it was mine on the line—my work, my name—and it cost me years of second-guessing every instinct I had. I swore I wouldn't let him close enough to do it again. And yet here I was, shoulder to shoulder, daring the fire to burn me twice.

The lights shifted, heat blooming across the stage.

"Good afternoon," I said, and the room hushed the way a room does when it's already decided to like you.

We were a machine. Hand-offs like baton passes, tempo in perfect rhythm, as easy as a chorus we'd rehearsed a hundred times—*and my sisters would be so fucking proud.*

Under the applause, heat pressed low and sharp—a private rhythm that had nothing to do with slides.

I wanted him—bad, immediate, hungry—and the thought made my pulse stutter.

Each judge had their own tic—linen-jacket lady tapping a pen, expensive-watch guy balancing his glasses low on his nose, navy tie staring like he was waiting for someone else to walk through the door. They sat in a perfect line behind a white conference table—tablets, poker faces, posture so straight it made you want to fix your own. Jerrick and I stood opposite on the small stage, our deck glowing behind us, the air-conditioned chill at odds with the heat under my collar.

I led with guest experience—arrival, first-touch, sensory hook—then Jerrick slid in on market segmentation, catching my last sentence and turning it into a runway for his charts. The slide transitions kissed our timing; the laughs hit where they were supposed to; the quiet hits landed where I wanted throats to tighten.

Then the mic crackled once, sharp as a gunshot, forcing me to pause mid-sentence. A ripple of unease rolled through the audience before the sound tech gave me a frantic thumbs-up. My smile didn't waver, but my pulse did. When I rolled out the vendor ecosystem—small-batch cacao, conservation partners, local guides paid above-market with profit sharing—the air changed.

Even Axel, sprawled in the audience three rows back with a shell necklace hanging lopsided like it had survived three too many conga lines, actually stopped fanning himself long enough to squint at the slide as if he was giving me a silent thumbs up. A miracle worth canonization.

Heads tipped forward. Linen judge even lowered her pen.

Jerrick took the momentum and sharpened it. "We're not selling itineraries," he said, voice even, eyes on them, not me. "We're selling a story guests tell themselves for the rest of their lives."

The judge in the middle—navy tie, square jaw—didn't write that down. He hadn't written much of anything. His pen lay capped on the table, untouched. He didn't fidget, didn't mark margins—just sat too still, like someone waiting for a cue that hadn't come yet. Even the way his gaze flicked sideways carried the weight of someone working off a script. He stared past us toward the aisle where sunlight cut a perfect blade across the hardwood.

I clocked it, then let it go. Don't spiral. Stay present. *Something's off about that fucker. He doesn't fit.*

We moved through the case study like rehearsal hadn't eaten half our afternoon: a couple who thought they wanted adventure-lite, the friction point, our fix. The room laughed where they were meant to laugh. They went soft where I meant to make them soft. Jerrick delivered the cost-value slide with the precision of a man laying Calacatta marble—every word deliberate, every number in place.

Slick. Sexy. Mine.

Questions. The front row woke like snakes in the sun. One leaned into the mic as though auditioning for a courtroom drama. Another creased the edge of his program, slow, like the pause itself was part of the test.

"What's your risk plan for weather volatility?" from the woman in linen.

"Define 'above-market compensation' with a percentage," from the man with the watch probably more expensive than a Ferrari.

I answered, precise. Jerrick answered, precise. Our answers respected each other like we'd done this for a decade. Another judge coughed deliberately, flipping through his notes as if searching for holes. He asked nothing, but the silence stretched long enough to scrape against my nerves. By the time navy tie finally leaned toward his mic, my spine was already braced for impact.

Then navy tie cleared his throat. "The vendor partnership network is... impressive," he said, flicking his gaze—not to me, where it belonged—but to Jerrick. "Adventura Luxe's commitment to community reinvestment is a model here."

Heat flashed the back of my neck. *Oh, fuck no. Not again.* History repeating itself in real time—my work, my idea, sliding straight into his column like it had his name stamped on it. My gut flipped, fury sparking with humiliation, and the ugliest thought hit first: Jerrick fucking stole it. Again. And worse? I'd let him close enough to pull it off.

My mouth smiled anyway. "I'm happy to expand on the structure if it's useful."

Navy tie lifted a hand, already moving on. "No, no. It came through."

It came through. As Jerrick's, not mine.

Jerrick's jaw moved like he might speak, then didn't. A tiny muscle flickered near his ear.

Did I just miss something? Or was that him swallowing words he didn't want me to hear?

We wrapped on the origin slide—my favorite: why we do this, why we care—and the applause felt big enough to stand in. People were smiling. A coordinator at the back gave a small, unprofessional fist pump. Even the sound tech grinned at us like we'd just bought him a puppy.

We'd killed it. Together.

Which is why the stillness at the judges' table was so loud.

Something felt off.

Navy tie looked toward the side aisle again, as if a cue might arrive in the light. A strange chill slid under my ribs, like something in the room was shifting where I couldn't see it. Beside me, Jerrick's fingers flexed once at his side, then stilled.

The head judge rose with a smile built to sell a time-share. "Wonderful work," she said. "Truly compelling. Scores will be posted in a moment, and the contract will be announced immediately after."

We stepped back, stage-left, into the soft dark where cables snake and nerves live. For a heartbeat we were just two people sharing a single, stunned breath. The stage smelled of hot wires and cologne, the hum of the projector filling the silence louder than applause ever could. My throat was dry enough to crave the untouched water still sweating on the judges' table.

"You were brilliant," he said quietly, not looking at me, eyes on the lighted digits of the timer as if it might confess something.

"So were you," I said, and hated the wobble in it. "But Jerrick, that judge thought—"

The big screen flickered to life, black background and sterile white numbers, as cold and impartial as a lab report. The screens behind us blinked to a tally board. Numbers populated row by row—experience strategy, operations, marketing, vendor partnerships, feasibility, budget integrity. A tight race, a photo finish, numbers that could launch or bury a career.

Wilder Horizons: 94

Adventura Luxe: 95

A single point. On vendor partnerships. *My* fucking vendor partnerships.

The board glowed sterile and certain. The lie was in how easily everyone accepted it.

The applause that went up was for us, for the show we put on, but the contract slid—as cleanly as a card from the bottom of a deck—right into his column.

People surged toward us with congratulations. The organizer took my hand in both of hers and said, "You two were electric." Then she pivoted to Jerrick with a gleam. "And Adventura Luxe—what a statement."

Navy tie was already shaking his hand. His grip lingered a fraction too long, his smile all polish and no pulse—pure performance.

I smiled like I was composed, because I am a professional and because I refuse to let anyone see me bleed in a ballroom. The noise rose—glasses clinking, congratulatory back-slaps, the pleasant roar of a job well done—while a small cold space opened in my ribs, patient as frostbite.

We stepped off the platform into lights and heat and people.

A stranger brushed my arm. "Inspired framework," he said, then leaned toward Jerrick with a wink. "Smart man to make it yours."

Frost spread slow along my ribs, patient, precise. I found a laugh from somewhere. It sounded like it belonged to someone charming on television.

"Brynn—" Jerrick started, finally turning to me.

"Champagne," I said, and a tray appeared as if I'd summoned it with a spell.

I took a flute and didn't drink. Across the room, navy tie angled again toward the side aisle, toward that slice of sun. I followed his gaze out of reflex and caught only glare—white, blinding, like something stepping out of reach.

Fear unspooled quiet as a pen scratching—methodical, disciplined, already keeping score.

Chapter 22

Teeth Behind the Smile

JERRICK

I F VICTORY HAD A taste, it was copper, like blood. This wasn't just about a contract. It was years of circling each other, of half-wins and near-misses that blurred into regret. Every pitch, every boardroom, every almost—we'd dragged our history into this ballroom, and now it was keeping score louder than the judges.

We'd made something undeniable. I knew it. The room knew it. Brynn's hands during that last slide had not trembled. When she spoke about paying local part-ners above market, about dignity written into contracts and profit shares instead of PR statements, three judges had leaned in like plants toward a window.

Then Navy Tie looked past us. And when the numbers posted—Adventura Luxe by a single point, in her category—the air shifted wrong.

Say something, jackass. Say it's hers. Say it out loud. But I don't. Coward.

I could have said it was dirty. I could have said the lattice was hers. But I didn't. If I were nineteen, maybe I would have. But I've lived long enough to know when not to.

So instead, I found her face.

She was smiling the way you smile when you've learned to keep your teeth covered around wolves. Her smile stayed, but her focus drifted past me, past the room, like she'd already walked out.

People pressed in. A judge told me the word "scalable" like it was a compliment. Someone from a luxury magazine asked for a quote. A microphone shoved too close caught my shoulder. A camera flash painted white across my vision. Hands clapped my back as if silence were confidence, as if not answering made me wise instead of gutted. I delivered a sentence I would not remember later, then excused myself with a nod I'd perfected against my will.

"Don't," I said under the noise, to no one and to myself.

Captain Cufflinks didn't appear—of course he didn't—but navy tie glanced right where he'd glanced before, toward that slash of light, as if reassurance lived there. He wasn't just a judge—he was a messenger. The kind of man who carried other people's power in his pocket and pretended it was his own. Every tilt of his head toward that light wasn't habit—it was signal. As if a decision might be confirmed by glare.

Across the table, Miguel caught my eye. Just for a breath. A fractional nod toward navy tie, then the kind of look a man gives when he's already told you once to keep your eyes open. My gut went cold. His hand flattened once against the tablecloth, deliberate, like a stop sign. No mistake: he'd seen this before. And he wanted me awake to it.

Watch closely tonight. Don't assume the scorecards will tell the whole story.

I watched Brynn instead.

A guest—somebody's spouse with sharp cheekbones and the self-satisfaction of a person who believed they understood power—tipped her glass toward me. "To legacy," she said, and the word legacy burned like acid.

"That's not—" I started, then strangled the rest because the ballroom is not a place to bleed either.

The guest drifted away, already bored, already hunting the next anecdote to weaponize at dinner parties.

If victory tastes like this, spit it the fuck out.

"Brynn," I said.

She lifted the champagne to her mouth and didn't drink. "Congratulations," she said, so beautifully I almost believed her.

I'd come to do this the right way: evidence, witness statements, a paper trail that couldn't be argued away. But "the right way" often looks like doing nothing at all.

"On the performance," I started. "On the room—"

"On the contract," she cut in, smiling that careful smile I'd learned to distrust. "Enjoy it."

I could feel every argument I'd rehearsed sliding farther away. I stayed silent.

"Walk with me," I said, low. It was a request with teeth.

She looked at the line of people waiting to congratulate us—waiting to congratulate me—and the light off the champagne made tiny suns in her eyes. "Later," she said. "After your interviews."

She turned away and the floor dropped like I'd missed a step.

"Brynn," I said again, because I didn't have a better word, because the other words in my mouth were dangerous and true.

Her gaze flicked toward navy tie, toward the place he kept checking, then back to me with a clarity that hurt. "It came through," she said softly. "Loud and clear."

Her smile was a blade, and I deserve every inch of it. The worst part wasn't her anger—it was knowing I'd earned her silence. She'd given me trust in slivers, hard-won and fragile, and I'd let the moment pass when I could've defended her. Now the distance between us was a canyon, and I was the one who carved it.

She moved away into the architecture of celebration—palms, glass, praise—and I stood still in the middle of it and tried not to burn the whole thing down.

***

BRYNN

You don't break in front of clients. Dad burned that in with one look when I smashed a glass at thirteen. I've had my pretty game face down ever since.

A coordinator framed us in her phone with both logos lined up. "On three," she chirped. "Say nailed it!"

"Nailed it," I said, and the phrase soured as soon as it left my mouth.

Because nothing screams billion-dollar professionalism like a caption fit for a college keg stand.

I found a corner where the shadow of a palm frond cut across the floor and looked like prison bars. I refused to see them that way. I didn't want them to. I wanted to be generous and adult and proud of what we'd done together.

We'd won the room. We'd won the night.

And then the scorecards lied. The applause still rang in my ears, bright and hollow, while my pulse dragged low in my chest. Whiplash hurts more when it comes wrapped in sequins and champagne.

Somewhere near the front, a man in a navy tie checked his watch and smiled like he knew a punchline the rest of us didn't. The smile wasn't for us—it was for whoever sat in the wings, pulling strings. He didn't look like a man weighing ideas. He looked like a man confirming an order had gone through.

My idea—my network—had been traced over with a heavier hand and awarded to the wrong name. It wasn't the first time. Back in Dubai, I'd watched him walk away with credit that should've been mine, and the bruise of it had never really faded. I thought this week might rewrite that story. Instead, the same script played on a bigger stage. Maybe the judge simply didn't clock the ownership in the moment. Maybe the judge was coached, cued, bought, or charmed. I can chase maybes until my shoes wear out.

A cheer went up near the stage. Jerrick stood in it like a person who'd been told a funny story that wasn't funny. He wasn't gloating. He wasn't basking. He looked like a man trying to hold a wall up with his back.

The sight should've steadied me. Instead, it twisted deeper. I kept scanning for edges—fair, foul, honest, rigged—and every version cut.

My phone buzzed the second I ducked offstage. Of course it did — the whole damn thing had been streamed, which meant my sisters were back in Maris Key with popcorn and opinions.

Summer, naturally, had beaten Rayann to the punch. Of course she had—Rayann would've sent memes and fire emojis. Summer sent verdicts.

SUMMER: Smooth delivery. Tight slides.

Another bubble popped before I could answer.

SUMMER: But he edged you out. By one point.

Summer's texts didn't pause for emojis. Three stabs in a row, straight to the vein.

SUMMER: Do you trust him?

The reply glowed. I killed it with a swipe.

But I didn't send it. Because I didn't know the answer. Because the man who made me feel seen on that rooftop was the same man whose shadow now stretched over my work. And if I couldn't untangle the two, then maybe I didn't know him at all.

When I looked up, he was there—close enough to touch, not touching.

"Later," I said, because the champagne in my hand had become a prop and my dress had become armor and my heart had become something I would not hand anyone in a crowd.

He nodded once, as if that settled it.

Applause swelled, big and warm and meaningless.

Someone offered me another glass. I took it. Didn't drink.

Across the room, navy tie laughed at something that wasn't funny—the same man Jerrick had been watching during the scores.

I smiled for a camera and let the stranger on my left believe I was happy. Inside, I braced like for an undertow—muscles tight, lungs holding—waiting for the next move.

Chapter 23

The Knife Between Us

JERRICK

THE CELEBRATION HAD THINNED to background static—laughter echoing off marble, bass bleeding under the doors—by the time I spotted her slipping down the hall. She hadn't meant for me to follow—her posture screamed "don't"—but I followed anyway.

"Brynn," I said, low.

She didn't stop. Didn't run either. The slit in her dress flashed with each step, champagne still in her hand, and the night pulled taut between us, like a fault line ready to open.

She cut into a side corridor where the palms and lights thinned and the music dulled to a hum. She pressed her back to the wall as if it were armor.

"You wanted me to walk with you?" she said. Her voice carried the kind of edge that cut cleaner for being quiet. "Fine—walk. Talk. Say what you came to say."

I stopped a pace away. "That win wasn't clean."

Her laugh had no humor. "Clean? Don't insult me. Tell me the truth—was I just a strategy? A pretty little distraction while your father laid the groundwork?"

"No." Too fast. Too raw. "Brynn, you know me. I didn't steal your ideas. I didn't invite him into this."

Her chin lifted, steel in her eyes. "Didn't invite him, or didn't stop him?"

The accuracy stung worse than the accusation.

And fuck, she wasn't wrong.

"Because that's what it looks like from here, Jerrick. You get the benefit. I get the scraps. I built that section from the ground up. And when that judge credited it to you, you didn't have the balls to correct him."

I let it land. Took the bruise. Miguel's warning flashed in my head—"keep your eyes open"—but I couldn't give that to her. Not without burning a man who'd trusted me.

"I need you to believe me." My throat worked around the rest, the part I couldn't say.

"Believe what?" she asked, voice flat.

I didn't answer fast enough. Her eyes narrowed. "Didn't know, or didn't say?"

"Brynn... " I shoved a hand through my hair, nerves frayed. "Not here. Please—come with me."

She hesitated, then followed. We cut through the hallway in silence, past the elevator bank and up the short flight of stairs that led to the rooftop bar.

The rooftop bar was nearly empty. Just a scatter of tables lit by hurricane lamps, the sound of the ocean in the distance. Most of the guests were still downstairs, drunk on post-panel glory, leaving this place to stragglers who wanted air more than company. A pair of businessmen hunched over cigars near the rail, the bartender polished glasses with the kind of disinterest that promised she wasn't listening.

It was private enough. The lamps burned low, throwing more shadow than light. A gust rattled the flames, shadows cutting across her face. Her hair whipped against her cheek, then stilled. The air went thick.

From up here, the ballroom felt like another world—laughter muffled to nothing but a dull throb underfoot. The night air cooled my skin, but my chest burned. The champagne I'd choked down earlier curdled like acid. My starched collar felt like a noose.

She set her untouched glass on the table between us like it was evidence.

"Talk," she said.

I dragged a hand over my face. "I'll tell you everything."

Her shoulders stayed squared, her gaze hard as flint

"The first call I got this morning was from my father," I said, the words scraping out like rust. "He didn't say it outright—he never does—but the message was clear: *Don't worry about the outcome.* That's when I knew the board was tilted."

Her breath hitched, sharp through her nose. She set her glass down with a click too precise to be casual.

"I thought I could head it off before it touched you. I went looking for proof. Made calls. Pulled favors. Found an email chain that didn't belong: a transfer, an altered ownership line, timestamped the same morning."

Her jaw ticked, that muscle below her ear twitching—the same spot I'd kissed two nights ago when her sighs had melted instead of locked me out.

"I stopped in for a quick bite before the panel and saw a few of the judges at a corner table. No laughing. No small talk. Locked in, serious, as if something was being decided. And there was a man with them who didn't fit. Expensive suit, navy tie, but he didn't read like press or staff. When I walked past, one of the judges looked up and caught my eye. Whole table froze. Then they pasted on polite smiles, as if I'd imagined it. But I hadn't. I know guilt when I see it."

Her lashes sliced the air. Fingers clamped the table edge, knuckles white.

"One of my contacts warned me. Told me to keep my eyes open. Said it wasn't just about one contract—something bigger was going on. But I couldn't give that to you without burning him. So I stayed quiet, thought I could fix it myself."

Her mouth pressed flat, shoulders shaking once with a breath she didn't let out.

"I wasn't hiding it from you to protect him—I was trying to protect you. I thought if I could stop it before it hit the stage, you'd never carry the stain. But by panel time, it was too late."

Her stare locked me in place, chair legs suddenly iron. "That's why I'm not accepting the contract," I said, voice low. Raw. "Not when it was rigged. Not when it was stolen from you."

Something flickered across her face—too fast to catch. Almost belief. Almost. Then her jaw set, shoulders squared, and the steel slid back into place. Whatever part of her wanted to trust me, she smothered it before it could breathe.

Her eyes widened for a heartbeat, then shuttered. Her jaw ticked like she was swallowing rage. Half in shadow, half in light. And I had no idea which side had already written me off.

"You'll forgive me if I don't take the word of a Thorne at face value."

Fucking deserved.

Her fingers loosened from the glass, curled against her palm, as if she had to hold herself back from reaching for me. The war played out in her eyes before the steel slid back in place. "If that's true... prove it." A whisper meant to wound. A challenge, not a request.

I didn't look away. Couldn't. The air between us felt loaded, like one wrong breath would set it off.

"The email chain. The altered ownership. The name of your contact." Her tone had gone cold, precise—the one she used when she was gutting people in negotiations. Worse than her anger. "You give it all to me. Now. Not later. Not when it's safe. You hand me the knife, Jerrick. Then we'll see who you're really protecting."

She was right. Handing it over meant turning the blade on my own name. My own blood. Choosing her anyway. If she took this public, Adventura wouldn't just lose the contract. My father's grip on the board would fracture. Every client who still bought the illusion of our legacy would see the strings yanked into the light. And me? I'd be branded either as the traitor who exposed it—or the coward who let it stand.

I didn't hesitate.

Pulled my phone from my pocket, thumbed open the encrypted folder I'd been carrying like a dossier. Slid it across the damp tabletop until it stopped at her clenched hand.

"It's all there," I said, voice rough. "Passcode is the date of our first kiss."

Her breath caught, sharp. That detail—intimate, exact, *ours*—wasn't business. It was trust. More binding than any contract I'd ever signed.

Her eyes flicked from me to the phone, back again. For half a beat the steel cracked. Just a hairline, but I saw it.

Her fingers hovered over the screen. Not touching. Not yet.

Then laughter burst from the stairwell door, too loud, too close. Spell broken.

Her hand jerked back as if the phone burned. Then, at the last second, she snatched it off the table like she didn't trust herself to leave it behind. "I'll look at it," she said. Voice sharp again, but aimed at herself as much as me. "But don't follow me."

She walked. Didn't touch the glass. Didn't look back. She had the proof in her hand now, and I had no fucking idea which way it would cut.

Chapter 24

Between Fire and Fury

BRYNN

THE PHONE WAS TOO heavy, too hot, contraband in my hand. My hands were damp, slick, and the champagne fizz still in my veins turned sour. My chest was tight. My stomach did a flip I couldn't call nerves or nausea.

I slipped into a half-lit lounge, Tommy Bahama prints, soft fabric, a breath of salt and mango. I wanted to hurl the damn phone into the wall. I opened it instead, hands shaking.

The passcode was easy. Too easy. The date of our first kiss. My hands shook so hard I almost blew it. Out of every number in the world, he'd picked that? Either manipulation at scale or the most reckless truth he could hand me.

And then the files hit.

Email headers stacked in neat, damning lines. Transfers. Altered ownership. Signatures that weren't ours. Timestamps printed like bruises.

I looked away and back. The numbers waited, patient and undeniable. Too clean to be a mistake, too dirty to be Jerrick.

The tighter I scrolled, the cleaner it got. My brain rejected it, insisting it was a setup, a fake, a Thorne play. But every time I blinked, I knew the truth: this wasn't his hand. This was his father's. And I'd been punishing the wrong man.

For weeks, I kept him in the enemy column. A rival to crush. A distraction I couldn't afford. I'd tried to file him under mistakes—like that almost-kiss two years ago I'd spent every day since pretending to erase. But staring at this evidence, I knew the truth I'd been fighting harder than him: I already believed him. God help me, I did.

What now?

This wasn't us alone. This was bigger. His father's fingerprints smeared across everything. If he could rig a panel, what else was he playing?

Summer—shit, I should call Summer. No. What would Summer do?

Breathe, Brynn. Think.

Except I couldn't think. My brain ricocheted between fury and relief. He hadn't betrayed me. But his father had. And Jerrick—oh God, Jerrick—had been standing there, taking hit after hit from me while trying to hold this back.

I clicked the screen dark and held it to my chest as if I could hold the whole damn world in. My lungs stuttered. My heart raced. This wasn't okay. None of it was okay.

What the hell were we supposed to do?

***

JERRICK

I shifted to the bar.

What if I lost Brynn?

"Zacapa. Neat," I muttered, voice rough.

The bartender glanced up. Older woman, maybe sixties. Hair streaked silver and pulled back in a braid that looked like it could double as a weapon. Skin browned by years of sun, lines from laughter and storms, eyes sharp enough to cut through bullshit. Lines bracketed a mouth that had laughed through storms and shut down nonsense without raising the volume.

A brass name tag flashed: Maritza.

She poured the rum without asking questions, slid the glass across. I caught the faint scent of citrus and vanilla clinging to her, warm and clean, like comfort layered over steel.

I lifted the glass. Nothing registered. Thought sparked and popped, no clean line to ground it.

My brain ran plays like I was back in a fight I couldn't win on points. Judges locking eyes with me and freezing. Navy tie asshole who didn't belong at the table. The email chain with its too-perfect timestamps. Every move stank of my father's fingerprints, neat and tidy as if he'd gift-wrapped the win for me. That was him in every arena—stack the deck, polish the edges, make the victory look inevitable. He'd spent my whole life treating me like a project to manage, not a son. A Thorne wasn't supposed to bleed, only win. And if I didn't play along, he'd make sure I lost in ways that cost more than contracts.

Which meant no clean victory. Brynn should've had the contract. She deserved it, and they stole it out from under her. I refused it, but that didn't erase the theft—or the fact my father would make me pay for walking away.

No trophy waited at the end of this. Only smoke and alarms. And through it all—her face. The way she'd looked at me when she walked off with my phone. Like she wanted to believe me and hated herself for it. That look burned hotter than the rum in my hand.

Maritza moved down the bar, wiping without hurry, not looking at me long but somehow still seeing too much. "You love her."

Not a question.

I huffed out something between a laugh and a curse. "That obvious?"

Her mouth curved, not unkind. "Men drink that way when they win or when they lose. You drink as if you are afraid." There was no judgment in her tone, only a kind of weary recognition. I wondered how many men had sat at this bar before me, spilling secrets into her rum, thinking they were unique. Maybe she'd known men like my father. Maybe she'd known women like Brynn—sharp enough to scare men stupid.

She wasn't wrong.

"Afraid I fucked it all up."

Her towel stilled. She leaned in, close enough that I caught the scent of lime, woodsmoke, and a long day. "Then fix it. Don't wait for her to forgive you. Earn it."

"It's complicated."

Her laugh was short, knowing. "Complicated is a word men use when they are scared to bleed for something." The way she said it made me think she'd bled once, too. For what—or who—I didn't know. But it gave her words weight.

"You think love is clean? No. It is messy. It is work. It is deciding the same thing again and again: *her.*"

I stared at the glass, the amber light catching, and tried to swallow. Still tasted like ash.

She tapped the counter, eyes cutting through me. "I saw the way she looked at you, when she left. Angry, yes. But not done. That is the face of a woman who already sees you as hers—even if she hasn't forgiven you yet."

"The way she looked at me... " I shook my head, jaw tight. "It wasn't hate. Not all of it. But it sure as hell wasn't trust either. I'm not sure I've earned the right to be called hers."

Her head tilted, braid sliding over her shoulder. "You are already that. She doesn't know yet. But she will. Unless you are stupid enough to let her walk away."

That hit harder than the rum.

I tipped the glass back. The liquor burned this time, finally. Maybe I needed it to.

***

BRYNN

He was still at the bar when I came back to the rooftop, phone clutched in my hand, evidence and weapon.

I set it down between us. Didn't give it back. Didn't throw it at him either. Just placed it there, screen dark, a heartbeat pulsing between us. Dead center.

"I looked." My voice was steadier than I felt. "And for once, I don't have a clever comeback."

His eyes lifted, guarded, hungry. "You believe me."

I crossed my arms. "I believe this issue is bigger than me. Or you."

His shoulders dropped a fraction. The tendons at his throat unstrung. And damn me, I liked that look on him. Like he was ready to fight for more than himself.

"You should've told me sooner," I added, sharper than I meant.

"I know." His jaw flexed. "I'll take the hits. You won't carry this alone."

The retort I had ready thinned to air. I crossed my arms tighter, but my breathing gave me away, hammering like it wanted out.

He pushed his chair back, stood. He closed the space with deliberate slowness, as if giving me the chance to shove him away. I didn't.

Behind him, I caught movement. The bartender, polishing a glass, glanced our way—just long enough to give him that all-knowing look women his mother's age seemed born with. Like she already knew exactly where this was headed. His shoulders shifted under it, but he didn't break eye contact with me.

"Brynn." My name came out low, wrecked.

Nope. You're still pissed, Brynn. Bail now.

Instead, I grabbed his shirt and yanked him down.

The kiss hit hard, all teeth and fury, like we were trying to win even here. His mouth crashed against mine, and I hated how much I needed it, hated how fast my body betrayed me. His hand clamped the edge of the bar for balance, the other bracing the back of my neck, dragging me into him as if I'd given him no choice.

I bit his lip. He growled into my mouth, low and guttural, and angled closer, hip pressing into mine where the barstool pinned me in place. Rum on his breath, champagne on mine, sharp and combustible.

"You're still pissed," he muttered against my mouth.

"Damn right I am." I kissed him harder, punishment and permission in one.

His laugh was ragged, swallowed by another kiss. One hand slid into my hair, tugging just enough to make my pulse jump. The other gripped the bar as if control lived there. My fingers fisted in his shirt, pulling him closer, neither of us giving ground.

Glass clinked behind him. Out of the corner of my eye, the bartender kept polishing, unbothered, but when she caught his profile in the lamplight I swore I saw her smirk. Like she'd seen this whole train wreck barreling toward her bar and wasn't about to stop it.

I finally tore back, breath jagged, lips swollen. "This doesn't fix anything."

"No," he said, forehead nearly brushing mine, voice raw. "But it sure as hell reminds me what's worth fixing."

My chest heaved, torn between fury and something far more dangerous. "We still have a problem, Jerrick."

His thumb grazed my cheek, rough and reverent at once. "Then let's take it apart. Together."

Chapter 25

Weapons on the Table

BRYNN

WE DIDN'T LINGER AT the bar. Too many eyes, too much noise, the world too ready to intrude.

Jerrick slid a folded bill across the bar with a quick wink toward Maritza, a silent thank-you, before jerking his chin toward the stairs. No discussion, just *decision*.

I ducked into my suite first, grabbing my laptop and a notepad, because if I was going to war tonight, I needed my weapons. My champagne-sticky dress hit the floor, replaced by yoga pants and a soft, off-the-shoulder t-shirt. It was going to be a long damn night. They weren't comfort. They were armor. A uniform for the real fight, stripped of sequins and masks, ready for battle in cotton and attitude.

When I slipped into his suite, he already had on a t-shirt and gym shorts, hair a little wild from running his hands through it. Laptop open, files spread across the table like a general laying out battle plans. He looked like the poster boy for controlled chaos.

When his eyes met mine, his focus faltered—just for a heartbeat. His gaze skimmed over the yoga pants, the bare line of my collarbone, heat flickering before he snapped it back to the screen.

Good. Let him suffer. We had work to do.

I slipped into the corner chair with my phone and dialed Summer before I lost my nerve. It was late with the time difference, but she picked up on the second ring, her voice groggy.

"It's late. What's going on?"

My throat was tight. "Something's happened. Something dirty." My palms were slick against the phone, stomach sinking cold even as the heat from Jerrick's body across the table bled toward me.

Of course this would happen on a trip where I wore sequins.

"Define dirty."

I laid it out: the judges, the blue-tie interloper, the ownership lines not just altered but watermarked—re-coded, as if someone had planned this fraud weeks before the first pitch. Not every detail—God forbid I hand her Jerrick's name outright—but enough to paint the picture.

The edits were too clean, margins aligned like a scalpel cut. Whoever did this cleaned their fingerprints—then left the knife in plain sight.

There was a pause on her end, bedding rustling. "Christ. That's actionable. If Adventura Luxe tampered with contracts and panel outcomes, Wilder has grounds to pursue damages."

"Legal?"

"Absolutely. And before you say anything—no, this isn't about your feelings. I don't give a damn about your history with Jerrick Thorne. If this goes legal, you separate. Distance. Cut communication. I won't have Wilder Horizons exposed because you couldn't draw the line."

If I blurred the lines, I wouldn't just drag Wilder into the crossfire—I'd torch my career, my reputation, the proof that I'd built something without anyone's name but my own. My pulse spiked. "You think I'd put the company at risk?"

Her voice softened. Barely noticeable.

"No, Brynn, I don't. I think you're smarter than that. But I also think you're human. Rayann mentioned something in passing. Made me wonder." A sharp exhale. "Listen, Brynn. If he's involved—even tangentially—you let me handle it. You don't get caught in the blast zone."

I stared at the phone like it had just slapped me. "Summer, it's not that simple."

Simple would be nice. My life is never on the simple menu.

"It is. If this goes legal, the optics matter more than your instincts. Trust me. You don't want Wilder's name tied to a Thorne scandal. Clear?"

Her tone brooked no argument. I nodded, even though she couldn't see me. "Clear."

"Good. Get on a plane. Send me everything you have. I'll talk to Juliette and line up counsel." Her voice softened just a notch, steel with velvet. "Brynn... don't be stupid."

Her voice echoed down years. I flashed to nineteen, Summer dragging me out of a disaster internship I'd sworn I could handle, her hand firm on my elbow while she cleaned up the mess I wouldn't admit I'd made. She'd always been the one to pull me back from cliffs I pretended weren't there.

The line clicked dead.

I sat there a minute longer, phone heavy in my hand, pulse hammering. When I looked up, Jerrick was watching me from across the room, jaw tight.

"Well?" he asked.

"She wants me to cut you off." My voice was steadier than I felt. "She said if this goes legal, I need to keep Wilder out of the crosshairs."

Something flickered across his face—hurt, quick, gone. "And what do you want?"

The mask slipped, quick as a blink. His eyes caught mine, not with hunger but with something rawer—fear, stripped bare. The kind that made my chest ache before he slammed the door back on it.

Protect him, don't protect him—pick a lane, Brynn.

I exhaled. "To fix this. Tonight. Before we both get on planes and this spirals into a mess neither of us can control."

He raked a hand through his hair. "For what it's worth, I didn't sign anything after the panel. Told them I needed final legal review on the IP clauses. Bought us a few days without raising suspicion."

We spent the next two hours buried in files, chasing not typos but fingerprints of corruption. Blue light from the screens carved shadows across his face, coffee gone metallic bitter on my tongue. My pen scratched furiously against paper, the sound too loud in the charged quiet, while the hum of the AC failed to cool the heat rolling off our shoulders. Email threads scrubbed but not erased cleanly enough. Metadata on contracts that traced back to Adventura Luxe servers. Calendar invites mysteriously "forwarded" to Adventura executives. Each breadcrumb pointed to foresight, not accident. A rigged game with his father's brand stamped across the rulebook.

Screens glowed, notes piled, our hands colliding when we reached across the table. Each spark dragged my attention off spreadsheets and back to him, forcing me to trace columns of numbers instead of the lines of his arms. My brain fought to stay locked on strategy, but my body betrayed me with every graze, every shift too close.

And the more we uncovered, the tighter the walls closed in. If these files went public, they wouldn't just scorch Adventura Luxe—they'd torch Wilder with them. A single clause made it look like I'd approved Jerrick's name swap. Another line suggested Wilder Horizons had "consulted" on the change, as if I'd signed off on the fraud myself. They'd forged my approval so neatly it almost fooled me.

Jerrick froze mid-scroll, lips parting. "Jesus." He turned the screen toward me. A memo buried in the appendix—clean formatting, perfect grammar, too perfect. His voice cracked. "This is my father's assistant. She doesn't just copy notes, she writes policy." His jaw flexed hard enough to ache. "He didn't just run Adventura Luxe. He built the entire scam with her hand on the pen."

No wonder it smelled off. He's been laundering his lies through loyalty.

I saw the boy he must've been—watching contracts get redlined at the dinner table, his father's voice smooth and merciless as ink erased lives. This fraud wasn't new. It was inheritance.

For a flicker his face went flat with panic, then his shoulders bunched and anger folded it into something coiled and dangerous. The shift coursed through him, fear sparking into a brutal need to own the space, to own me. He leaned back with a groan, rubbing his neck, eyes cutting toward me. "You have no idea how hard it is to sit here and not throw you on this table."

The room stilled. Laptops hummed. My pulse drummed. My gut twisted. I trusted Jerrick, but I didn't trust the gravity his father carried. Men like that didn't need chains to drag you back—they used blood, power, and promises you couldn't refuse. And what scared me most wasn't that Jerrick was guilty. It was that one day he might not have a choice.

"Focus, Thorne." My voice cracked like a whip, though my heartbeat thundered.

His grin was feral, sharp. "I am. That's the problem."

By three a.m., exhaustion made every touch electric. His leg pressed into mine under the table. We reached for the same page, fingers colliding and locking for a beat too long. Neither of us moved. The evidence of fraud lay crushed between our hands, the air so thick I could barely drag in a breath.

The evidence blurred; the only thing sharp was the heat between us.

I shoved the laptop aside, reached over the table, and kissed him like I'd been starving for weeks. He met me head-on, mouth hot, tongue rough, hands sliding into my hair and fisting like he'd been waiting all night for me to snap.

The chair screeched against the floor when he pulled me around and yanked me into his lap, my top riding high. His cock was already hard, thick against me through layers that suddenly felt like too much.

"Brynn," he growled against my neck, voice wrecked. "Give me the order. Tell me to stand down."

"Shut up," I gasped, grinding down. "We don't have time."

"Fuck," he bit out, dragging the straps of my bra down hard enough they nearly tore. His mouth closed over my breast, teeth scraping, and my head slammed back on a moan I couldn't swallow.

I pulled his tee over his head and reached for his waistband. His laugh was low, dangerous, swallowed by another kiss as he hooked my thigh over his hip and slid his hand into my pants and beneath the lace of my panties.

"Already wet," he muttered, thumb circling cruel and perfect. "Knew you'd break before me."

I bit his shoulder, hard enough to leave a mark. "Cocky bastard."

"Yours," he rasped, and pushed two fingers deep.

The stretch was too much, not enough. I clawed at his boxer briefs and shoved them low enough to free him. He hissed when I wrapped my hand around him, thick and heavy, pre-come slicking my palm.

"Now," I demanded, desperate

"Say it," he ordered, teeth at my ear.

"I need you to make it all go away. Five minutes. No strategy, no judges—just this."

He pulled down my pants and panties simultaneously, reached for his wallet, and pulled out a condom, fumbling with a curse. He tore it with his teeth, rolled it on in one rough stroke, and was inside me before I could draw another breath.

The stretch stole my cry, swallowed by his mouth and the frantic rhythm of skin and breath.

It was quick, rough, merciless. A chair half-toppling, his hand clamped on my ass to drive me down on him, my nails raking his back like I wanted to peel him open. The world narrowed to this—his cock pounding into me, the burn of it, the sweat slick between us, the wet slap of bodies that couldn't get close enough.

"Come for me," he demanded, and I did—sharp, fast, tearing through me like a firework. He followed, teeth sinking into my shoulder as he came hard, deep, holding me pinned to him like he'd fuse us together if he could.

When it was over, there was no collapse into softness. We were both still shaking, half-naked, breathless, clothes askew, but our laptops were waiting. The notes, the evidence, the plan. The cool air licked at sweaty skin, raising goosebumps where his hands had branded me. Coffee went bitter on the table beside the sharp tang of sex. For a long second, our eyes locked—no satisfaction, just a grim recognition. Our laptops glowed like judges, waiting, reminding us nothing had changed but our sweat-slick skin.

For half a heartbeat, his hand lingered at my waist, thumb dragging slow against my skin like he wanted to say something he couldn't. Fear flickered in his eyes, gone as fast as it came, but it landed in my gut heavy as stone. We'd slapped sex over an open wound and called it Saturday night.

And that's exactly what we pulled back toward us, skin cooling in the night air, sex still clinging to us like a brand.

Because this wasn't done. Not yet. We had the evidence. What we didn't have was time. The plan was simple, if brutal: catalogue everything, lock it behind redundancies, and put it in Summer's hands before anyone could erase the trail. Only then could we even think about how to cut Adventura Luxe off at the knees.

Chapter 26

She Chose Wilder

BRYNN

WE WORKED UNTIL THE numbers blurred, pushing the hotel Wi-Fi so hard it choked on warnings about heavy use. My tabs were a graveyard. .. my eyes chasing ghosts across endless screens: admin consoles, cloud drives, email exports, revision histories, payment processors, resort portals. Jerrick's screen reflected in the window—a cage of spreadsheets and time-stamps.

My eyes burned, cursor streaking every time I blinked too slow. My vision kept melting into pixels. I blinked and the spreadsheet blurred into a smear of numbers I couldn't trust.

Every trail was worse than the last. Wire transfers routed through shell companies tied to a Cayman account. Calendar calls with "consultants" who matched two of the judges' personal emails. Twin proposals in a shared drive—ours with Wilder's name in the document history three weeks earlier, theirs rolled back with a scrubbed author field and a fresh "initial upload" note that didn't match the server clock.

Between the recycled logins and the cut-and-paste countersigns, it was less cloak-and-dagger and more lazy paperwork—careless in a way that made my skin crawl.

"This isn't one mistake," Jerrick muttered, scrolling a ledger. "It's the foundation. It's all of it."

His cursor hovered, then clicked open an internal memo thread. Certain phrases lit up like warning flares: *controlled outcomes, alignment dinners, external influence secured.* Corporate code that wasn't nearly as subtle as it thought it was.

I kept going. Catalogued the files, cross-checked every detail, recorded the screens. Backed everything up twice and stashed copies in a secure drive far outside Adventura Luxe's reach. Only when the evidence lived in three places and none of them touched Adventura Luxe would I feel safe handing the sword to Summer and our attorneys.

A line item stopped me cold in a financial permissions report—an old payout buried under "Legacy HR." Wrong category. Wrong era.

"Jerrick?" I pinged the link into our shared chat. "Does this mean what I think?"

God, no. Don't let it be what I think.

He opened it. Silence. His video tile, forgotten in the corner of my screen, went very still.

Settlement Agreement – J. Thorne (Spousal). It had to be his mother. Not his father. Not Jerrick.

Confidentiality: enforced.

Custody stipulations: voided.

Educational fund and trust: secured.

His voice came rough. "This... was my mother."

"You've never talked about her."

"There's nothing to talk about. She left." The words sounded practiced. A script he'd been handed and never questioned. The timestamps, the countersignatures, the routed accounts didn't care about his script.

"Jerrick, if I'm reading this correctly, she didn't just leave," I said quietly. "She found something. And your father paid for silence."

He clicked into the attached NDA. Metadata flashed: created by external counsel, uploaded from a private device, shared only to his father and two execs. Seventeen years ago. The same month an internal risk memo flagged "exposure via domestic party" and then vanished from the index—except the difference still showed a deletion.

Jerrick froze. His eyes darted across the screen like if he blinked, it would all rewrite itself. His throat worked, a sound catching that never made it into words. For a second I thought he might hurl the laptop across the room, or put his fist straight through the table. Then all that fury collapsed inward, leaving nothing but shock.

Seventeen years of lies cracking open in real time. *Jesus*.

He sank back, out of frame. "He made me believe she didn't want me. That she chose another life."

The words hit like a body blow. I couldn't move, couldn't speak—just sat there, staring at the truth gutting him in real time.

"I was seventeen. Old enough to hate her. Not old enough to know better."

My chest burned. This outgrew the usual corporate stink; it had line items that belonged in criminal ledgers. Someone had taken property—ideas, credit, the clean arc of other people's lives—and filed it as a business expense.

I dug further into the "Legacy HR" vault and found a misfiled folder—no preview available. It was password-protected, but someone had recycled the same login they'd once used on a travel booking portal. Sloppy. I tried the pattern, and the files unlocked.

Old email exports. Scans named by whatever office scanner had spit them out years ago. The text recognition had only half-worked, garbling words but catching just enough to make the files searchable. I sorted by "contains: Wilder" and got more hits than I wanted. Most were contracts. One wasn't.

A scanned photo of a handwritten note sat buried in an attorney's "personal reference" folder. The text recognition was messy, but the preview pane still showed enough to make out the words:

She chose Wilder, but she'll regret it.

My blood iced. This wasn't business. It was obsessio n... and obsession was so much worse.

The cursor shook under my hand, like even the machine knew this was poison.

I sent the image to him with a single "?" because anything louder felt wrong.

Jerrick's tile reappeared. He didn't look at the camera; he kept reading the note, then the adjacent email headers from the same week—nights of messages to himself forwarded to counsel with subject lines stripped to single words: *Oath. Debt. Correction.*

"This isn't about business," he said. "It never was."

The suite went quiet. The ocean outside might as well have been on mute.

He scrubbed through more headers, building the picture in real time. His father's calendar the month of the separation. A private dinner with a panel chair years later. Donations timed to the week of a pitch. Every piece connected with a grudge masquerading as strategy.

"All of this," he said, eyes on the screen. "Every contract, every stolen pitch, every sabotage. It wasn't about winning. It was about her. About punishing the man she chose instead of him."

My mother—my soft, untouchable memory—suddenly cast in a harsher light I didn't ask for. *Don't make it true.* But the metadata didn't blink.

Jerrick finally looked up. He was wrecked—eyes bloodshot, face carved tight like he was holding himself together with sheer force of will. Guilt clung to him, heavy and suffocating, for sins he hadn't signed but was still made to carry.

"I'm not him," he said, voice rough, desperate. "Brynn, I swear. I'm not him."

The air in the suite seemed to thin. My chest ached like I'd been holding my breath with him.

I did. Because the next tab he opened wasn't another buried contract or email thread. It was a retainer agreement builder—for outside counsel. Not the company's lawyers, not anyone on Adventura Luxe's payroll. His hand hovered only a second before he started filling it out, name after name, line after line.

Jesus fuck. He was actually doing it.

My pulse kicked, sharp and hot—shock and awe colliding.

He wasn't just saving evidence. He was drawing a line in the sand. Breaking from his father's protection, from the firm that had shadowed every decision he'd ever made. Choosing strangers—independent counsel—over the empire stamped with his name.

Then he copied the evidence index into a clean folder and gave me sole permissions, locking his own family out. Once, I would've killed to keep him out of my files. Now I was giving him my trust, handing him proof I'd never have shared if he were still my rival. A timed release to Summer and Wilder's legal team followed, with a digital fingerprint to prove nothing had been altered.

He wasn't hedging anymore. He was choosing a new future, knowing exactly how ugly it would get.

His shoulders dropped, just a fraction.

We moved like a unit. I set the auto-send to Summer for 0700 ET with a separate key sent by text. He drafted a formal notice to Adventura Luxe's compliance inbox—timestamped but unsent—so our counsel could control first contact. I wrote the handoff memo: what we had, what we suspected, what to lock down before anyone started wiping logs. We mirrored the entire package to an offsite drive with zero-knowledge encryption and confirmed the check sums matched.

By the time the clock crept past four, the evidence lived in three places Adventura Luxe couldn't touch. Redundancies armed. Sword sharpened.

"We should get some sleep," I said, the room tilting from fatigue. His gaze flicked to the evidence still glowing on the screen, jaw tight. Sleep wasn't what scared him—it was what would come after.

He didn't answer right away. The glow of the monitors made him look younger and older at once.

"Stay with me," he said finally. "Until morning." He didn't ask me to trust him. He asked me not to leave. Not a command. Not a test. A request with all the arrogance stripped out of it. I could have gone to my own suite. Pretended this was still a rivalry, still safe. But we'd crossed the line when he chose the truth over his legacy. We were in this together now.

"Okay."

The air changed—pressure releasing in a quiet, invisible way. Jerrick reached across the table, fingers brushing mine, then curling firmly around them like he was anchoring himself. "Come on," he said quietly, not as a command but as a plea.

We shut the lids and let the room go dark, the only light a blink from the router. The hum of the AC, the distant crush of waves against the shore—ordinary sounds, cruelly at odds with the wreckage we'd dragged into the light.

We didn't touch at first. I stood there, listening to his breath steady, the quiet stretching between us. Tomorrow is war. But not tonight.

Then he reached for my hand, steady and sure, and drew me toward the bed. When we sank onto the covers, he didn't reach for more—he reached for less. For quiet. For stillness. His arm curved around me in a way that felt protective instead of possessive. His fingertips skimmed my cheek, slow enough to trip my pulse but not a move toward anything more. He leaned in, pressing a kiss to my forehead, the kind that said thank you without breaking open the words.

"Stay," he whispered, voice roughened by exhaustion and something heavier. "That's all I want." Minutes—maybe an hour—later, his hand found mine on top of the coverlet. Not gripping. Not claiming. Present.

Before sleep dragged me under, I saw the note again—four words from a man who couldn't let go. *She chose Wilder, but she'll regret it.*

Morning would come. Flights. Lawyers. Summer with a list and a plan. But right then, in a dark room over a ruthless ocean, the truth was simple: he wasn't his father. I wasn't alone. And together, we'd stop being pawns.

Chapter 27

The Weight We Carry

BRYNN

T HE AIRPORT GLEAMED WITH polished tile and sunlight streaming through wide glass walls, the humid air carrying the faint salt of the ocean even here. Travelers drifted past in linen shirts and resort wear, all bronzed skin and souvenirs, oblivious to the weight we carried, heavy as chains no one else could see.

We stood near the gate, neither of us saying much. What was there to say? We'd spent the night dismantling an empire—slumped over keyboards, eyes glazed in the glow of blue light, coffee cups sweating rings into the table—and now we were being split apart at the seams.

Me heading back to Maris Key, him north to Austin, into the shadow of his father.

He reached for my hand, thumb brushing over my wrist, a secret only we knew. His eyes were bloodshot, exhaustion etched deep, but the way he looked at me still managed to undo me.

"See you soon, Wilder," he murmured. Not bravado. Not rivalry. A promise.

My throat tightened. I wanted to answer with something sharp, something clever, to keep the armor between us. But the words wouldn't come. All I had was truth. "Yeah. *Soon.*"

His hand lingered against mine, warm, steady, reluctant to let go. Then he leaned in, pressing a soft kiss to my lips. "Thank you," he whispered, so low I almost didn't catch it. For what—staying, fighting, believing—I wasn't sure. Maybe all of it.

I stood frozen as he pulled away, every cell screaming not to let him go. But the boarding call crackled overhead, final and merciless. He turned, shoulders squared like a man walking into battle, and disappeared into the stream of passengers.

I stayed behind, carrying evidence on my laptop, my bag suddenly heavier with decades of damage—and futures it could still blow apart. He was walking into his father's storm. I was walking into mine. And neither of us knew when the next time would be.

Figures. I spent two years fighting it—telling myself he was the asshole who stole Dubai out from under me—then five days finally giving in. And the universe's answer? Sorry, sweetheart, no refunds, no returns.

Boarding blurred past in a mess of tangled earbuds, fumbling my passport, and a stranger's suitcase clipping my shin—ticket check, overhead bins slamming, the shuffle of sandals and rolling bags. A blast of chilled air hit me as I stepped onto the plane, a jarring contrast to the damp heat of the terminal.

I collapsed into my seat near the window, tugging the seatbelt across soft black joggers and a clean white tank layered under a light cardigan. Comfortable, not corporate. My hair was pulled into a loose braid, damp from the quick shower I'd forced myself into before leaving the hotel. At least I felt human again, even if exhaustion still pressed behind my eyes. Not exactly Wilder Horizons chic, but it would get me home.

The cabin smelled of citrus cleaning spray overlaid with the faint musk of sunscreen and too many people packed close, the low thrum of the engines under it all. Across the aisle, a family wrestled a toddler into a seatbelt, the kid already sticky with juice. Behind me, someone coughed into the recycled air vent.

I tried to zone out, pressing my forehead to the cool window, but my bag dug into my legs. With a sigh, I shifted it into my lap. That's when I saw it—smooth leather peeking from the unzipped side pocket.

Not mine.

Jerrick's journal.

My stomach dropped. We'd been running on fumes, laptops and notepads piled together while we catalogued Adventura Luxe's rot. In the scramble, I must have grabbed it with my things.

I turned it over in my hands. Smooth leather, edges softened with use. Heavy in a way that didn't come from pages. It smelled faintly of sandalwood—Jerrick. The scent curled through me, as if he were still here, close enough to touch.

Hell, I missed him already.

I shouldn't open it. I knew I shouldn't.

But the weight of it... the weight of everything—my sisters, Wilder Horizons, the mess we'd uncovered, and the shadow of his father—itched at me. One look could change everything. One look could confirm if he was truly clean.

My thumb hovered on the edge.

Don't fucking do it, Brynn.

Nope. Not like this.

I shoved it back in the bag, but the temptation burned. On the flight, my hand cramped around the pen as I scrawled notes for Summer and Juliette. I flipped the same magazine page three times without seeing it, clouds outside blurring into one endless white smear. None of it stuck. Every time I glanced down, the journal sat there like it was daring me—open me, see what he really thinks.

And underneath it all, one memory kept looping—his mouth on mine, the kiss that had felt less like strategy and more like surrender. Like I was worth burning for.

By the time the wheels hit the tarmac, I'd convinced myself the journal was radioactive. Do not touch. Do not peek. At least not yet. The bag thumped against my shin, heavier with temptation. I swore I could feel the words humming inside, every page daring me to crack it open. Lists, sketches, secrets—it could be nothing, or it could be the one truth that decided whether I'd trusted the right man.

Emme was waiting outside baggage claim, leaning against her spotless white Lexus SUV, black hair glossy even under the fluorescent lights. She waved the second she spotted me, then slid back behind the wheel as I climbed in.

The interior gleamed, spotless as always, with a green smoothie tucked neatly in the cupholder between us. Emme, however, was all Sunday casual—Tampa Rays baseball cap pulled low over a ponytail, silver hoops flashing when she turned her head. Fitted tee, broken-in jeans, sneakers. She looked like she should've been sliding into a ballpark seat with a hot dog instead of chauffeuring me to an emergency meeting.

She caught my glance and snorted. "Yeah, I was supposed to be at the game right now. Front-row seats, perfect weather, nachos the size of my head. Instead, I'm driving your ass to a conference room."

"Um, I love you too?"

"Straight to the office," she said, buckling her seatbelt with a sigh. "Summer's called an emergency meeting. Juliette's already there."

"Of course she did," I muttered, settling my bag at my feet. Sunday or not, I should've known.

Emme shot me a quick side-eye, cheerful but sharp. "So. What kind of mess are we walking into?"

"It's big," I said. "Messy. Legal-level messy."

Her jaw dropped. "Please tell me Jerrick Thorne didn't—"

"He didn't. He's one of the good guys." The words came out sure, no hesitation.

Emme blinked. "Wow. You sound certain."

"I am."

She didn't push. Instead, she flipped the radio to some peppy indie-pop station and grumbled, "Guess who's being shipped to Patagonia next week? Me. Summer says it's the new playground for the über-rich. Who the fuck goes to Patagonia? Shoot me fucking now."

I snorted, tension cracking. "Vendor Relations Barbie can handle glaciers."

"Vendor Relations Barbie does *not* do glaciers," she muttered, pulling into the Wilder Horizons lot. "But fine. I'll survive on kale chips and trauma bonding."

I glanced over, filing that away. I'd been digging into Patagonia's rise for months now—the new playground for clients with more money than sense, all wrapped up in eco-bullshit about "sustainable luxury." If Summer was sending Emme down there, it had to mean potential vendor contracts. Maybe the first step in staking our claim.

"Vendors?" I asked, sweet as sugar. "Nothing like watching you charm a pack of frostbitten hoteliers."

Emme groaned. "Apparently. Because nothing says luxury travel like subzero winds, penguins, and a lecture on carbon offsets."

We pulled into the garage beneath our building—Wilder Horizons on the fourth floor—the glass tower catching the last stretch of late-afternoon light off the bay. Emme muttered something about missing her favorite player's ass in motion as I slung my bag over my shoulder and headed for the elevators.

Daisy nearly skidded into me in the lobby, notepad clutched to her chest.

"Welcome back, Brynn! Hi, Emme. Juliette's here with Summer. Rayann and Annie are on their way. Conference room's prepped. Do you need coffee? Water? A full blood sacrifice to the copier?"

Her words tumbled out in one breath, all fresh energy and wide eyes.

"Keep the printer alive and you're a saint."

She bolted, already dialing three numbers at once.

It was strange, seeing them stripped of their armor. No sharp suits, no blowouts or heels—just jeans, soft sweaters, hair pulled back in a way that made them look younger, almost girlish. Pretty in a way I usually missed when they were in full work mode. Summer and Juliette, the two oldest, usually carried themselves like commanders, distant even when they were kind. But right then, casual and raw, they felt more like my sisters than the executives who shared my conference table.

I didn't realize how badly I needed that right now.

"Let's hold until the others get here," Juliette said, though her pen was already moving.

Emme ducked into her office for a minute, leaving the three of us in the war room. Summer slid a folder across the table—hard copy, because of course she had one. "We've been with legal all morning. They've outlined next steps, drafted language for injunctions, and prepped the press angle if this leaks."

I scanned the bullet points, each one sharper than the last. It was everything Jerrick and I had unearthed—our messy screenshots now lined up as neat bullet points in Summer's color-coded folders.

Summer's gaze was unflinching. She flattened her palm over the folder as Juliette's pen clicked twice in restless rhythm. "This is going to get ugly, Brynn. But we're ready."

I nodded, no hesitation. "Agreed."

I didn't know it then, but while I sat in that glass room with my sisters, Jerrick's phone lit with his father's name.

He didn't take it. Not yet. Tomorrow would be soon enough. Jerrick had never been simple—part fighter, part strategist, part son clawing free of a father's shadow. The man who kissed me at the gate was the same one now staring at a screen he refused to answer, every choice carving him further from the name he carried. And I wasn't sure which version of him scared me more—the one breaking free, or the one still chained.

Chapter 28

Collateral

JERRICK

THE SKYLINE LOOKED DIFFERENT when you were walking into battle. Austin glass and steel cut sharper than jungle thorns. My reflection in the tower's doors barely looked like me—suit pressed, jaw set, no trace of the man who once bent under his father's shadow.

He was waiting when I walked in. Same office. Same skyline stretched wide through floor-to-ceiling glass, the sun catching on towers of steel and glass that he claimed like personal trophies. The room smelled of money and polish—leather, bourbon, and a cologne that lingered like a dry threat, the whole place carrying the weight of a bank vault with a grudge.

Charles Thorne didn't rise to greet me. He never did. He sat in that high-backed leather chair like it was a throne, silver hair sharp as the lines of his tailored navy suit, his cufflinks winking under the recessed lights. He moved with surgical economy—fingers flipping cufflinks, no wasted warmth, a smile that did its job and nothing more.

My fists reflected back at me in the lacquer, doubled and sharp. Behind him, the skyline blurred in the glass like a painted backdrop, Austin at his feet.

Fuck, he loved this view. Loved the feeling of everything beneath him, including me.

His eyes flicked over me—cool, gray, unreadable except for the disdain tightening at the edges. His jaw was clean-shaven, lips pressed in the kind of line that had once kept me silent at twelve, at fifteen, at twenty.

"You've embarrassed me," he said finally, his voice deep and deliberate, a blade sharpened on every syllable. "You've embarrassed this family."

I didn't sit. "I'm not signing your contract."

His brows twitched, the smallest fracture in his composure.

"You think I don't know what this is?" My voice cracked like a whip. "You've built your empire on intimidation, on payoffs and closed doors. But this—" I jabbed a finger at the folder on his desk. "This isn't business. This is you asking me to sell my integrity. *Me—your own fucking son. You want me to do your dirty work, to be the one who drags myself through the shit you don't want on your shoes?*"

I leaned in, the mahogany biting into my palms. "Brynn doesn't deserve that. She built her agency from the ground up with nothing but grit, brains, and sleepless nights. She earned every win, every client, every damn word in her pitch. I respect her too much to let you piss all over it because you're afraid of losing."

She wasn't just the rival I once swore to beat. She stood on broken sleep and stubborn willpower and still smiled like she'd already won. Brynn was proof that strength didn't always come in fists—it came in refusing to quit when the world tried to write you off.

And I sure as fuck won't tell you what else I've found—judges in your pocket, scorecards rewritten, the kind of corruption that bleeds when you cut it open. Let the lawyers pull that thread. I'll hold my cards until it's too late for you to bury the mess.

His eyes narrowed. "Ungrateful. Disloyal. After everything I've given you, this is how you repay me?"

Given me? You mean bought me, branded me, tried to make me your fucking clone.

My pulse hammered, but I kept my voice steady. I thought of Brynn — her hand on my wrist that night, her voice daring me to fight. That was the anchor. That was the reason I didn't break.

"I don't want your empire," I said. "I don't want your money. And I won't throw Brynn under the bus to save your reputation."

The corner of his mouth curled. "Brynn Wilder? She's a liability. A distraction. The sooner you cut her loose, the sooner you'll stop dragging my name through the mud."

Say her name again, old man, and I'll put my fist through your perfect, goddamn teeth.

I shoved the words back across the desk. "She's not the distraction. She's the fucking reason I'm still standing. She's smarter than half your board combined, and she built something from nothing while you were busy buying off judges and padding your empire. You want to call that weakness? You don't know the first thing about strength."

The temperature in the room dropped. His hand tightened on the armrest, knuckles white. "You're getting soft—just like your mother. She's wasting away in Florida, pretending her little life means anything."

There it was—the nuclear option. He always knew how to aim below the belt and smile while he twisted the knife.

You smug, heartless bastard. You gutted her, you gutted me, and now you've got the balls to sneer about weakness? Fuck you. Fuck every inch of this empire you've built on blood and silence.

My throat burned. "Florida?"

"She's been there for years," he sneered. "Pathetic."

The rest blurred. His voice rising—threats of cutting me off, disowning me, stripping me of every advantage. I barely heard it because one thought drowned out the rest.

My mother.

Not gone. Not dead. Not across an ocean.

Florida.

Alive. Breathing.

For seventeen years, I'd lived with his version of her—selfish, restless, incapable of love that lasted. I'd stopped trying to find her after the first few years, when every trail went cold and every question earned that look from him, the one that said weakness was worse than failure. So I buried it. Buried her. Told myself I didn't need the woman who walked away.

But she hadn't walked away.

He'd written a check to make her disappear. Paid for silence. Paid for absence. And I'd spent half my life defending him for it.

The ground didn't just shift—it vanished.

When he finally spat his last warning—"You'll regret this, son"—I walked out without looking back.

The parking garage was too quiet. Fluorescent lights buzzed overhead, echo rattling off concrete like static in my teeth. Oil fumes clung to the air, sharp as acid. My hands shook on the steering wheel of my Cadillac CTS-V—not from fear of him anymore, but from the fire crawling under my skin, eating me alive.

Seventeen years. Seventeen fucking years of silence. Seventeen years of believing she'd walked away from me like I wasn't worth the fight.

I pulled out my phone, screen glowing too bright in the dim. Searched. Found a number I wasn't sure would work. My thumb hovered, sweat slicking the glass, heartbeat pounding so hard I almost dropped it.

One ring. Two.

Then her voice—soft, breathless, Florida sunshine wrapped in syllables. "Hello?"

Air caught sharp in my throat. "Mom."

A pause. Then a sob, strangled and thin, as if she was afraid to breathe me away. "Jerrick?"

The syllables scraped down my spine. My grip on the wheel went white-knuckle, pulse hammering in my ears. *Seventeen years, and she still had the right to say my name like that?* Anger hit, hot enough to blister. "Why did you leave me? Why didn't you fight?"

"I did." Her voice cracked like glass under weight. "You don't know how many times I tried. Your father—he had the courts, the money, the power. I th ought... I thought staying away would keep him from punishing you more."

Her words slid under my skin like acid. I pressed my forehead to the steering wheel, metal cold against the heat rising in me. *So that was it. Not protection. Not sacrifice. He bought you off with my future.*

My voice shook. "So it's true. He made you choose—either walk away or he'd bleed you dry."

Her breath caught, ragged. "He told me if I fought, if I stayed, he'd ruin me. And he would have, Jerrick. I had nothing. No lawyer, no money, no way to stand against him. He promised you schools, connections, a future I could never give you. I told myself letting him raise you was better than dragging you into poverty with me."

Better? Christ. You thought leaving me with him was better?

For a moment, I imagined her then—alone in some Florida apartment, the glow of a secondhand lamp over court papers she couldn't afford to fight. Maybe she'd rehearsed these words for years, whispering them into the dark, hoping one day she'd get the chance to tell me. Maybe she'd convinced herself the lie was mercy.

I slammed my hand against the wheel. "So you abandoned me and called it opportunity? You let him turn me into a fucking pawn so you could scrape by somewhere else?"

Her voice cracked, splintering through the line. "You don't understand. He was prepared to cut you off right along with me. Said if I fought, if I stayed, you'd be dead to him. No rationale, no sympathy. He's not a man who loves, Jerrick. He's not a man who ever wanted to be a father. But he had the power... God, he had the power to make sure you had every opportunity. The schools. The money. The future I couldn't give you."

Her words rang hollow against the concrete around me. Opportunities. Futures. What the fuck good were they if you couldn't breathe, couldn't trust, couldn't feel anything real?

The word *love* burned like acid in my chest. I'd spent years chasing it—four with a fiancée who needed more than I could give, four trying to build something I didn't understand. In the end, all I had were pieces I couldn't fit together, because the only blueprint I'd ever had was silence.

"My whole life, I never knew love outside of you—and you stripped that from me. I tried, God, I tried—there was a woman once, a fiancée. I gave her everything I thought love was supposed to look like. But it wasn't enough. I didn't know how to give her what she needed, because no one ever showed me how. You took that from me the day you walked away."

Silence stretched, raw and suffocating.

Her voice wavered. "Jerrick…"

I pressed my fist to the wheel, knuckles aching. "And it wasn't just you. I didn't understand how fucked up he was back then—what kind of husband he must've been to you. I only saw the father who controlled everything, who made the rules. I thought his power was normal. I didn't realize he was gutting both of us."

And now I don't even know if I can give that love. Not the way other men can. Every time I try, I hear his voice, feel his hand turning me into something sharp and cold.

Brynn deserves more than a man who has to learn love like it's a second language.

Silence. Only the buzz of fluorescent lights, the faint hiss of air vents. Then a broken whisper: "I thought I was giving you everything. And in doing it, I gave you nothing."

I swallowed hard, but it scraped like gravel. "I don't know how to forgive you."

Her answer came back like glass underfoot. "I don't know how to forgive myself either."

The line hummed between us, thin and merciless, until it broke with a click that left me alone in the hum of the garage. The stench of oil. The stale reek of concrete. The salt sting of tears I couldn't hold back anymore.

All I had left was Brynn—her voice in my head, sharp as a blade and soft as salvation.

Fight.

So I would.

I stared at the empty screen until my vision blurred. Then my thumbs moved, quick and reckless.

ME: Confronted him. Told him I'm done. Fighting for us.

I hit send before I could think better of it. Brynn deserved to know she was the only thing keeping me steady.

Chapter 29

Fighting for Us

BRYNN

MY PHONE BUZZED ACROSS the conference table, a quick rattle against wood. I didn't move at first. Juliette's pen clicked again—twice—metronome to Summer's steady, lethal calm. Emme's office door stayed open, a sliver of light and the faint clatter of her keyboard down the hall.

I dragged the phone closer. Jerrick.

My heartbeat did that stupid, traitorous lurch. I opened the message with my thumb, breath held tight enough my ribs pricked.

JERRICK: Confronted him. Told him I'm done. Fighting for us.

Heat flashed up my chest, a match held too close. *You idiot. You beautiful, infuriating, necessary idiot.* My thumb hovered. I didn't answer. Not yet. The room had teeth again.

The war room gleamed with polish that cost extra—a slab of walnut stretched long and heavy, its surface dark as molasses and slick enough to throw back every glare from the recessed lights. The walls were dressed in whiteboards crowded with ink, blue and green lines weaving into knots of strategy. A scatter of sticky notes feathered the edges, neon squares curling at the corners like they'd been peeled and slapped down in fury.

At the far end, a built-in LED panel spanned nearly the width of the wall—black glass now, waiting. When powered, it would spill every receipt and screenshot across the wall in high-definition clarity, sharp enough to cut. Its sleek frame caught the overhead lights, cold and merciless, like a mirror that never blinked.

Cords still trailed underfoot, black coils from chargers and laptops, a reminder that even in Horizons' fortress of order, chaos leaked in through the seams.

Emme reappeared, a stack of folders hugged to her chest, the scent of eucalyptus lotion threading through. "They're on their way."

Footsteps in the hall. Voices. Annie slipped in first, cheeks flushed, braid sliding over one shoulder, soft floral that never announced itself until she was close. Rayann ghosted behind her, eyes cutting straight to me and sticking there, reading too much in one sweep. Summer didn't look up as she slid an extra tabbed folder toward each chair—hard copy, color-coded, edges perfectly aligned like a deck of cards ready to cut a throat.

"Legal's been tearing through this since sunrise," Summer said, fingers drumming on the folder's edge. "They've got injunctions ready, press talking points queued—everything short of a miracle."

I scanned the bullet points as the sisters found seats, the leather sighing under each of us. My fingertips came away dusty from the paper—too many hands on the printer today. The list was a row of knives. *We did this—Jerrick and I—wild text threads and messy screenshots turned into weapons in clean font, tight margins, and Summer's merciless highlighters. God, I need this to hurt someone who deserves it.*

Summer lifted her gaze. No blink. Her nail tapped once on the page. "This is going to get ugly, Brynn. But we're ready."

I nodded. The motion felt like a bone setting. "Agreed."

Juliette capped her pen with a click that sounded final. She leaned forward, forearms on the table, voice low enough it hummed through the grain. "Here's legal's position."

We all stilled.

"The lawyers are going straight for an emergency order to lock Adventura Luxe down. No moving money, no shredded files, no contracts slipped under the table. Charles gets named, along with anyone who touched this—hit for stealing our work and sabotaging the panel." Her voice cut each word like it was meant to bleed. "We'll force preservation of evidence—no deleted texts, no 'lost' emails, no burned notebooks. Subpoenas go out to the judges, the organizers, the hotel. Then we move to void the results and disqualify every bid tied to interference."

Emme slid a page out and added, "We've got a forensic firm on standby. If there are edits to scorecards or swapped slides, they'll find them. If someone breathed on a spreadsheet, we'll know."

Annie's hands twisted in her lap. She stilled them, chin up. "Press?"

Summer's mouth did that small, satisfied curve that never reached her eyes. "Statement ready to go—facts only, no adjectives. We lead with integrity of process. We don't accuse; we 'ask questions publicly' while naming the court filings. If they come for us, we look like the adults in the room."

Rayann's knuckles rapped once on the table. "What do we want out of this?" she asked, voice silk over steel. "Besides blood."

Juliette and Summer shared a look that lasted a breath. Summer answered. "Three things, minimum. One: a permanent injunction—no use of our materials, no ghosting our lattice into their proposals, no approaching our vendors with stolen strategy. Two: a public correction and apology from Adventura Luxe and the event organizers, plus a formal nullification of this panel's outcome. Three: damages and fees that sting—enough to make settling their best option, not trial. We negotiate from a position that assumes they settle out of court to avoid discovery."

"And if he doesn't back down—" Annie started, then cut herself off, throat working. Nobody filled the silence. We all knew what she meant. Men like him always thought they were untouchable.

Juliette steepled her fingers. "If he doesn't settle, we welcome discovery. We let the light in. He has more to lose."

My phone warmed against my wrist where it lay against the table—another buzz. The conference room air smelled sharp with toner and lemongrass, heat from too many bodies pressing close. My water glass had gone lukewarm, and the faint tang of Juliette's espresso still clung like a warning. The secure link pinged. A second later, Summer's laptop lit with intake chimes from the shared drive. She didn't look surprised. "That him?"

I swallowed. "Yes."

Rayann glanced at Summer, then pinned me again. She didn't bother with *Are you okay?*—she went straight to: "Does it corroborate what we've got?"

I tapped the first audio file and held my breath because the room had already learned to stop asking permission.

The playback filled the LED panel in small waves of sound—voices compressed into clean, clinical clarity. His—Charles Thorne—came through like a blade, slow and deliberate.

"You've embarrassed me," he said finally—deep, precise, teeth wrapped around every syllable. "You've embarrassed this family."

Jerrick's laugh cut—short, flat. "I'm not signing your contract."

A rustle of paper. A chair squeak. Then Jerrick, voice sharpened by whatever it takes to stand up to monsters.

"You think I don't know what this is? You've built your empire on intimidation, on payoffs and closed doors. But this—" he jabbed at a folder—*I can hear the slap of it*—"this isn't business. This is you asking me to sell my integrity. Me—your own fucking son."

Own fucking son. The phrase landed, a bucket of ice down my spine.

"You want me to do your dirty work, to be the one who drags myself through the shit you don't want on your shoes?" Jerrick said. Closer to the mic now—the rasp of breath, a chair scraped back, wood creaking as he leaned in. "Brynn doesn't deserve that. She built her agency from the ground up—grit, brains, sleepless nights. She earned every win." His voice cracked—anger or something softer. "I respect her too much to let you piss all over it because you're afraid of losing."

A throat cleared—polished. "Ungrateful. Disloyal. After everything I've given you, this is how you repay me?"

"I don't want your empire. I don't want your money. And I won't throw Brynn under the bus to save your reputation."

A long beat—too slow—and then Charles's mouth tightened. "That girl? She's a liability. The sooner you cut her loose, the sooner you'll stop dragging my name through the mud."

Someone in the room—Rayann, I guessed—whistled; a sharp, involuntary sound. Juliette's pen paused mid-sweep. Even Summer's jaw ticked. Annie's braid slipped forward as she ducked her head, cheeks blotched red like she couldn't stand hearing a father spit his son's name like that. Emme, usually quick with a barb, went still—folders clutched to her chest as if bracing against the blow. For once, even Juliette's pen stilled without clicking, silence louder than any verdict.

Jerrick's line—low and lethal—hit the LED like a shard of glass. "She's not the distraction. She's the fucking reason I'm still standing. She's smarter than half your board combined, and she built something from nothing while you were busy buying off judges and padding your empire."

The air left my lungs in a rush. No one had ever said something like that about me—not like that, not with that kind of fire. It wasn't a compliment. It was a confession dressed as defiance.

Charles reached for the knife that always sat on his tongue. "You're getting soft—just like your mother. She's wasting away in Florida, pretending her little life means anything."

The room shifted—the way people do when someone points at the floor and the truth is under their feet. My throat went hard. *Florida.* The syllable landed and exploded—my fingers went white around the edge of the folder.

The last thing in the clip was his slow, poisonous promise—"You'll regret this, son"—and then a chair pushed back, footsteps, a door closing with a soft, terminal click.

I rewound once and listened again—he never said *I did it.* He never named the judges. He showed how far he'd go to keep the machine running—the threats, the sneers, the casual contempt. Enough for a jury to hate him; not enough for a confession. *Yet.*

This is perfect and infuriating. It's enough to map the thread; it's not a smoking gun.

"Christ," Rayann said under her breath. Someone—Annie, I think—let out another low whistle that sounded like a warning.

Juliette clicked her pen closed. "Audio of a confrontation with his son—recorded in his office—puts witnesses on notice and gives forensics a place to start. We still need corroboration—timestamps, matching hotel comps, messages to judges. But this shows motive, method, and malice. It's not a confession, but it's a roadmap."

Summer's face, in the LED glow, was a blade. "Good. Counsel will pull logs, subpoena the hotel, and match phone pings to his movement. If we can place him and show third-party contact, forensics will stitch this together."

They'll stitch it together. Something in my chest unclenched, just a fraction—hope measured and legal, not cinematic. *He risked everything. He walked into a tiger's den with a recorder in his pocket. He could have been shredded. He did it anyway.*

I closed the file and the room felt louder—folders slapped, leather chairs sighed, phones bright like small moons. My hands were steady enough to hide the tremor.

"Everything I needed," I said, and this time my voice didn't wobble. "Everything we needed."

Juliette's mouth tightened. "Send this to counsel. Label the files—date, time, *Thorne office*. Attach the hotel comps. Tag judges' names where we can. Forensics on the audio—clean it, amplify timestamps. If this lines up with the other dots—if a pattern emerges—we litigate from a place of proof."

Rayann's hand brushed mine—brief, solid. "You did good," she said—no flourish, no softness, the kind of praise that counts because it's rare.

He did this for me, and the heat behind my ribs wasn't just adrenaline. It was gratitude and terror braided together, a match near dry brush.

Outside the war room door the world kept spinning; inside, on walnut and LED and sharp paper, we started to make a map of how to bring the light.

Chapter 30

Severed Legacy

JERRICK

THE TOWER'S LOBBY SMELLED of chilled polish and glass. Marble so clean it held the bruise of every shoeprint until a man with a cart wiped it away. Somewhere behind the front desk espresso hissed. I could taste it—burnt bitterness and scorched bean—staining the back of my throat as the elevator doors slid open with a polite chime.

Don't pace. Don't flinch. Finish it.

Thirty-eight floors up to my father's office. His assistant's chair sat empty; her orchid remained untouched—white and perfect. The door stood cracked, a small open seam that tasted like a dare.

He didn't look up when I walked in. His pen scratched once, twice. My chest squeezed, heart beating fast enough I could feel it in my teeth.

"Close it," he said.

I shut the door. The room folded itself around the sound of our breathing. Cold air crawled down my forearms through the starched sleeves; gooseflesh rose along the crease of my shirt.

"Let's not make this theatrical," he added, still writing.

"It isn't," I said. "It's simple."

The pen stopped. He capped it with two fingers and finally lifted his eyes. Steel—forged and polished. The lines at the corners went shallow then vanished, erased by the set of his mouth.

"Go on."

"I'm done." I slid the envelope across the blotter; the paper settled with a soft, final thud. "Formal resignation. Effective immediately."

Silence shifted. Out on the glass, a hawk coasted between towers, wings barely moving. I swallowed. Dry. Bitter. *Do it clean. Don't give him anything to twist.*

He didn't touch the envelope. "You're not serious."

"I am."

"That contract—"

"Reviewed. Paid out what needs paying. I'll resign the club membership today. The cards are already dead." My jaw tightened. The tooth I'd cracked years ago hummed. "This isn't a tantrum."

His laugh was a sharp exhale. "Tantrums are for children. This is vandalism."

"Of what?"

"Your life." He stood. No rush, no stumble. Even his suit breathed better than mine. "Everything you are has been built under this roof."

"Everything I am," I said, heat rising under my collar, "survived despite this roof."

His temple twitched. "That woman."

My fists clenched at my thighs. "No."

"Don't insult me by pretending this isn't about her."

It's about me. It's about breathing without tasting his fucking shadow. "This is about me refusing to sell myself in pieces to make your books balance."

I thought of Brynn—standing there, unshaken, fire in her eyes and conviction in her voice, like she'd decided I was worth believing in long before I ever did. She'd been my rival, my thorn, the woman I swore I'd outwork. And yet she'd become the proof that I could be more than the shadow my father carved. Walking away wasn't just about me—it was about being the kind of man she believed I could be.

My father stepped closer, light catching the silver in his hair. He didn't smell like home. He never had. "You're walking away from a company with your name on the brass."

"My name's a rental here."

"Your name," he said, each word plated in ice, "was given to you by me."

I felt the old ache rise—nights spent learning how not to want his approval, years of building muscle over bone he'd forged thin. The envelope lay between us. I nudged it with my fingertip and felt the space close a little.

"Take the paper," I said. "Or don't. I'm done either way."

"Because of a girl with a travel company and a pretty mouth?"

My vision narrowed. "Say her name again and we won't leave here with this just being words."

His smile had no teeth in it. "There it is. The temper. You never learned how to use it for anything but breaking what you love."

"I'm trying not to do that anymore."

He slid the envelope back with one finger. Not far—just enough to mark possession. "You were meant for larger rooms than this."

"I don't want larger rooms. I want honest ones."

The bird disappeared into its own reflection. Something inside my chest tried to follow it and slammed ribs on the way out.

He nudged the envelope with his fingertip. "You'll be back."

"No." I didn't ask for the words to leave my mouth—they did.

"You think you'll open one of those sweat-stink studios and be happy? As if happiness belongs to the broke."

"I know where happiness doesn't live." I didn't whisper it. "Here."

The moment stretched—taut, whine in the wire. He picked up the envelope at last. Weighed it. Didn't open it. "Then we're finished."

"We are."

He didn't offer his hand. I didn't either. The office felt colder.

"You leave this family today." Each syllable clicked. "Don't bring my name into whatever gutter you choose next."

I let the words hit, one after another, hard little stones. *There it is. The last inheritance.*

"If the name meant as much to you as you pretend, you'd have worn it better," I said. Quiet. Not a strike. A truth.

"Get out of my office."

I went for the knob and hesitated. He stayed framed by glass and skyline—perfect and immovable. My mouth tasted of rage and disgust.

"You taught me how to stand still while someone tried to own me," I said. "Good lesson. I learned the rest somewhere you've never been."

I didn't wait for the reply. Out. The hall. The elevator. The brushed-steel mirror showed someone I knew—eyes bloodshot, jaw bristled, tie strangling his throat.

It's done.

The elevator hummed. The drop hit my stomach, sour and clean. On the ground floor, the espresso hissed again, sharp as a cat. Outside, heat soaked the concrete and climbed instantly into my suit.

I walked three blocks because the car would smell like him and I needed sweat to scrub the office from my skin. The street hit me—taco smoke, hot tar, and the faint sweetness of cut grass. My phone vibrated once. A message lit the lock screen from the one person I could pick out of a crowd of ten thousand.

Brynn.

My ribs cinched. *Not yet.* I typed, deleted. Typed, deleted. My hands shook but I slid the phone face-down and kept moving.

The academy's door stuck halfway, swollen from last week's rain. The bell above it jangled cheap. Inside, the air hit me—a wet blanket of human heat and disinfectant, eucalyptus from someone's muscle rub. Mats hummed with bodies—bare feet slapping, gis rasping, breath bursting in little animal grunts. The sound settled something ragged in me. Home smelled like sweat and laundry detergent and old tape.

"Professor in?" I called, tugging at my tie.

"In back," our purple-belt desk kid said, not looking up from taping his fingers, tongue trapped between his teeth in concentration. "He's murdering blue belts with pressure passes."

"Perfect."

The world narrowed to texture—tatami biting through thin socks, chalk-dry palms on my collar as I tore off the tie, the sharp relief of cotton loosened at my throat.

"Shoes," someone snapped. I kicked them into the cubby. The rules mattered, here. Rules kept the chaos honest.

Professor Ríos finished sprawling across a blue belt who made dying whale noises and tapped. Ríos sat back on his heels, dark hair damp, gi pants streaked with white tape glue. He had the kind of forearms that lived in rope climbs and farmers' carries, a face cut blunt by years of doing the hard thing instead of talking about it. His eyes flicked to me, took in the lack of gi, the suit pants, the throat.

"Uh-oh," he said, voice dry as chalk. "Funeral or job interview?"

"Both." My voice rasped. I cleared it. "Got a spare?" I nodded at the loaner closet.

He studied me for a beat longer, reading the tension in my shoulders the way he read grips. "XL top, A3 pants. Go."

In the back, the closet coughed a mothball gust when I pulled it open. The cotton was rough, stiff with too many washes and bleach. I didn't care. The gi settled on my skin with a weight that made the noise in my head drop a register. I tied my belt—twice around, ends even. The knot sat against my stomach like a promise. That knot meant more than rank. It was the opposite of my father's contracts—this one I tied myself. No witnesses, no signatures, no ledger keeping score. Just fabric and breath, a promise that every time I walked onto these mats, I chose discipline over power, resilience over fear.

When I stepped back out, he was waiting at the edge of the drilling line, one eyebrow up. "Rounds?"

"Hard."

He nodded, as if I'd said *please* and *thank you* at once. "Shark tank. You're the bait."

"Good." I rolled my neck until it popped. "I could use teeth."

"Everybody!" he called. The chatter dimmed, curious eyes cutting over. "Professor Thorne needs to remember where he puts his breath. Two-minute rounds, rotations on my clap. If he dies, you're all doing burpees."

"Nice incentive," I muttered.

He grinned, a flash. "Try not to suck."

The first white belt came at me nervous and wild-eyed, collar-grabbing with that newborn moose energy. I let him drive, absorbed, closed the space and felt his weight, his breath— cheap protein bar and mint gum—on my chin. Frame. Hip escape. Knee slice. The mat whispered against my toes. My chest burned. Something opened.

The second round, a blue belt with wrestler ears tried to neck crank me from top half. I gator-rolled, came

up in his guard, and the sweat on our forearms made a
slick new language between us. I could taste salt, chem-
ical clean, adrenaline turning metallic at the back of my
throat. Tap. Clap. Rotate.

Purple belt next. He was patient. He waited out the
storm. I felt the patience and respected it and crushed it
anyway, pressure settling like weather on his ribs until
his hand patted twice. The tiny, helpless slap echoed
through my bones.

There you are. Hello.

By the time Ríos slid in, my gi clung to me and I could
wring fluid from my hair. We touched hands. His grip
was dry and deliberate, a teacher's promise: *I'm not here
to hurt you. I'm here to show you where you break.*

"Breathe," he said.

We moved. He let me take the first dominant position—his charity was precise, educational. I took side
control, crossface deep, felt his jaw set against my bicep.
He didn't push. He made space in places I didn't see
until he was already there. A shrug, a frame, and I was
floating, feet searching for floor that had become air, and
then the mat kissed my back hard enough to bark the
breath out of me.

"Post," he said.

I braced my arm, trying to block the sweep. He trapped it anyway—*took the post.* Shoulder of justice—his term—settled across my sternum like a benediction that hurt. Black at the edges of my vision, stars tinkling. I found the frame, put my knee in, chased a thread of space, and built a bridge with my hips that swung my chest clear an inch at a time.

"Better." His voice was close to my ear, warm and steady, the way a lighthouse would sound if it had words. "Again."

We didn't speak for the next minute. We argued in pressure and frames and breath. When I finally caught the armbar, his hand landed on my thigh with a light, satisfied tap.

"Water," he ordered, rolling to sit with me.

We sat there, legs pretzeled, sweat darkening the mat. The room noise swelled and receded around us. I sipped, plastic bottle pliant in my grip.

He cocked his head, watching something in me unclench. "You look lighter. Or like you got run over. Which is it?"

"Both," I said. The laugh that leaked out of me was ugly and clean. My lungs felt rinsed in salt. "I quit."

"Adventura?"

"Effective now."

His eyes didn't widen. He'd been expecting this more than I had. "And Daddy Dearest?"

"Disowned me." I let the words sit between us. They didn't weigh as much as they should have. Or maybe the rounds had shifted my spine enough to carry them differently. "Said don't bring his name into my gutter."

Ríos scratched his jaw with taped fingers. "Sounds like freedom dressed as insult."

"It fucking stings."

"Good. You're alive."

It hit me—no one could hand me a life anymore. I had to build the next one myself.

Noise flicked up by the front desk—some white belt laughing too loud; the fan gargling hot air. A zipper somewhere rasped. A kid complained about mat burn in a stage whisper.

"What's next?" he asked.

The question rattled the scaffolding I'd just erected. The answer rose without permission. *Her.*

Chapter 31

Opening Moves

JERRICK

My chest answered before my brain could veto it:

Her.

Her mouth—brave and stubborn. The pulse I remembered under my thumb. The way she looked at me when she thought I wasn't watching: hungry, wary, all in. The memory hit like a body shot—deep, slow ache that made my breath hitch. We started as a problem set—fluorescent lights, bad coffee, a Dubai vendor summit where I undercut her on price and she cut me to size with facts. She didn't flinch then, not when I won ugly, not when I tried to smile it pretty. She just filed me under enemy and got sharper. Somewhere between rivalry and respect, I started wanting to be the man she argued wasn't real.

"She is," I said before I could stop it. I shook my head. "I can't call. Not yet. Not with my head like this." *My father's voice is still hot in my mouth.*

Ríos nodded, as if he'd heard the second, unsaid name anyway. "Then don't. Build something you can invite her into that won't collapse."

"I've wanted my own space." The admission warmed me, like a door easing open. "Studio. Kids' classes. Self-defense for women. Maybe competition, someday. Clean mats. Good coffee. No bullshit."

"Good coffee," he echoed, amused. "That'll bring them in."

"I'm serious."

"So am I. Name. Location. Partners." He ticked them on fingers. "You have capital?"

"Enough to start if I don't set it on fire." I rubbed my sternum where his shoulder had pressed promise into me. "Not sure about partners."

"You don't. Not now." He leaned back on his hands, looking at the ceiling's peeling paint as if it were a map. "Find a storefront that smells like dust and potential. Windows. Foot traffic. You make it a room where people learn they can do hard things, and they pay you to remember it."

Something in me notched into place. A simple machine. Lever. Fulcrum. Motion without loss. "You make it sound easy."

"It isn't." He looked at me again, eyes crinkling. "But you've done harder for worse."

My phone was a coal in my pocket. I palmed it, thumb frozen over Brynn's name.

Say nothing you can't back with action. The rule tasted like a reprimand I'd learned long before. *Don't hand her a half-built room and call it shelter.*

"I need a day," I said. My voice didn't shake. "To go home, throw away the pieces with his fingerprints. To make a list that's more than rage."

"Make three," Ríos said. "One for grief. One for business. One for her."

"Professor," the purple belt called, jogging up, cheeks pink. "We setting up for women's class?"

"Ten minutes." Ríos grunted to his feet and slapped my shoulder—firm, friendly, bracing. "Wash the loaner. We don't share that much DNA here."

"Yes, sir."

He cocked a brow. "What did you call me?"

"Yes, Professor."

"Better." He walked off, already chewing some poor blue belt's posture just by looking at him.

I sat a second longer, letting the fans drag prairie air across my overheated skin. The mat under me was a living thing—scuffed, stained, sworn to a thousand small deaths and resurrections each week. I slid my phone out and opened her thread. Her last message sat above the keyboard, sharp as a blade and bright as she was.

Brynn: *I'm here. Say nothing if you need to. Or say everything if it helps.*

I typed, deleted. Typed again.

I did it. I'm out. It hurts like hell, and I've never breathed cleaner. I want to hear your voice. I'm not going to ask for it until I deserve the time I'm asking you to spend.

Delete. Too much. Too soon. I went simpler.

ME: I'm here. Can't discuss yet. With you otherwise.

You've turned my world upside down, and I fucking need you.

I hit send. The whoosh was ridiculous and thin. My chest eased anyway. I shoved the phone back in my bag before her dots could start mocking me.

On the way to the laundry sink, I peeled the loaner gi off at the sink and ran cold water over my skin until it prickled. Chlorine bit my knuckles. The cotton drank.

Soap foamed under my nails. The smell chased the office from my nose. When I wrung it out, water ran to the drain in a rhythm that felt like the start of something. Hammer on a frame. Work beginning.

I hung the gi on a line near the open back door. Outside, heat leaned in. The alley exhaled sour and sweet: yeast from the bakery two units over, rot from an open trash can. I stood in the doorway with my belt in my fist.

"Next moves?" Ríos called from the floor without looking.

"Find a space," I said. "Then find the words."

"Order works," he said. "Or don't. Just move."

I smiled at nothing. My ribs hurt. My father's voice was a hundred miles away even if it lived down the street. I could taste salt, rubber, water, and underneath them all—something clean.

The academy door stuck again when I left; this time I shouldered it open and didn't apologize to the bell when it cried out. Outside, the sun hit my eyes hard enough to make them water. I let it. I didn't wipe my face.

Next move.

***

BRYNN

The war room emptied in waves; chairs scraped, coffee cups hit the trash, Juliette's sneakers squeaked a steady retreat. Summer fielded a call before the door even shut, Emme stretched long like she'd finished a marathon instead of an afternoon in corporate combat, and Annie slung her canvas bag over her shoulder with that unbothered smile that said she could survive anything.

Ray leaned against the frame, knowing in the way only a twin could understand. "Bar in ten?"

I nodded, tugging my sweater tighter across my chest. "I'll catch up."

They didn't press. Sisters never did when the cracks showed. They just filed out, voices fading toward the lobby, leaving me with the echo of Juliette's pen still ticking in my head.

I sat back. Black joggers creased under me, my tank clinging to clammy skin. Adrenaline had bled away; my pulse staggered in the hush.

That's when I saw it—the corner of my tote gaping open, leather peeking between folders and a half-dead pen.

The journal.

Air left my lungs in a small, sharp hiss.

I pulled it out like it might burn. Plain cover, softened edges, the ghost of Costa Rica clinging to the leather. My throat went dry.

Don't.

I cracked it open anyway.

His handwriting slashed across the page, cramped and pressed deep enough to dent the paper.

Tap is not fail, tap is learn

Clean mats. Good coffee. No bullshit.

Teach kids to fall safely. Teach adults they still can.

My chest hitched. This wasn't a pitch. It wasn't a speech. It was him—unvarnished.

I turned another page.

Slow down. Smile at someone today. Fucking mean it.

Discipline = Freedom

Ink: Kanji, chess knight, raven, compass...

Words blurred. Tears rose hot and stupid. I swiped them away and kept reading.

And there I was. My finger trembled when the name hit.

Wilder. Her laugh = life. Need more.
Rattles me. Worse than sparring. Better than winning.
Better man when she's near

My breath snagged. I clutched the journal, leather cool under my palms, as if pressure could stop the cut. I flipped again, greedy now, chasing him across the paper.

Ask first, shut up more
What breaks first—body or mind?
Let small go, guard the big

Guilt hit next—a hard, public-panic in my stomach. This wasn't mine. I had no right to be inside his head like this.

I snapped it shut and pressed it to my thigh, as if pressure could erase the words. My pulse thudded in my throat, loud enough to drown the room.

The clock ticked. Ten minutes gone. My sisters would be at the bar already, Emme ordering a lemon drop martini, Ray sipping wine like it was reconnaissance, Annie laughing at nothing and everything. Waiting for me.

I slid the journal back into my tote, buried under folders it didn't deserve to hide behind. My hand lingered on the leather before I forced it away.

My phone buzzed—twice.

Subject: **Request for Comment — Adventura Luxe Inquiry**

From: investigations@travelwire.news

Another notification stacked on top of it from an unknown number: **Can we speak on background about panel irregularities?**

Heat climbed my neck. The circle was widening.

Later. Or never. But not now.

I stood, smoothed my sweater, dragged air deep enough to mask the wreck of my face. Then I unlocked the door, squared my shoulders, and stepped into the hall.

Time to meet my sisters.

Chapter 32

Lock It Down

JERRICK

T HE HEAT SLAMMED INTO me on the sidewalk—a furnace door opening. Blackbirds heckled the parking lot like they'd been hired to. A delivery truck hissed past, brakes screaming, yeast air from the bakery folding over exhaust. A kid across the street licked an ice cream cone, a single drip hitting the pavement. Nothing out here knew my life had just cracked clean down the middle.

Good. Let it not notice. Build under the noise.

I crossed to the car, top button loose, collar gaping where the rules used to sit. Steering wheel skin-hot, the smell of conditioned leather rising to meet me. The seat belt bit my collarbone, pinning the starched cotton to my skin. I pulled out with the kind of calm that used to scare interns—a quiet that meant the decision was already made and the paperwork was playing catch-up.

The phone buzzed in the console. Not looking. Not yet. Brynn's name sat there like a pilot light. I wasn't going to set myself on fire in a parking lot.

Downtown blurred into the river, into a strip of sun-faded stucco and glass. My townhouse sat at the end of a block trimmed within an inch of its life—lawns clipped, hedges squared, mailboxes standing at attention. I keyed in and dropped my shoes by the door. The silence inside was neat, predictable—the hum of the refrigerator, the tick of the clock on the mantel. Leather couch, stacks of books, a leather chair with a permanent dent in the cushion that matched the curve of my spine. It wouldn't be silent for long.

She'd been more than a distraction. Every time I wanted to fold, her voice cut through the noise—sharp, relentless, calling me out until I stood straighter. Brynn didn't just push me; she held up a mirror and dared me to become the man I swore I could be. Even now, a single line from her on my phone carried more weight than my father's entire empire.

I didn't sit. Went straight to my office, needing my journal. Ríos's words were still in my head, and I wanted them on paper before they slipped. My backpack slouched where I'd dropped it yesterday, half-unzipped, yesterday's mess still shoved inside. The journal wasn't there. Should've been—plain cover, unmarked spine, hiding everything. Notes. Timelines. Sketches of mats. That two a.m. list that started with *if I ever get free.*

My gut hollowed. The pack felt wrong in my hands—too light. *Fuck me. The resort. Did I leave it there?*

Breathe, Thorne. Control what you can.

The phone finally earned my attention. Brynn's text.

BRYNN: Here too. Breathe. I've got you—on mute until you're clear.

A raw, useless laugh scraped out and turned into a breath that finally reached my ribs.

You have no idea what that did to me.

The laugh died when the phone rang. Unknown number—no, not unknown, just new. My attorney.

I picked up. "Thorne."

"Jerrick. Dexter Blackwell. You good to talk?"

"Now's good."

"Quickly: I filed the notice of representation. All communications to you go through me. Do not respond to your father or anyone acting on his behalf. You are not to discuss proprietary information with any third party. You understand."

"I do." My tongue tasted like copper from biting back everything I wanted to say.

"Second," he continued, voice like a stapler—efficient, final, a little mean. "Your employment contract has three landmines—noncompete by radius and client list, a confidentiality clause with a bad-faith carve-out, and an intellectual property ambiguity your father thinks is iron. It isn't. But you will not be teaching, consulting, or launching anything for sixty days unless I say otherwise."

"Got it."

"I want a full inventory. Financial accounts you control, passwords changed, two-factor authentication enabled. Devices—remove any company profiles. If you have physical documents, lock them up and send me a scan sheet. If anyone contacts you directly, you text me first, yes?"

"Yes."

A pause. Paper in the background. "One more thing. Do not contact your... romantic entanglement about any of this. The less they know, the safer they are."

"I already told her I can't discuss it."

"Good. Keep it that way. We aim for boring. Boring wins."

He clicked off before reassurance could get awkward. I stood in that tiny room and realized I was squeezing the phone so hard my hand hurt. I blew it open and flexed until the ache changed shape.

Kitchen next. I rinsed a mug that didn't need it, ground beans, breathed through the bitter bloom. First swallow—burn, then smoke, then the sweet undernote that hits once your tongue stops flinching. Heat slid down and lit up empty spaces inside me. I leaned on the counter and watched the setting sun through the blinds.

Make the lists, man. Ríos wasn't wrong. Three of them.

I tore a page from a yellow pad. At the top: **Grief**.

-the father joke that was never funny

-the last time he hugged me

-the way he loved winning more than he loved anything that could love him back

My hand didn't shake until the pen caught on the word *father* and tore the paper. I flipped the sheet and didn't press as hard. For a second I couldn't breathe. The word alone carried more weight than any subpoena, more bite than the fights we'd had across boardroom tables. I was still the kid who wanted him to say *good job* and mean it. Every round on the mat, every contract signed, every mile run—it had all been me trying to outgrow that ache. And here I was, paper ripping under my hand like proof I hadn't.

Business.
-bank separation
-passwords
-LLC (not yet), Florida State requirements?

I froze. *Florida.* My pen had gone rogue, scribbling what I hadn't planned, what I hadn't even admitted yet. Florida wasn't the plan. *She was.*

-Mats, rent, insurance, release forms
-coffee that doesn't taste like regret
-childcare corner by the front window
-scholarship jar

I stopped when the letters started leaning forward like they could run ahead without me.

Her.
Under it I wrote nothing for a long time. The word looked ridiculous by itself—too small for the thing it tried to hold. Finally:
-call when cleared

-bring nothing half-built

-build the room first, let her open the door if she wants it

-be the man, not the son

-don't fuck this up

I tore the page loose and stuck it under a magnet on the fridge shaped like a whale from a tourist shop I'd sworn I wouldn't buy anything at. My hand left a coffee thumbprint on the edge. *Good. Proof you were here.*

I hit my bedroom closet next. Needed a fucking cleansing. Now.

Suits first—charcoal, navy, all of them reeking of boardrooms, bullshit, and compromise. Into the bag. Not the trash—donation. Let someone else get a fresh start out of what used to choke me. Shirts next—white gone dingy under bad lights, collars stiff like chokeholds. Into a fucking trash bag. Ties by the handful, the silk slithering through my fingers. Boom. Gone. Corporate fucking costumes. I'd worn them long enough. I kept one suit, my favorite. A couple shirts. A tie or two. Because life still demands the occasional mask.

The entry camera pinged. Motion. My name on the intercom in a voice I knew down to the bone.

I didn't move.

"Jerrick?" My father. Calm. Casual. Like he'd brought goddamn muffins.

The phone lit—Blackwell, again.

"Don't answer it," he said without hello. "He's at the door."

I froze. "How the hell do you know that?"

"I've got people watching."

Well, fuck me. I'm impressed.

"Let him talk to a camera. Do not open. Document everything. If he gets out of line, you're going to the police station later for a report."

"For what."

"For a log. Paper trails aren't romantic, Mr. Thorne. They're effective."

His voice clicked out. I stared at the door that had my father on the other side and had the brief, insane thought that it didn't feel like much of a barrier anymore. Charles knocked once more—knuckles like a gavel—and left.

I stepped back, unlocked the deadbolt, and locked it again just to prove to my nervous system that the decision was real.

Back in my office, I opened the safe—steel mouth yawning. Passport. Birth certificate. A thumb drive with a strip of blue tape labeled *dooby snacks* because seventeen-year-old me thought he was funny.

My phone buzzed again.

Not a call. A voicemail transcribed.

Unknown: Mr. Thorne, this is Officer Delgado with APD. We received a request to log a no-contact notice related to a familial dispute. If you'd like to make a statement in person, we're at—

Blackwell moved faster than I did. I smiled without showing teeth.

Back in the kitchen, I poured the rest of the coffee cold over ice and drank it like punishment. The bitterness cut through everything soft. Good. No soft until it's safe.

The phone chimed, a single bird-note.

Fuck's sake. What now?

Not a text. Email. Subject line: *Notice of Key Card Deactivation.* Adventura Luxe's company tone chirped cheerful as a hostage video. I filed it and then created a new folder called *Petty Shit* and put it there. Then I laughed—once, loud enough to startle me.

Keep your teeth, Thorne. You're going to need them.

Chapter 33

Still Here

BRYNN

WEDNESDAY NIGHT, THREE WEEKS into no-contact. The bar smelled like lime rinds and salt-sticky wood. Lights were low. Glasses sweated. Voices hummed like static. Our favorite bartender knew our order without asking and still asked—respect. We said yes to chips, no to queso, yes again because queso existed. My sisters crowded the booth like a small army—Rayann halfway through her new whiskey habit, Emme nursing a lemon drop martini, Annie building a garnish hoard at her elbow.

I folded myself in beside them, shoulders tight. The leather sighed beneath me; someone's perfume—citrus, expensive—clung to the seat.

"You look feral," Annie said, lime slice already between her teeth.

"Earned," I muttered. The first sip of tequila burned enough to taste like proof of life.

Rayann pivoted her glass, ice clinking like distant windchimes. "You want space, I will bulldoze space. You want noise, I will hire you a marching band."

"Both," I said. "Alternating. Every other hour."

I sipped margarita, salt scorching the split on my lip. My thumb rubbed the sting, worrying the cut like it might turn into something else.

They talked—vendors, trips, who owed who a call-back. I nodded where I was supposed to. Rayann was already carving a Patagonia contingency that cut Ferox out clean. Juliette had three attorneys on leash and a press plan with no adjectives. Emme was hunting vendors who couldn't be bought, and Annie—quiet, steady—was building a reader list big enough to make noise if we needed it. My pulse stayed synced to the vibration in my pocket. Warm. Waiting. His name.

I slid the phone free beneath the table. One line typed, my thumb hovered on the edge of send—like a cliff.

ME: *Here too. Breathe. I've got you.*

I hesitated before pressing it. Same words as before—back when everything between us was chaos. Only now, it felt like a promise instead of a lifeline.

Screen face-down. Margarita glass clinked against Rayann's in a toast I didn't hear. My throat was already too tight.

We'd circled each other for years—airport lounges, midnight calls, vendor mixers where his shadow cut too close to mine. Every time I swore I hated him, some part of me still watched—how he never broke posture, how he studied a room before he moved. Even then, buried under rivalry, I think I was already measuring how close I could stand without falling.

Words spooled around me until the room softened. I let their voices carry me like a river that knew where it was going. A phantom buzz bit my thigh; maybe real.

I wanted to hear his voice, not words—just the sound of him. *You're fine. I'm fine. We're fine.* I wanted to tell him my chest was locked, the key buried somewhere neither of us could reach.

Instead, I sucked salt from my thumb and asked Rayann if we could rework the Patagonia vendor map. It felt safe to want things that were logistical.

On a cocktail napkin, I clicked the pen three times, then carved out three rules in ink that bled too fast:

1. Don't peek past page three in the journal

2. Eat actual food—coffee and tequila don't count as a food group

3. Stop running doomsday drills I'll never get to command

***

JERRICK

That same week, with the no-contact clock still ticking, I signed my name until it looked wrong.

The townhouse echoed in a way it never had—pictures off the walls, rug rolled into a tired body, the air carrying the faint tick of pipes that had always been muffled before. The realtor's pen scratched faintly across paper, printer still radiating residual warmth. We shook hands. Her bracelets chirped like nervous birds.

"So fast," she said, smiling too hard.

"So done," I answered. My jaw clicked. The keys left a small dent in my palm before I dropped them in her hand. *Fuck the corporate life.* The phrase landed heavy and right. I didn't say it out loud. I didn't need to that day. I capped the pen, uncapped it, capped it again—small control over a day already stripped bare.

Outside, Austin heat hit like an open oven. Asphalt popped faintly under tires. A cicada screamed from the live oak like it was arguing with God. My shirt stuck between my shoulder blades. Sunlight carved hard lines across the sidewalk until my eyes watered.

By dusk, I had keys to a furnished short-lease apartment—month-to-month, nothing on the walls. Austin. I had to stay through the hearings, finish what my father started before I walked away for good. The rest of my life sat in storage, boxed and waiting—for what, I wasn't exactly sure yet.

Blackwell called while I was unloading groceries. "Hold," he said. "Don't call her. We're almost there."

We both knew my father would try to bleed me in court out of spite—corporate theft, breach, whatever he thought might stick. Blackwell was there to make sure it didn't.

"Define almost."

"Not your kind of almost," he said, chair legs scraping across concrete. "The cautious kind. I'll ring when I can move the ball. You write. You don't reach."

Static bled through the line.

"Prelim filings are in—temporary restraining order on data destruction, notice to preserve devices, and a motion to compel third-party records. Your father's side will posture. We let the paper do the talking." A pause, then softer, almost reluctant: "And Thorne—keep breathing."

Somewhere in his office a fan clicked at the end of each rotation. "I'm breathing," I said. The lie tasted like copper on my tongue.

After he hung up, I opened a fresh notebook because I didn't trust laptops for dreams.

Title: **STUDIO—FOUNDATION**. Ink scratched, steady and grounding.

Mission: discipline as freedom

Values: safety, respect, grit, joy

Ages: core 6–18, adults evenings

Scholarships: 10% spots—no questions asked

Calendar: belts quarterly, tournaments optional

Staffing: two blue belts with patience, one admin mother hen

I kept writing until the apartment stopped sounding like nothing. I kept writing until my heartbeat slowed into sentences. I folded my gi belt on the couch arm, edges lined sharp, the way I'd been taught.

I picked up my phone. Her message waited.

BRYNN: *Still here. Breathing. With you when we're clear.*

I set the phone face down, screen to wood, and went back to line items. The silence dried me out faster than the Texas heat ever could.

***

BRYNN

Home was quiet in that way a house got when you stopped making noise to test if it made some on its own. Bali thumped her tail twice—permission to be human. I dropped my keys in the bowl and they rang too loud, the sound shivering down to somewhere tender.

Shower. Water pressure strong enough to drown thought if I stood with my forehead to tile. Shampoo smelled like coconut and someone else's vacation. Steam blurred the mirror and blurred my resolve. *Don't open the journal.*

I cracked the journal anyway, a sliver. Three pages became four before I forced it shut. My pulse collected at the base of my skull and tapped—tap tap tap—accusation in Morse code. I shoved the book into the tote beneath invoices and a half-melted lip balm because shame liked to be buried. I twisted the thin ring on my middle finger until the skin beneath ached.

My phone lit a halo under a stack of mail. One text sat there, careful, not asking, not pushing.

JERRICK: Breathing. With you when you're clear.

I didn't answer. I held the phone in my palm until the heat became mine. *With you when we're both allowed to be the same sentence.* I plugged it in across the room like it might burn through the nightstand.

On a fresh page: **HIM.**

-Had he slept

-Did his father's face break or stay stone

-Was he safe

-Was he writing lists the way I was

-Did his hands shake after he walked out or did he lock it all down

-Did he miss me in the quiet, or only when the phone buzzed

-Would he recognize himself when this ended

The list steadied me like a balustrade in the dark. Ink smudged across my thumb where I'd pressed too hard. I wrote until the edges blurred.

***

JERRICK

Gym at dawn. Air heavy on the skin. Mats tacky under bare feet, yesterday's sweat refusing to leave. I taped a kid's ankle because he was brave and stupid and *both* belonged on the mat. "Light drills," I told him. "Show me you can follow before you try to fly."

He nodded, eyes too serious in a small face. My hands remembered how to be gentle. My voice remembered how to be loud without being cruel. When he nailed the shrimping drill on the third try, his grin cracked a door in my chest, fresh air sliding in. Between drills I re-wrapped the tape roll tight, the habit automatic as breathing.

I was helping out at my professor's academy, covering a before-school kids' hour here and there—cash slipped into my hand, no fanfare. I bowed to him each time I stepped in, a spine-deep thank-you for the opportunity. Respect lived in my body like bone.

Between afternoon classes, I stayed after to wipe down mats, to tape the edge where the foam split, to run drills with stragglers who didn't want to go home yet. The rhythm steadied me—counting shrimps, tightening belts, reminding kids to bow before they bolted for the door.

Florida was already in my bones. Instinct, not logic. The next step wasn't Austin strip malls or warehouses with skylights. It was sunlight through palms, mats ten wide, twelve deep. My own door. My own wall of framed photos—kids laughing, belts tied right, sweat-slick smiles.

My phone rang. Blackwell again. "Paperwork moving," he said. "Still—hold."

"Define moving," I said, breath fogging in the refrigerated hush of an empty space.

"Think tectonic," he said, and I heard him smile like a man who played chess with other men's disasters. "Any trouble on your end?"

"Quiet," I said.

I hung up. My hands remembered a choke I didn't teach beginners. I exhaled. I taught it to the wall instead, grip on invisible gi, step, turn, finish without a body. It was enough to remind my muscles who they belonged to now.

The phone hummed. Her name. One line on the screen before it faded.

BRYNN: Still here. Chaos intact. Heart too.

I locked it without touching it. My chest clenched hard, a three-beat refrain pounding through bone—want, wait, worth.

I bought a donut and didn't eat it until I was sitting on the bare floor of the apartment, sugar caving under my teeth, coffee going cold in a cup that wasn't mine. The sweetness hurt good. I let it.

***

BRYNN

Conference room today. Emme clicked through Patagonia slides—snow peaks, endless sky, a contract draft waiting to be signed. Juliette's shorthand left no room for excuses. Summer cut in, clean as a blade, and I backed the strike with the twist. Annie lounged in her chair, tossing out commentary that made Emme groan but still laugh.

At lunch, I sat in the courtyard with a cowardly plastic fork and a salad steeped in discipline. A breeze carried hot-dog smoke from somewhere sinful, and I considered defecting to a life where mustard was a food group. *Run away. Open a sandwich shop. Meat In Your Mouth*. I speared a tomato and pretended it was good enough.

Afternoon. Marketing calls. Someone tried to sell me "authentic Costa Rican jungle vibes" in the form of plastic monstera leaves. I ended the call before I set myself on fire with a stapler. Emme cackled from down the hall like a gull who knew where all the french fries lived.

Rayann dropped off a tea I hadn't asked for and said, "Don't apologize for needing anything." Annie followed with a Post-it that read: *Eat actual food*. They parented me sideways because straight-on made me feral. I filed it under adored and kept moving.

At six, the building was too quiet. The auto-lights hummed like bugs too stubborn to die. The city outside smeared into gold through fingerprinted glass. I put my forehead to the cool pane, pressed until the glass stole some of the heat out of me.

My phone lit up once. I didn't look. I breathed long enough my back started to loosen.

When I finally checked, it wasn't him. It was a notification telling me to stand. I laughed and did. Then I went home and ate leftover pasta because carbs don't lie.

***

JERRICK

The dive bar around the corner from the studio. Low thrum of voices, chairs scraping concrete. I exhaled into the familiar comfort. Two friends waited like I'd never vanished. We claimed a corner table carved with initials, beer rings layered like old ghosts. I gave them the skeleton of the story, enough to be understood. They answered with laughter, with easy jabs, with a hand on my shoulder that said more than words. For an hour, I felt normal.

Back at my sterile apartment, I unclipped the key fob I'd carried for years—the leather tag stamped with my initials—and dropped it into the small bowl that came with the place. The sound was wrong. Good. Let it stay wrong until the new sound became right.

I opened the notebook again. Wrote down more lists.

Voicemail from Brynn I hadn't noticed. I listened because I was human, failing, and also doing my best.

Silence first—her breathing, a sea. Then: "No need to call back. Just... I thought you might need to hear my voice." A soft laugh that tasted like salt even through a speaker. "Breathing."

My chest hurt in a way that was blessedly alive. I kept it. Let it live there—a secret heartbeat between my ribs and the drywall.

My text sounded.

BLACKWELL, late: Hearing tomorrow. Don't be heroic. Be invisible.

ME: Copy.

I added nothing, and it was the bravest thing all night.

***

BRYNN

Night. The ceiling fan ticked like an old watch. Bali purred at my feet, paws twitching as if she were running in dreams where she caught every mouse and forgave them. I lay on my back and bargained with the dark. One more day. One more hour. One more breath without cracking.

The voicemail from Jerrick glowed like a small eye. I held the phone above my face and watched the blue light turn my hands into someone else's. I listened.

His silence came first. Then: "I needed your voice. I needed to smile." The tiny catch on the last word. The weight he wasn't putting on me. The weight I carried anyway.

My eyes burned. I pressed my knuckles to them until stars burst under my lids. I breathed low and slow until my ribs finally took over.

***

JERRICK

Hearing day. The courthouse smelled of paper, old varnish, a stale promise. The hallway air was cooler than it should have been and warmer than I wanted it to be. Shoes on tile clicked a hard rhythm. I sat on a bench that had seen too many gods prayed to and too many deals cut. Blackwell's tie was the color of a bruise and his eyes were amused in a way that said he ate stress for breakfast with grapefruit.

"Don't posture," he said. "Don't twitch. Don't win today. Just don't lose."

Opposing counsel looked pressed and polished, suit sharp enough to cut and gum chewed like it cost too much. He rattled off phrases—breach of fiduciary duty, misappropriation—words designed to stain, not stick. The judge listened without blinking, a statue in a rented robe. Words stacked into towers that looked steady but could have toppled at a touch—if consequences didn't exist. My tongue tasted of copper.

When it was over, it wasn't over—but the air was different. Blackwell lifted one eyebrow, the international sign for *we didn't die.* He leaned sideways as we walked.

"Hold."

"Now?" My voice sounded scraped raw.

"Now especially," he said. "We're almost there."

Outside, I bought a bottle of water from a cart that should not legally have existed and drank until my stomach sloshed. A busker's guitar note skimmed the air, sharp then gone. I took it as a benediction.

Back at the apartment, I pressed my forehead to the doorframe, letting the wood pull the day's heat out of me. I yanked off the tie, peeled the shirt until it hung from one hand, then kicked free of slacks that still reeked of courthouse drama. Bare skin, bare floor. I dropped and did pushups until my arms shook and my brain surrendered. Sweat stung my eyes; salt crawled into the cut on my knuckle from yesterday's fight with the heavy bag at the studio.

Don't reach. Don't reach. I reached for the notebook instead.

-Opening weekend—fun, not fear

-Sparring rules—consent language for kids

-Partnerships—school counselors, shelters

-Community center outreach

-Local PD youth program tie-ins

I started to text Brynn. Stopped. *Held*.

***

BRYNN

Morning. Coffee was bitter, honey sweet. The mug warmed my fingers and I let the heat travel up to where I had been cold. The house smelled of citrus cleaner and vanilla because I had cheated and lit a candle that promised calm. It almost delivered.

No text that day. It was his hearing day. I wanted to reach out but I didn't. I wondered if he knew I was falling for him. I told myself it was only corporate mud-slinging, but mud still drowns if it sticks.

The sisters' thread pinged—Rayann wanted a beach walk, Summer wanted thirty minutes on the quarterly, Juliette wanted blood. Emme sent a meme that made me snort-laugh and unclench my jaw. I chose all of them because I could be plural.

Before I left, I stuck a Post-it to the journal's cover. *When cleared.* I drew a small box beside it and left it unchecked.

I grabbed my tote, my lists, my keys. The door clicked shut, and the morning air was soft as a vow. I turned the lock, and I knew what it sounded like when a key fit.

Somewhere, miles away, another door was closing behind him. I didn't know yet the next one he opened would be mine—in Maris Key.

Chapter 34

One Hell of a Hello

BRYNN

JERRICK: SEE YOU SOON. Don't run.

Like I could. My pulse hadn't slowed since the news that Charles folded—the settlement signed, Horizons' terms met. Done. Over. Yet I'd been vibrating in my skin like an over-wound clock, ticking louder every hour I knew I'd see Jerrick later.

A knock shattered the quiet before the sun had burned the dawn away. I wrenched the door open. There he stood—rumpled from travel, stubble sharp, eyes wrecked and hungry. He'd slung a duffel bag carelessly off one shoulder, his shirt clinging with a Florida humidity he hadn't shaken.

His flight was scheduled to arrive at 6:03 PM. It was still morning. Early. Asshole muscled his way onto an earlier plane, just to catch me off guard at my own door. *Typical Thorne move.*

"Brynn." My name was gravel in his mouth. His gaze dragged over me—bare feet, tank top, the joggers I'd pulled on as pathetic armor.

"You're early," I said, my voice already shredded.

"Didn't want to wait." His bag hit the floor with a thud. His hands claimed my hips before I could remember what air felt like.

His mouth crashed into mine. No hello, just a desperate claiming. His tongue slid hot against mine, teeth catching my bottom lip until I tasted copper. He drove me back, slamming me into the wall. He fisted a hand in my hair, angling my head back until a gasp tore from my throat, and he swallowed that, too.

"Miss me?" The words were wreckage against my jaw.

"Asshole," I rasped, my own hands clawing at his shirt. Buttons pinged against the floor.

"Yeah," he growled, teeth scraping my throat. "But I'm *your* asshole now."

My hips bucked up to meet him before my brain caught up. He shoved my joggers down, and I realized I was already lifting my hips to help. His fingers slid inside me, thick and greedy, while his other hand pinned my wrist above my head.

Bali bolted, tail a blur, like even she knew better than to witness this.

"Fuck, Brynn," he muttered, pressing his forehead hard to mine. "I've been losing my mind without you."

"Yes. I've been insane without you," I gasped.

His thumb circled, perfect and ruthless. My legs shook, the wall cool against my spine, heat everywhere else. Each ragged breath sawed out of me, ribs straining until I broke.

"Not done," he rasped. His zipper fell while foil tore. He spun me, palms bracing my hips, and then he was inside—hot, thick, filling me in one thrust that stole every sound from my throat. His chest pressed against my back, his hand a brand on my waist.

"Feel me?" His voice broke. "I needed this. Needed you."

"Everywhere. You're everywhere," I whispered.

His pace was frantic, a raw, hungry rhythm. His mouth found my ear, the words a torn prayer. "Missed you. So fucking much, baby."

"Say it again."

"I missed you, baby." He nibbled my neck.

Baby.

"I need you, baby." A bite on my jaw.

Oh, Jerrick. You beautiful bastard.

Release ripped me open, divine and filthy all at once. My thighs quaking, his name spilling from my lips in pieces. He groaned, buried himself to the hilt, and came with me, his forehead pressed to the wall beside mine. We stood there, shaking.

Silence pressed in, the drywall cool against my cheek, our breaths the only sound sharp enough to cut through it. For a moment, nothing moved. Just his heartbeat crashing against mine, the smell of sweat and travel clinging to his skin. No words. No rush. The kind of silence that felt like survival.

Finally, he eased back, his hands still holding me up when my legs refused. He kissed my temple, a soft, desperate gesture that gutted me more than all the wild urgency that came before.

"Guess that's one way to unpack your bag," I whispered.

He grinned, wrecked and wild. "Hell yeah."

He eased out of me slow, a hiss catching in his teeth, and for a heartbeat I thought my knees would just quit and dump me on the floor. "Up," he murmured, palms steadying me like I was a weapon he wasn't ready to set down.

I tipped forward, expecting him to let me slide, but he hooked an arm behind my knees and lifted me instead. My head thunked against his chest, sweat-slick cotton clinging to my skin. His heart hammered like a fist through his ribs.

The duffel still sat abandoned by the door. He carried me past it, into my bedroom, past curtains bleeding early light. Outside, gulls screamed over the water, a reminder the ocean was just beyond glass and stucco. Inside, the air held traces of salt and detergent, tangled with the musk of my perfume. Sheets twisted from the night before waited, and he set me down in the middle of the mattress—I sank as if it were quicksand.

He followed, weight pressing me deeper. His mouth caught mine, softer now—still greedy, but edged with something wicked. The scrape of stubble along my chin burned in the best way. His tongue brushed mine, coaxing instead of conquering.

"Hi," he whispered into my lips.

"Hi?" I laughed, breath shredded, voice wrecked. "You fucking broke into my day like a home invader, and now you're saying hi?"

He smirked, forehead still resting against mine. "Would you rather I said *surprise*?"

"Try *sorry I almost killed you against drywall*."

His chest rumbled with a laugh, low and dark. "You liked it."

"Screw you."

"Working on it," he said, already sliding his hand up my ribcage.

His palm skimmed sweat-slick skin, catching on fabric, knuckles grazing my nipple through the tank. I arched without meaning to. He caught the hem and peeled it up slow, exposing goosebumps in the draft from the ceiling fan. The cotton hit the floor, and his mouth followed, open and wet down the line of my sternum, teeth catching the underside of my breast.

"I missed this," he murmured into my skin. "Missed *you*."

The word *missed* caught in my chest harder than his thrusts ever had, leaving me clutching at his shoulders like I could hold it there, proof against the dark. "Don't get sentimental now," I said, though my voice cracked.

His head lifted. His eyes—bloodshot from no sleep, darker than they had a right to be—met mine. "Too late, baby."

Heat punched through me again.

He shifted lower, palms sliding down my thighs until he caught behind my knees.

"Jerrick—" My voice cracked.

His hands pressed me open, steady and unyielding. "Mine to touch now," he murmured, breath hot where I needed him most.

A shiver bolted through me, sharp and helpless. I grabbed the nearest pillow and smothered the sound tearing up my throat.

He yanked it away, tossed it somewhere, eyes dark and hungry. "I want to hear you."

"Bossy."

"Always." His grin was feral, but his voice—rough silk, unraveling me.

Then his mouth was on me, sliding lower, tongue hot and relentless, beard scraping tender skin. I choked his name, hands clawing sheets. The ceiling fan creaked overhead, lazy and oblivious, while he worked me frantic. The taste of him still clung to my tongue, the sound of him breathing me in like oxygen, the smell of sweat and sex permeating our space.

My hips jerked, thighs trembling around his head. He didn't let up, not until my body bowed off the mattress, scream ripping raw from my throat.

When I collapsed, chest heaving, he dragged himself up over me, his chin slick, his mouth hungry. He kissed me deep, made me taste myself on his tongue.

"Still bossy," I rasped, clinging to his shoulders.

He smirked against my mouth. "Still yours."

His weight blanketed me, heat still clinging between us. The mattress creaked under us, springs protesting every shift. My chest heaved under his, my skin slick, hair plastered to my temples.

He shifted, braced on his elbows, but didn't move far. Just close enough that his stubble scratched my cheek, his breath hot at the corner of my mouth.

"You're heavy," I muttered, voice a wreck.

"You love it."

God help me, I did.

I shoved at his shoulder anyway. He rolled, pulling me with him, and I landed sprawled half across his chest. His heartbeat thudded hard and uneven, still chasing the moment. I pressed my ear there and let it pound into me, wild and real.

Silence stretched. Not awkward—never that. Just heavy, filled with the sound of the fan, our breaths, the faint hum of traffic blocks away.

Finally he exhaled, rough. "Coffee?"

I laughed into his skin, the sound muffled. "That's your aftercare?"

"That's my survival." His hand skimmed lazy patterns down my spine. "Unless you want me to keep running on fumes."

I lifted my head, met his eyes. Bloodshot, rimmed in exhaustion, but still burning. "Coffee, it is."

He kissed my forehead, sudden and soft, before pushing upright. The sheet slipped down his hips, and I caught the line of his abs, the V of muscle dipping low, and holy hell—*coffee might not be the first order of business.*

I grabbed his wrist before he could stand. "Bed first. Coffee later."

His laugh rumbled, low and dangerous, as he leaned back over me. "Feed me coffee first, and you can have whatever you want."

"Deal."

"Hungry, too." He kissed the tip of my nose before rolling out of bed, bare-ass naked, strolling toward the door like he owned the place. His duffel still sat where he'd dropped it, and he snagged a pair of gym shorts on his way past. Bali poked her head out from behind it, suspicious glare locked on him.

"Traitor," I muttered at her, dragging myself up and tugging the sheet around me like a toga. My legs hated me. My thighs burned, my knees ached, and my lungs still stuttered. But damned if I wasn't grinning like an idiot as I padded after him.

"You don't know how to work that machine," I warned, leaning against the counter, sheet knotted precariously over one breast.

He shot me a look over his shoulder. "I can fly halfway across the country without sleeping, but I can't push a button?"

"Pretty sure you'd break it out of spite."

He fiddled with the settings anyway, and I winced when the machine hissed like it was insulted. He glanced at me, lips twitching. "Black? Or should I dump half a carton of sugar-free hazelnut creamer in there?"

"Touch my creamer and you'll never walk again."

He laughed, poured two mugs, slid one toward me across the counter. His hand brushed mine—still hot from earlier—and it was ridiculous how that tiny contact shot down my spine.

We sipped in silence at first. The coffee was strong, bitter, grounding. His shoulders finally seemed to unclench, muscles relaxing under the weight of the morning light spilling through the blinds.

I broke first. "So you just...what? Bullied the gate agent until they let you on an earlier flight?"

His smirk deepened. "Charm. Persistence." A shrug.

The coffee had barely hit my bloodstream when he leaned one hip against the counter, all lazy menace, mug dangling from his fingers. Stubble shadowed his jaw, his hair was a mess from my hands, and his eyes—God help me—were already sliding lower, like I was breakfast.

"You got eggs?" he asked, voice smooth, a little too casual.

I narrowed my eyes. "That better not be a euphemism."

His grin was criminal. "Depends. You offering?"

"Asshole."

"Your asshole?" His grin cut sharp, dirty. "Say the word and I'll eat *that* before breakfast."

I threw the nearest spoon at him. "Kitchen. Focus."

"Still sounds like a yes," he muttered. Already he was at the fridge, casual as hell.

"Why?"

"Because I'm making breakfast." He batted those dangerous lashes, mock-innocent while his voice stayed pure filth. "You let me in your bed. Let me in your fridge, too."

"Big mistake," I muttered, but I was already tugging the sheet tighter around me and pointing at the fridge. "Bottom shelf. Don't break them."

He crouched, pulled the carton free, inspected it like contraband. Bali crept closer, sniffing suspiciously, tail flicking like she knew better than to trust him.

He cracked the first egg one-handed, shell snapping against the rim of the pan like he'd done it a thousand times. Show-off. The sizzle hit instantly, sharp and savory, filling the kitchen with the smell of hot oil and promise.

"You can cook?" I asked, incredulous.

"Baby, I can do everything." His voice was low, rough, and absolutely not talking about eggs.

Heat shot up my neck. "Stop flirting with my skillet."

He slid me a look over his shoulder, wicked and slow. "Thought I was flirting with you."

I sipped my coffee, trying not to smile. The pan hissed, butter popping, and his broad back moved with easy precision as he stirred, flipped, plated. Like he belonged there. Like he'd been doing this every morning for years.

When he finally set a plate in front of me—toast, eggs, bacon I didn't even know I had—he leaned down, voice hot in my ear. "Eat up. You're gonna need your strength."

My fork clattered against the plate. "Oh, for fuck's sake." I should've been furious, or at least pretending. Instead I found myself grinning into the steam rising from my plate, the absurd domesticity of it all cutting through the wreckage of the last hour. The bed would come later. For now, there was coffee, eggs, and the dangerous comfort of him at my table.

He kissed my temple, smug bastard, and sat across from me like we weren't about to destroy the bed again in thirty minutes.

Chapter 35

Where I Stay

BRYNN

T HE SHEETS LAY WRECKED around us, heat and scent baked into cotton—him everywhere. I should've shoved him off, demanded coffee, salvaged a shred of dignity. Instead, when he slid back inside me—slow, steady, unhurried—my body arched, breath catching as every shred of resistance dissolved.

It wasn't collision anymore—it was a tide, deep and patient, rolling slow enough to claim me. His mouth burned a trail down my throat, his hands holding me open like a prayer. Each deliberate grind was measured torture, restraint that ripped sounds from me I didn't know I could make.

"Brynn," he murmured, voice hoarse against my mouth. "This—fuck—this is all I thought about."

I clung, nails tracing desperate lines down his back. When I broke, it wasn't a scream but a sob. He swallowed it with his mouth, groaning his release into me, forehead pressed to mine as we fell apart together.

Silence pressed heavier than his chest on mine, filled with the weight of weeks that nearly broke us. His chest hammered under my cheek, the air sharp with all the words we hadn't spoken.

Finally, his voice, ragged. "My father pushed until the end. He made it hell, Brynn. Never easy."

I held him tighter. My thumb worried at the split in my lip, the sting nothing compared to what sat like a stone in my chest.

Tell him. Tell him about the journal.

"Jerrick, I have your journal." The words scraped out of me before I could stop them. "I didn't mean to take it—I just... it ended up in my tote. I tried not to, but I opened it. Read more than I should've. Then I snapped it shut and shoved it away. I shouldn't have." Heat prickled under my palms until I had to curl my fingers to keep from pulling away. "I know things I shouldn't know."

His shoulders dropped, a breath escaping as if he'd been holding it for weeks. "So you have it." His thumb brushed my temple. "I thought I'd lost it. And Brynn—there's nothing in there I'd hide from you. Every word's yours if you want it."

"It's not..." I faltered, heat climbing my throat. "It's not dirty secrets or anything. It's... you. Pages of routines, lists, half-sketched logos, quotes scrawled in the margins. You write things like 'Discipline is freedom' and 'Fail forward' in Sharpie. I shouldn't have seen it, but I did. And Jerrick—it wrecked me, because I realized how much of you I've never let myself see."

His mouth curved, not quite a smile. "That's all it is, Brynn. My reminders. My anchors. I've been writing them since I was a kid, long before the business deals and the fights with my father. It's how I keep my head straight. If you read it, then you already know—I wasn't lying when I said I wanted more than winning with you."

He traced a slow line at my hairline, unbearable tenderness in the touch. "We can be together now, Brynn, if that's what we want."

My breath hitched.

If? After everything, it still came down to if?

"I want it," I whispered, the words tasting equal parts terror and truth.

His gaze lingered, unreadable. "I've been thinking a lot while I've been stuck in limbo. About what comes next." He didn't elaborate. Just dropped the words like stones into water, leaving ripples I couldn't yet see.

I opened my mouth to press, but his hand on my hip held me off. *Not now. Later.*

We barely made it through takeout menus before he was opening drawers like he belonged here.

Later, we ate straight from containers on the counter, Bali lurking like a thief at our feet. Empanadas, plantains, grilled chicken, rice laced with herbs—too much, overwhelming. But all I saw was him—barefoot, half-dressed, completely at home in my kitchen.

"Baby, pass me that fork," he said absently.

The word detonated in my chest. I tossed the utensil his way, aiming for casual. "Stop trying to soften me up with food."

"Worked this morning." He winked, biting into an empanada.

"Menace."

"*Your* menace." His grin split wide.

We didn't even bother cleaning up—forks abandoned, Bali licking crumbs—before he pulled me toward the bathroom.

Heat curled low again, traitorous. Steam blurred the mirror, thick with grapefruit shampoo and rising heat. His hands were firm on my hips, his mouth finding the soft place beneath my ear. My gasp tangled with his rough laugh, a sound that dragged hot across my skin.

"Mmm, on your knees, baby." His voice vibrated against my neck—command, promise, and that dark, asking sweetness that always undid me.

Steam curled between us as I sank down, my palms flat to the wet floor. His stare seared through me, all restraint and hunger, before I closed my lips around him. His groan was a wrecked thing, his hands fisting in my wet hair, not forcing, but holding, guiding, as I loved him with my tongue until his thighs trembled and his breath came in ragged pulls.

"Enough," he growled, his voice stripped raw.

He reached back, water streaming down his chest, and tore open a foil packet with his teeth. A pause—brief, deliberate—before he rolled it on and caught my mouth in another kiss. In one fluid, powerful motion, he hauled me up, pinning me against the shower wall. The tiles were cool against my back, a stark contrast to the scorching heat of his chest. He hooked my leg high around his hip, entering me in a single, devastating thrust that stole the air from my lungs.

"Look at me, Brynn," he commanded, his voice a low rasp against the drumming water.

I forced my eyes open, meeting his intense, unblinking gaze. This wasn't a frenzy; it was possession, deep and deliberate. Each powerful surge of his hips was a punctuation to his earlier words—*'We can be together now.'* My name was a prayer and a curse on his lips as he drove into me, his forehead pressed to mine, the water sluicing over us like a baptism.

When I shattered, the sound broke from me against his shoulder. He followed with a guttural groan, his body shuddering as he came, holding me fast against the tile and the relentless strength of him.

After, he gently lowered my leg, his hands softening, roaming my back in slow, soothing circles. He turned off the water and wrapped me in a thick, warm towel, kissing my hairline with a tenderness that made my chest ache. In the fogged mirror, I saw us—his body solid, his eyes unbearably soft, standing behind me like he belonged there. The image hit like a blow. Like home. *Fuck.*

Back in bed, too wrung out to move, we lay tangled in sheets that had given up hours ago. Bali huffed from the floor, finally reclaiming her spot at the foot of the bed, as if to remind us he'd survived the chaos too. Jerrick's arm lay heavy across my waist, my fingers tracing idle circles on his chest as sleep found us.

***

JERRICK

The bar buzzed with low music and glass-on-glass percussion. Perfume, whiskey, salt from the rim of a margarita—the air thick with a mix of things designed to loosen people's edges. Brynn threaded ahead in black jeans and a silk tank that caught the light like spilled ink. My hand stayed at her back; she leaned into it—a quiet line of heat that didn't ask permission. Anyone watching could see it—she wasn't alone tonight.

The table shifted as we approached. Six sets of eyes. Five shockingly beautiful sisters and their equally pretty intern, Daisy. Every one of them carried a different kind of sharp.

Juliette rose first. Blazer and sneakers—CEO dressed down, but calculated. She extended her hand, grip sharp as a contract. "Mr. Thorne." Firm grip, cool gaze. "Thank you for your cooperation. Not every man would've made this as smooth as you did."

Smooth. If only she knew the blood under that settlement.

I matched her grip. "Appreciate that. And it's Jerrick."

"We've heard a lot about you," Summer said, not bothering to stand. She leaned forward, arms crossed, eyes dark as rifle sights.

Brynn stiffened beside me.

I didn't. "I'd be worried if you hadn't."

Her mouth tilted. Not a smile. More like a test. "We'll see."

Sniper eyes. I've fought men who stared the same way before throwing a punch.

Before Brynn could cut in, Emme leaned forward with a grin like a match strike. "Holy hell, Brynn. You dragged this one straight off a romance cover?" She gave me a long once-over, shameless. "Points for drama. And the jawline."

Brynn groaned. "Emme, for God's sake—"

"What? I'm being thorough." Emme winked at me. "That bone structure should come with a warning label."

I let my mouth tick upward. "Guess I'll take it."

I like her. No filter. The one who keeps the rest of them from chewing each other's throats out.

Annie lifted her pint, cheeks pink already. "Ignore them. Welcome to the circus. We don't get out much."

"Or we get out too much," Rayann countered, her smirk lazy, eyes sharper than her tone. "So this is the infamous Jerrick Thorne."

I let the corner of my mouth lift. "Depends who you ask. You want the résumé or the rumors?"

"Careful," Brynn muttered. "He'll get a bigger head than he already has."

"Impossible," Rayann and Emme said in near-unison, sparking a round of snickers.

The man beside Rayann stood. Broad. Military stamped into his posture. His handshake was firm, no squeeze, no bullshit.

"Max," he said. "Whiskey?"

I arched a brow. "You read my mind."

He slid a glass across, neat pour already waiting. "Figured as much."

Our glasses clicked—solid, clean sound that landed like an understanding. *Good. One ally at the table. Maybe the most important one.*

Daisy tried to sip her martini, choked halfway through, and sputtered into her napkin.

"And that's our cue," Emme announced. "The intern is dying. Someone get this man a chair before the real interrogation starts."

We settled in. Brynn's knee pressed against mine under the table, a solid line of heat. Juliette's gaze tracked the movement, her lips a thin line.

"God, you two," she sighed. "Could you try to hide it for more than five minutes?"

Brynn's chin went up. "Nothing to hide."

"Oh, there's plenty," Rayann drawled. "We've just all got a pretty good idea what it is. She's been... distracted."

"Irritable," Summer added, swirling her drink.

"Defensive," Emme finished with a triumphant point of her glass. "All classic symptoms of a high-grade man infestation."

Annie giggled into her beer. "Stop, you'll scare him off."

I leaned closer to Brynn, my voice low but carrying. "Not a chance."

Brynn turned, her lips brushing my ear. "You smell like sex."

Not wrong. My hand found her hip under the table, the heat of her skin cutting through denim. "So do you. They've already figured it out."

Emme whistled. "See? Filthy. And almost sweet."

"Sweet?" Brynn scoffed, pulling back to look at her sister. "He's the furthest thing from sweet."

Emme waggled her brows. "That tracks. Definitely doesn't look like a man who does missionary."

Annie shrieked with laughter. Summer dropped her head into her hands. "Christ, Emme."

Max choked on his whiskey and shot me a look that was half-sympathy, half-amusement.

I shrugged, sipped mine. "She's not wrong."

Brynn jabbed me in the ribs. I caught her wrist under the table, held it until her pulse hammered against my thumb.

Juliette pinched the bridge of her nose. "Children. I'm surrounded by children."

"Speak for yourself," Emme shot back, lifting her glass. "Some of us are just getting started."

My hand held her there, grounding us both. The noise blurred around us, but her heat at my side marked it clear—*this is where I stay.*

Chapter 36

Epilogue: Tied To You

BRYNN
Eight months later

T HE RIBBON WAS A shredded memory on the
floor, the balloons starting to sag like tired lungs.
But the air in Jerrick's studio still crackled—a live wire
of energy and new-beginning sweat. The scent was a
layered punch to the senses: the sharp, honest stink of
hard work, the rich oil of tanned leather, the chemi-
cal-clean bite of detergent on fresh mats. Our mats. The
polished floor gleamed like a dark ocean under the lights,
those pristine white walls now broken by the bold, fucking beautiful banners of Wilder Horizons. Seeing them
here—my world stamped bright inside his—hit harder

than any boardroom win. At the center of it all, the logo I'd drunkenly sketched on a cocktail napkin—a black belt knotted tight over a rising sun—now blazed larger than life. His. Ours.

God, it worked. He worked. We fucking worked.

The place was a glorious zoo. Parents packed the wall benches, a sea of proud, blinking faces. At the far end of the row, one face stood out—so familiar, yet tentative, like she wasn't sure she had the right to take up space here. Jerrick's mom. Her hands twisted the strap of her purse, but her eyes never left her son. Pride shone there, soft and raw, like sunlight breaking through cloud. My chest ached knowing he'd let her back in—and that I'd nudged him to try. A herd of kids in brand-new, stiff white gis shrieked and chased foam pads like deranged, sugar-fueled puppies. And Jerrick—calm as a goddamn mountain in the center of the storm, his black belt a slash of absolute certainty—moved with an anchor's gravity.

I've orchestrated luxury launches and multimillion-dollar pitches, but watching him command a room of sugar-drunk eight-year-olds? This is the real high-stakes shit.

"Block high! Kick low!" His voice, rough silk, cut through the chaos.

A dozen tiny limbs flailed in chaotic unison. A pad slipped, skittering toward me. I lunged, my hip clipping the cold, unforgiving metal of the equipment rack. The world tilted. Gloves, headgear, shin guards—it all came down in a cacophony of clattering plastic and thudding foam that echoed like a gong.

Every single head swiveled my way.

Perfect. Wilder sister, certified slapstick prop.

My thumb dragged over the split in my lip—a nervous tic I'd never shaken—before I squared my shoulders.

"Smooth, Wilder," Jerrick's voice carried, a grin in every syllable. "I'll put you on demo duty."

"Bite me," I shot back, my cheeks burning.

He didn't bite. He lifted the whistle to his lips—my whistle. The one that meant you're up.

I stepped onto the mat. The coarse cotton of my gi pants rasped against my damp palms. "Alright, you tiny kickers," I called out, forcing my voice over the racket. "Eyes here."

I dropped into a stance, hip-checked the stubborn pad upright with a solid thwump, and sent it flying clean across the mat with a kick that cracked like a whip. A beat of silence, then gasps. Giggles. Then a tidal wave of kids trying to imitate the move. Pads thudded, laughter spiked, and somehow—*fuck me*—it clicked. Organized, beautiful chaos.

When the class finally ended, sweat plastered my shirt to my spine. My hairline was damp, my voice sandpaper-raw. And Jerrick was just... staring. Like I'd reinvented oxygen.

He stepped close, his heat a wall against the air-conditioned chill. His hand caught my hand, calloused thumb brushing over the frantic pulse point. "I've never loved you more than watching you lead that pack of wild animals," he murmured, the words only for me.

My throat locked. *Fuck. He means it.*

Then his free hand went to his pocket. He pulled out a small strip of black belt cotton, edges still stiff. He wrapped it around my wrist, slow—so fucking slow—his fingers tying the knot with a deliberate precision that felt... permanent. Tight. Secure. Irreversible. He cinched the tail ends flat, the way only he would—methodical, exact, like every promise he made had to hold.

I tugged the knot once, grounding myself in the press of cotton against my pulse.

I blinked. And a small, black ring box slid across the mat, nudged by his thumb. His other hand folded mine gently over it, sealing the choice with touch before I even opened it. The studio noise—the shrieks, the chatter, the pop of a balloon—blurred into a distant hum. All I saw was him.

I flipped the lid open with shaking fingers. Inside, a platinum band cradled a brilliant diamond, flanked by two smaller stones—blue topaz and green tourmaline—the colors of Costa Rica's ocean and jungle. Light caught on every facet, scattering tiny sparks across the mat between us. It looked wild and perfect and completely impossible to say no to.

"Marry me, Wilder," he said, voice steady as stone but his eyes wide open, vulnerable. "Be my partner on every mat, in every fight, for the rest of our goddamn lives."

My laugh cracked on a sob. "You think I'm saying no?"

"Still waiting for the *yes*," he shot back, the corner of his mouth twitching.

"Yes." The word was a breath, then a declaration for every sister leaning against the wall, every parent watching us like the main event. "Yes!"

The studio erupted. Kids shrieking decibels higher than the popping balloons. Summer smirked like she'd been betting on this outcome all along. Emme's eyes spilled tears, hands pressed to her mouth. Juliette muttered, "About damn time." Rayann didn't cheer—she just slipped a steady hand over mine when the ring slid home, her grip grounding as stone. Annie, on the other hand, all reckless joy, shouted "Called it!" loud enough to startle the mini-kickers. Off to the side, Jerrick's mom pressed a trembling hand to her mouth, eyes swimming. When he caught her gaze, the corner of his mouth softened, just for her. The distance wasn't erased, not yet—but the bridge was built, one step at a time.

Later, he told me the only thing he remembered from that roar of noise was my face—messy hair, eyes wet, lips shaking around the word yes. He said it was the first time in his life a crowd could've vanished and he wouldn't have noticed.

The launch party bled into Wilder Horizons territory. Champagne flutes sparkled in hands, catered trays of sliders and sushi were picked clean, a playlist bouncing from hard hip-hop beats to the deep, resonant thrum of Costa Rican drums. Emme raised a glass in a toast that had everyone laughing. Summer handed out branded towels with a smirk. Juliette wrangled kids at a photo wall. Annie moved through the crowd with sparkling cider for the mini-kickers.

And Jerrick? He was in his element. Thriving. The sign-up sheet was booked solid, the waiting list a page long. Parents cornered him with questions, kids clung to his gi legs like human Velcro. He looked alive. Free. Exactly where he was meant to be.

I slipped into the shadowy gear room to catch my breath. The air was thick and cool, smelling of new rubber and dense foam. The door clicked shut. Then he was there—all heat and hard hands and hungry mouth, no patience, no pause, just collision.

"Jerrick—" I warned, my back against the shelves of shin guards.

"Brynn," he growled into the skin of my neck, pushing me deeper into the shadows. "It's our fucking party. We can disappear for five minutes."

His black belt hit the floor with a soft thud. My fingers clawed at the fabric of his shirt. A breathless laugh tangled in my throat as a helmet toppled from a shelf and bounced off my shoulder.

"Careful," I whispered, biting down on a grin. "Wouldn't want the kids to learn the advanced drills."

He answered by kissing me hard enough to make my knees buckle, his hands mapping familiar territory.

When we stumbled back out, cheeks flushed, lips bruised, and gi's crooked, my sisters didn't miss a damn thing. Annie raised a knowing brow. Rayann's smirk could cut glass. Juliette just muttered, "Predictable," into her champagne.

But I didn't give a single fuck. Because the studio was alive, buzzing with a future we'd built with our own hands. The man I loved was radiant, finally home. And the strip of black belt was still tied tight around my wrist—a vow, a claim, a goddamn promise.

Welcome home, Wilder.

***

Craving just *one more* moment with Brynn & Jerrick?

Yeah. You are.

Grab their exclusive **BONUS EPILOGUE** right here → https://shorturl.at/O6ngK

Pitch Battle: Overruled

Hey. Jerrick here.

I don't usually do this. But then again... I didn't plan on Brynn either.

If you made it to the end of our story—and you're still thinking about it—do us a favor. Leave Kate Sweden a review. She's the reason we ended up in the same jungle, the same pitch battle, and the same bed I swore I'd stay out of.

She'll call it "fate." I call it Kate, playing writer-God with tequila and bad decisions.

So if you laughed, cursed, blushed, or screamed into a pillow—let her know. Reviews keep this chaos alive.

Drop your review here. It matters more than you think.

And heads up—Kate's not done. Rayann and Max had Scotland. Brynn and I survived Costa Rica.

Next up?

Emme Wilder in Patagonia.

Snow. Ice. And penguins. Lots of penguins.

(Yeah, apparently they mate for life. Emme won't shut up about it.)

Brynn here.

Classic Thorne move—end with penguins.

Anyway. If Kate gave you even one moment of chaos-induced happiness, steamy distraction, or the urge to text your ex—leave her a review. She thrives on it.

You know what to do. Right here.

And as for what's next?

Patagonia. *Seriously, Summer—who the fuck sends us to Patagonia?*

Anyway, it's all about Emme's sunshine, a grumpy Frenchman, and way too many tuxedo birds.

Buckle up, lovelies. It's about to get chilly.

Afterglow, Extras, and Contacts

Come Kick Off Your Heels in the Lounge

Looking for sassy sneak peeks, steamy reader chaos, and wildly inappropriate group chat energy?

You belong in Kate Sweden's Reader Lounge.

I've got spoilers. I've got smut. I've got memes that will spiritually wound you (in the best way).

Basically, it's book club—but with less wine and more fictional orgasms.

Come hang out: → https://shorturl.at/qW1Sj.

Wanna Stay in the Wilder Loop?

Spoiler alerts, spicy extras, behind-the-scenes chaos, and the kind of newsletter that'll make your inbox blush?

Sign up for my newsletter here and let the Wilder shenanigans begin" → https://kateswedenromance.com/mailing-list

Craving More Chaos, Spice & Sneak Peeks?

Explore exclusive bonus scenes, upcoming release goodies, and the kind of behind-the-scenes extras that should probably come with a warning label—
Right this way, babe:

www.KateSwedenRomance.com.

Let's Get Social (Yo Know You Wanna)

Come for the chaos. Stay for the thirst traps, TikToks, unhinged reader theories, and late-night overshares.
Follow me here:

Tik Tok – @kateswedenromance

Instagram – @katesweden_author.

Goodreads – Kate_Sweden

Link Tree – https://linktr.ee/kateswedenromance

Your Review = Our Happy Ending

Your reviews? *They have superpowers.*

They help new readers find their next favorite spicy escape—and keep authors like me doing the happy ugly cry in public.

If Jerrick and Brynn challenged you (in the best way), I'd be wildly grateful if you'd drop a quick, honest review on **Amazon** or **Goodreads**.

You rock. You're hot. I adore you.

A   m   a   z   o   n   →
https://www.amazon.com/dp/B0F2GRPBMX

Goodreads → https://shorturl.at/XEfQl

Jerrick & Brynn's Afterparty

Finished the book and still emotionally compromised?
Same.

So I made you things.

Want to *see* the resort vibes, Brynn's chaos-core aesthetic, or that jungle situation in full visual glory?

There's a whole Pinterest mood board waiting for your unhinged deep-dive:

Pinterest Mood Board→

https://pin.it/4IYF71Nus

Want to *feel* every stolen glance, every slow burn, and every spicy disaster all over again?

The official Jerrick & Brynn Spotify playlist is basically a rollercoaster of tension, yearning, and sin:

Playlist → https://shorturl.at/TQCt4

Turn it on. Fall apart. Repeat.

Acknowledgements

To my Wild Magnolias team—thank you for cheering this book into existence, the second in the *Wilder Horizons* series, with endless pep talks, bags of salted potato chips (my other true weakness), and a suspiciously bottomless supply of coffee. You believed in this story long before it managed to put on pants.

To my son, who sat across from me during homeschool hours, sketching angles and triangles while I was over here trying to untangle the geometry of two fictional people falling into bed—thank you for being blissfully unaware of the utterly inappropriate chaos glowing on my laptop screen. May geometry always be your toughest equation, kiddo.

To my incredible beta readers—you were such an essential part of this journey. Your sharp eyes, big hearts, and endless encouragement made this book shine brighter than I ever could have on my own. I have had so much fun working with you! Aimee Lavigne, Cassie Springer, Cheryl Thigpen, Christina Miller, Glorymar Rosario Vicente, Jessica Aranda, Meagan Luton, Justine Plowman, and Taylor Parry, thank you!

To my ride-or-die street team: thank you for shouting about this book from the rooftops (and TikTok, and Instagram, and probably to random strangers in Barnes & Noble). Your passion, hustle, and hilarious messages kept me going. I couldn't have done this without you.

And to my family—thank you for your steady love, the kind that anchors me no matter the storm. Always.

To my mom, whose laughter is my favorite soundtrack and whose wisdom is stitched into everything I write: you are the heart behind every page.

About the author

Kate Sweden is a romance author with a flair for funny, a soft spot for slow burns, and a love of happily ever afters with heat. A former Air Force officer, educator, and lifelong book nerd, she traded briefing rooms and lesson plans for plot twists and first kisses. These days, she lives in Northeast Florida with her husband, their teenage son, and a very opinionated dog named Sailor—plus a pantry that's suspiciously short on chocolate.

Challenged by You: Book Club & Reader Guide

Drink + Snack Pairings

Buckle up! Make your book club spicy *and* delicious:

- **Pitch Battle Palomas** – Tequila, grapefruit, lime, and a salted rim sharp enough to cut a rival down to size

- **Namaste Nachos** – Jalapeños, queso, and enough chaos to spark a yoga studio scandal

- **Jaguar Jungle Mojito** – Rum, muddled mint, raw sugar, and a wild streak that might bite back

- **Power Suit Empanadas** – Crisp, golden pockets stuffed with spice—perfect fuel for a woman who can crush boardrooms *and* billionaires

Tropes Checklist

Check off your favorite romance tropes featured in *Challenged by You*:

Rivals-to-Lovers

Forced Proximity

Office Romance

Arrogant Hot Guy

Competition

Secret Past

Miscommunication

Comical Sidekicks

Family Dynamics

Spice Scale: How Hot Are We Talking?

Total Heat Rating: out of 5
(Your Kindle might need a fire extinguisher.)

Scene Breakdown:

- **Chapter 14 – Team Building**

  Location: Jerrick's suite

  Vibe: Relentless domination meets desperate surrender—filthy, punishing, and consuming, with a shockwave of tenderness after the wreckage

- **Chapter 15 – Nothing to See Here**

  Location: Jerrick's Suite

  Vibe: Raw, hungry, and emotionally destabilizing—equal parts carnal urgency and terrifying intimacy

- **Chapter 18 – Toucan Play That Game**

  Location: Brynn's terrace

  Vibe: Fast, filthy, hilarious

- **Chapter 34 – One Hell of a Hello**

  Location: Brynn's condo in Maris Key

  Vibe: Explosive reunion—raw, urgent, furious, and hungry, a kiss that's both punishment and homecoming

- **Chapter 35 – Where I Stay**

  Location: Brynn's condo in Maris Key

  Vibe: Baptized in steam and sarcasm—holy water never looked this filthy

Book Club Discussion Questions

Pour the wine. Grab the dark chocolate. Let's talk.
Bonus points if you share in our Link Reader's Group:
Kate Sweden's Reader Lounge (yes, please!)

1. Brynn and Jerrick start as rivals—at what moment did you first feel the chemistry between them shift?

2. Do you think Brynn's pranks are a coping mechanism, a form of control, or both?

3. Jerrick reveals his jiu-jitsu tattoos and their meanings. How did that layer of discipline and vulnerability change how you saw him?

4. Which scene best captured the tension between "professional rivals" and "personal desire"?

5. How does the Costa Rican setting heighten the intensity of their relationship? Could this story have worked anywhere else?

6. Brynn's chaos vs. Jerrick's control: which side did you relate to more, and why?

7. The pitch-off is central to the story. How do the professional stakes add to the romantic tension?

8. Did you sympathize more with Brynn or Jerrick during the misunderstandings? Why?

9. Brynn constantly weighs family loyalty against personal desire. How does that conflict shape her choices?

10. Jerrick's relationship with his father adds depth to his character. How does it impact the way he loves Brynn?

11. If you could step into one scene and watch it unfold in person, which would you pick?

12. Brynn often uses humor to deflect when she's vulnerable. How does Jerrick break through that defense?

13. Brynn and Jerrick's banter is sharp and relentless. Did you find it more funny, tense, or fore-

play in disguise?

14. How does "control" look different for Brynn versus Jerrick?

15. If *Challenged By You* were adapted into a movie or series, who would you cast as Brynn and Jerrick—and which scene *must* make it to screen untouched?

Author's Note from Kate Sweden

This story grew out of my own experiences in the jungle years ago—mosquito bites, unexpected wildlife encounters, and the kind of heat that makes even the most disciplined person unravel. Add in one rivals-to-lovers what-if, a few prank wars, and the delicious thought of what happens when control finally snaps, and *Challenged By You* refused to stay tame.

Jerrick and Brynn are fictional.
But the need to feel loved just as you are? That part's very real.
Thanks for reading. Thanks for swooning.

And if someone makes you feel seen, safe, and maybe just a little challenged in all the good ways... hold on tight. That's where the magic begins.

KATE SWEDEN

A Forbidden Reunion Romantic Comedy

Hooked by You

Wilder Horizons Series

Preview of Hooked By You (Wilder Horizons, Book 3) – Emme's Story

Chapter 1: Patagonia or Bust

The knock came before I'd even made it to my second cup of coffee.

Not polite. Not casual. One of those sharp, militarized raps that said, *open this fucking door or I will, and you won't like how I do it.*

I opened the door to our office suite—early, quiet, and blessedly empty except for me—and there she stood.

I blinked. Summer Wilder did not do mornings. At least, not at the office. She was a ten-o'clock arrival, calendar-blocked to the minute, blazer crisp, coffee waiting.

I was the early riser. Not because I liked mornings—God no—but because I liked claiming this slice of stillness before the day went feral. It was an unspoken arrangement between sisters: I opened, she closed. I got peace, she got control. It worked.

Until today. Summer Wilder. COO of Wilder Horizons. Eldest sister by seven years. Already dressed like a minimalist power icon—tailored black trousers, crisp white blouse tucked just so, delicate gold hoops catching the light, AirPods still in, manila folder in hand like it contained either a hostile takeover or a kingdom blueprint.

"Don't say no," she said by way of greeting.

I raised an eyebrow and backed up to let her in, the scent of burnt espresso and copy paper clinging in the air. My hair was still damp from the world's fastest blowout, a few polished waves pinned back with gold clips. Lip gloss, heels, tailored pink blazer—the full Vendor Relations Barbie starter pack. That's me—smile painted on, charm set to high. Charm's expensive currency, and some days the cost showed in my jaw, sore from grinning at ghosts, while my phone lit up with numbers I didn't want to call.

My shoes were off under my desk only because I'd swapped into fuzzy slippers for these sacred pre-nine a.m. hours, when no one was around to judge me for preserving my arches.

Summer marched straight to the kitchenette and glared at the coffee machine. She jabbed a button, twisted the wrong dial, and stared down the chrome beast like it had personally betrayed her. The machine sputtered, hissed, and blinked a red light. She kept jabbing buttons.

"Is this thing still broken?"

"No. You're just banned," I said, watching as she smacked the side like it was a vending machine. With a sigh, I slid in, shooed her aside, and coaxed the machine into purring within seconds. I handed over the mug—black with just a splash of cream, Summer's idea of indulgence. She took a long sip, grimaced anyway, and muttered about the death of decent caffeine.

I flopped onto the sofa, legs tucked under me, and flipped open the folder she handed me. Heavy cardstock pages. Stiff. Smelled like ink and recycled ambition. "You're in a mood. And early. Who are we conquering today?"

Summer turned with her mug, took one sip, and wrinkled her nose like it personally offended her. "You."

"I'm already conquered. HR has the paperwork to prove it."

"You're going to Patagonia."

I laughed. Then realized she wasn't laughing.

"Wait. Seriously?"

She nodded and leaned one hip against the kitchenette counter, all business now. She squared the folder's edges on the counter before she spoke. "We've got two scouting reports, three unaffiliated client pings, and a whisper from that freaky travel concierge Rayann blackmailed into sending us his 2026 high-wealth trends list. Patagonia's on it."

If anyone can sway a freak, it's my sister Rayann—Sales Director and goddess who could sweet-talk a cactus into producing vodka.

"Logistics aren't the problem," Emme said quietly. "Vendors are already courting me—someone pitched glacier-side wine tastings yesterday. I love the hustle. Access, though, is the real issue. Patagonia doesn't bend for outsiders. If Summit strikes first, they'll lock down the gates before we even book a flight."

If Summit landed Patagonia before us, they'd scoop our highest-paying clients, corner the luxury market, and brand Wilder as second-best. We didn't survive on second place.

"Trends list or not, Summit Expeditions is already circling," Summer added. "They've been sniffing at Patagonia for months. We move first, or we move out of the way. And don't waste your charm on him," Summer said flatly. "Rumor is, the last scout Summit sent came back after forty-eight hours—said he barely spoke a word. Just get the deal. "

I stared at her. "You want me to fly to the literal bottom of the planet—"

"Top of our opportunity funnel."

"—to freeze my ass off in the name of luxury?"

She gave me a pointed look. "Our clients want what's remote, curated, and impossible to replicate. Patagonia checks every box."

"Penguins and frostbite. Very aspirational."

"Don't forget status-driven suffering. That's trending hard. Think *cryotherapy meets altitude sickness.*"

I swore under my breath and shoved a throw pillow over my face. "I hate it here." And for half a second, I almost meant it.

"No you don't," she said mildly. "You love it. The negotiations. The thrill. The adrenaline hit of getting somewhere first."

She wasn't wrong. I pulled the pillow away and studied the top sheet again. Elevation stats. Micro-climate notes. Vendor portfolio. Then—

A lodge photo.

Jesus.

The place looked like a painting. Or a conspiracy theory. All stone and timber, perched on the edge of a cliff like it dared the mountain to move. Balconies jutted toward the horizon, glass walls swallowing every inch of view. A sweep of alpine forest spilled below it, roofs dusted white, smoke curling from a chimney like someone had staged the world's most decadent winter postcard. Even the driveway looked dramatic—cut into the rock face, winding up like it only allowed the worthy.

Dad had a map on his study wall once—faded paper, corners curling—where a red pin marked this very stretch of Patagonia. He used to say it was the one place that slipped through his fingers. Looking at the lodge now, I felt the pin prick me back. I remembered standing on a stool in his study, tracing the edges of that map while he swore one day he'd plant a flag there. It had been years since a place—not a person, not a paycheck—hit me like that.

"You're sending me *here*?" I asked quietly.

Summer nodded. "It's called *Refugio Cielo*. The owner's an ex-architect. French. Rugged. Off-grid since 2018."

"Why do they always have to be French?"

"Because you respond well to accents and sexual hostility."

"Fuck off."

She grinned. "He runs everything himself. No social media. No press. No confirmed affiliation. But he's booked out six months in advance with clients who sign NDAs just to get on the waiting list."

The corner bore a logo—mountain peak, crossed tools, survival wrapped in luxury. The paper cut into my palm, like it sensed the name it guarded: Luc Moreau.

Oh great. A name like a wine I couldn't afford—French, ex-architect, vanished from the design world a few years back. No interviews. No comeback. Just silence—and a lodge balanced on a cliff like defiance.

Summer was still talking. "You'll evaluate the property, secure a preliminary contract, and gather local vendor options for expansion. If he plays nice, we keep him solo. If not, we launch our own high-altitude outpost. Either way—"

"Wilder wins."

She toasted me with her mug. "That's the spirit."

I got up and walked to the window. Sunlight glared across the glass, Florida humidity pressing my blazer to my back, jasmine syrupy-thick in the air. Outside, a car horn bleated twice, lazy traffic edging past the square, petty noises that felt obscene against the silence I was already craving. Even the storm's aftertaste lingered on my tongue, metallic and damp. I pressed my fingers to the pane and imagined Patagonia instead: wind sharp enough to flay the skin awake, air so thin it scraped your lungs clean, silence so profound it roared. Miles of wilderness that gave no fucks about polished logos or curated guest experiences.

My skin prickled.

Not from cold.

From *curiosity*.

I flipped into hunter mode so fast it scared me.

Wilder Horizons wasn't just a company; it was our father's legacy. He'd started with nothing but charm, grit, and a refusal to settle for ordinary, building luxury adventure travel experiences in places most people couldn't even find on a map. After he died, the six of us inherited more than his contracts and client list—we inherited the mandate to keep it alive. Summer, the oldest, took COO, weaponizing calendars and color codes to keep the whole machine running. Juliette, next in line, stepped up as CEO, steering global strategy and turning his dream into an empire. And me? I was the one who knocked on impossible doors and made people open them. Which was exhilarating, sure—until you looked up and realized you were always chasing, never arriving.

"Flights?" I asked, already calculating layovers and luggage weight.

"You've got a little bit of time. Still a few deals to close and a PR mess to untangle first."

"Perfect. My favorite kind of vacation prep."

"Add it to your to-do list."

I turned back to the folder. There was a small note clipped inside in Summer's handwriting: *Don't try to charm him. Survive it, if you can.*

I smiled.

Too late.

I was already plotting how to melt the frost right off Mr. Luc Moreau.

Even if I had to do it in three layers of thermal underwear.

Hey loves —

Think that first chapter was fun? Oh honey, that was foreplay in mittens. Fall headfirst into the third book in the Wilder Horizons series, ***Hooked By You***—where the nights are cold, the kisses are hot, and a certain

Frenchman finally loses control.

Grab your copy here!

XO Kate

www.ingramcontent.com/pod-product-compliance
Lightning Source LLC
Chambersburg PA
CBHW032007110726
47901CB00004B/998